THE 13TH REALITY

BOOK 4
THE VOID OF MIST AND THUNDER

THE 13TH REALITY

BOOK 4
THE VOID OF MIST AND THUNDER

JAMES DASHNER

ILLUSTRATED BY
BRANDON DORMAN

SHADOW
MOUNTAIN

Library of Congress Cataloging-in-Publication Data
Dashner, James, 1972– author.
 The void of mist and thunder / James Dashner.
  pages cm — (The 13th reality, book 4)
 Summary: When an all-consuming void from the Fourth Dimension opens up, unleashing monsters throughout the Realities, Master George has one last weapon at his disposal—the mysterious and powerful Karma button, which might be even more dangerous than anyone imagined.
  ISBN 978-1-60908-055-6 (hardbound : alk. paper) [1. Space and time—Fiction. 2. Adventure and adventurers—Fiction.] I. Title. II. Series: Dashner, James, 1972– 13th reality ; bk 4.
 PZ7.D2587Vo 2012
 [Fic]—dc23   2012017338

Printed in the United States of America
R. R. Donnelley, Crawfordsville, IN

10   9   8   7   6   5   4   3   2   1

This one is for the Storymakers.

You know who you are.

CONTENTS

CONTENTS

CONTENTS

CONTENTS

ACKNOWLEDGMENTS

I can't believe the series has come to an end. It's been a long and sometimes tough journey, but I'm so proud of the story and thankful to the people who helped push it through to the finish. Particularly Chris Schoebinger and Lisa Mangum. Without them it absolutely never would have happened. Much appreciation to all my other friends at Shadow Mountain too.

As always, I'd like to thank my agent, Michael Bourret, for his tireless work.

Thanks to Liesa Abrams and all the good folks at Simon & Schuster for believing in the series enough to take it to a larger stage. Here's to many more people discovering the adventures of Tick and the other Realitants.

PROLOGUE

A VERY SPECIAL BOY

It was all about the soulikens.

Master George sat in his study, the lights dimmed, Muffintops purring in a corner, the first light of dawn's birth still an hour off. He stared at the wall as if the most fascinating thing in the Realities had been stapled there for him to see whenever he wished, but it was only a knot in the wood of his paneling. A knot that had two eyes and a mouth if you looked at it just right, and for some reason it reminded him of a boy named Atticus Higginbottom.

Atticus. Tick. The young man who changed everything.

The boy who'd disappeared from existence.

It was a shame. More than a shame. It was a downright tragedy. Master George had never ached in his heart so much for someone lost. Right when they'd finally begun to understand why the boy had such extraordinary powers, why he was able to harness and use Chi'karda as if he were himself a Barrier Wand—and a powerful Wand at that, even more so than Mistress Jane, who had a unique and tragic story of her own—he was gone.

But none of that really mattered anymore. It wasn't the *reason* George missed Master Atticus so much. He missed him—ached for him—because the boy had become like a son to him. So innocent, yet brave. So genuine. Such a kid, but so grown up. Oh, how he missed that dear, dear boy.

He was a wonder.

Sato had completed the mission George had asked of him. He had visited each Reality and searched until he had found the same thing in each one: a grave for the Alterants of Atticus Higginbottom—the boy's "twins" in the other twelve Realities. Never before had such an odd coincidence occurred, where only one version of a person remained throughout all the Realities. They'd never know if there was some deep cosmic reason behind it, or how it had happened.

But one thing was for certain: every one of those Alterants' soulikens had traveled to and collected within the body of the one remaining Atticus who had lived in Reality Prime. It had changed his structure, his makeup, his quantum mechanics. He was full of Chi'karda, filled beyond measure with the powers that bound and controlled the universe. Filled beyond anything mankind could ever hope to recreate or dream about.

He was lost now, gone from existence.

There'd probably never be another quite like him, in far more ways than one.

George called for Muffintops. He needed to hug a friend.

PART 1

THE NONEX

CHAPTER
1

A GASH IN THE FOREST

The forest smelled of things dead, things rotting.

Jacob Gillian paid the stench no mind, walking his merry way along the narrow path that threaded through the tall oaks and pines like a dried-out stream. Of course, the reason he paid it no mind was because he'd lost his sense of smell thirty years ago in an unfortunate spice sniffing contest. His grandson, Chip, had to tell him that the place stunk like a three-week-old dead rat stuck under the pipes.

The two of them had been hiking side by side for well over an hour, knowing full well that something horrible had happened deep within the dark woods. Exactly *what* had happened was still a mystery, and the reason they were out there. Jacob had heard the awful sound of ripping and shredding and booming. Chip had smelled the nose-wrinkling stench. Those two things together spelled trouble, and by golly, the source behind it needed finding out.

Jacob and his grandson had moved into the boonies

after Chip's parents had been killed in a train collision near Louisville. Ever since then, they'd learned to live with little and less, loving the wild freedom and exhilaration of being smack-dab in the middle of nowhere. Their closest neighbor lived a good thirty miles down the poorly maintained state road, and the nearest town was forty miles in the other direction. But that's just how Jacob liked it, and the life had seemed to grow on Chip as well.

One day they'd return to civilization and start learnin' Chip on the ways of society. But for now, there was time. Time to heal, time to grow, time to enjoy. Time to have time.

"I think I see something up there, Grandpa," Chip said, a little too enthusiastically, considering the circumstances that had brought them out into the woods.

"What is it?" Old Jacob couldn't see much better than he could smell.

"There's a bright patch. Seems like it goes all the way up to the sky!"

"On the path or off it?"

Chip grabbed Jacob's hand and started hurrying down the little ribbon of beaten leaves and undergrowth. "Just to the right of it. We're almost there!"

Jacob followed along as careful as he could while still keeping up with Chip's eager steps. Warning bells rang inside his mind, but he did what he'd done since the day he'd stepped out into the humid fields of Korea as a soldier—he ignored them. Curiosity always won out in his book, and courage came as naturally as a nice belch after dinner.

They'd just rounded a bend, skirting past two mammoth pines that looked like brothers, when Chip suddenly pulled up short. Jacob ran right past him, almost yanking his grandson's arm out of its socket when the boy didn't let go. But then Jacob saw what had stopped the kid, and all he could do was stand and stare. He felt Chip's sweaty hand slip out of his own.

Fifty yards ahead of them, a swath of the forest had been wiped from existence and replaced by a brushstroke of . . . something else. Starting deep in the ground and shooting all the way to the sky was a wide gash in reality, a window to another place. Jacob could see part of a beach, the deep blue waters of the ocean beside it, a sun where there shouldn't *be* a sun. The time was almost noon, and the *real* ball of fire was directly overhead. It was as if someone had clawed a rip in the reality of this world and replaced it with another.

"What in the great dickens are we lookin' at?" Jacob whispered.

"Grandpa?" was all Chip managed in reply. His voice shook with equal parts confusion and terror.

"I've been from one end of this world to the other," Jacob said, not sure if he was talking to himself or to his grandson. "And I've never seen a thing like that in my life."

"Let's go home."

"Home?" Jacob tore his eyes away from the spectacle and looked down at Chip. "Didn't you hear what I just said? This is a once in a lifetime opportunity! Let's go check her out."

Jacob took Chip's hand once again, and they started

marching closer to the impossible vision of another world streaked across their own. They'd come to within twenty feet when a person appeared on the beach, stepping into the picture from the right edge of where reality had been torn apart.

It was a lady, though Jacob could only tell that from the ratty, filthy dress she wore; a hood was pulled up over her head. A red mask, seemingly made out of metal, covered her face. The expression on the mask was one of anger.

She saw them just as they saw her, and she stopped to stare, the features of the mask *shifting* to create an expression of absolute shock.

Jacob took a step backward before he realized what he was doing.

"Who are you?" the woman asked, her voice raw and scratchy, like it came out of a throat scarred with acid. "Do you know how this happened?"

Jacob's mouth had turned into a bucket of dust, and he couldn't remember how his tongue or voice box worked. He tried getting words out, but nothing came except the slightest hint of a croak.

Surprisingly, Chip spoke up. "Lots of bad sounds came from over here, and the whole place is stinky. Me and my grandpa were just trying to see what happened."

Such bravery from the kid meant Jacob had to speak. He found his voice. "Where you from, miss? Um, if you don't mind me asking."

The lady's mask melted—literally, by the looks of

it—into a frown. "I'm from the Thirteenth Reality. Where are you?"

Jacob swallowed a lump the size of his big toe. "Um . . . Kentucky?"

Before the lady could respond, her image and everything around her suddenly spun into a tornado of colors that quickly merged and transformed into a mass of gray. It swirled and swirled, picking up speed and creating a wind that tore at Jacob's clothing. And then the sound of terrible thunder seemed to come from everywhere at once, shaking the forest and splintering Jacob's skull with pain.

When the spinning mass of gray mist expanded and took him, he had the strange thought that although he certainly wasn't a cat, curiosity had killed him all the same.

CHAPTER
2

A FORMIDABLE FOE

Mistress Jane winked herself a thousand yards down the beach as soon as the first sign of trouble appeared with the strange gash into another reality. She'd been talking to an old man and his boy, just beginning to wonder if she dared try to step through and escape the Nonex, when the whole thing collapsed into a spinning vortex of gray mist. It was all gone now, the echoes of the detonating thunder that had accompanied its short but catastrophic end just now rumbling away to oblivion.

Interesting. That was all she could come up with to describe what she'd witnessed. Very, very interesting. She had the faintest spark of an idea as to what had actually happened. It gave her something to contemplate while trapped in her bizarre new world.

She turned away and resumed her long walk down the never-ending beach. The salty breeze coming off the ocean waters stirred her robe, and she wished she could take off her mask and feel the wind against her cheeks once more. But it hurt to remove the thing, and even if she did, the result would be disappointing. The nerves of her skin were mostly burned away, replaced by the particles of Chu's Dark Infinity weapon. She felt things in a different way now. Not unpleasant, necessarily, but not the same.

Chu. Reginald Chu. Why did she have to think of the man?

She'd spent the last week with him and that upstart boy Atticus Higginbottom. In the Nonex, there was nowhere else to go. They were on an island that sometimes seemed small and other times, gigantic. Nothing made sense in this place. You could begin eating a piece of fresh fruit and have the thing turn rotten before you finished. Fish flew through the air, and birds swam underwater. Trees shifted in the night— or what passed for night. It had been three days since the sun last set below the horizon. Everything here was wrong.

Not to mention the bad company. Chu was nasty— always grumpy, always degrading in how he spoke to her, always arrogant. Atticus was nice enough, considering the three of them were bitter enemies, one to another, but he had his own kind of arrogance, as if his innocence and goodwill were tangible things that floated around his body, pointing out how everyone else wasn't worthy to be in his presence. The boy made her ill. And angry. And thirsty for revenge.

But none of that mattered right now. None of it. They all had the same goal at the moment, and that was to get out of the blasted nowhere they currently called home.

A flicker of movement to her right caught her attention.

She stopped just in time to see the boy come out from behind some trees, carrying some stray wood. He dumped it on the ground.

How sweet, she thought bitterly. *He's making a campfire. What a Boy Scout.* Same team or not, they all tried to keep their distance from one another as best they could.

When Atticus noticed her, a look of sheer disappointment painted his features. This both hurt Jane and made her angry.

"Where's Chu?" she asked, as though the boy were her servant and not her mortal enemy.

Atticus shrugged. "I don't know." He knelt on the ground and started arranging the logs in an orderly pyramid.

"You find some matches I don't know about?" Jane asked. "If you think I'm in the mood to help—"

The logs burst into flame, all of them. An instant bonfire.

Atticus stood up, gave her a glare. But then his look changed to guilt, as if it were against his nature to be mean. Then he smiled, which made Jane angrier.

"Altering the physical state of wood from a solid to a gas?" he asked with another shrug. "You think I can't do that by myself? Come on. That's as easy as lighting a match, Mistress Jane."

He didn't wait for a response, just turned and walked away, disappearing back into the woods.

Igniting fire. Such a simple thing, really. And yet, for some reason, it terrified her to see the boy do it without any obvious effort whatsoever. She flopped down onto the sand, staring at the waves as they lapped onto the beach and tried to ignore the icy fear trickling through her veins.

Atticus—the boy known as Tick—was a foe to be reckoned with.

⁓

Jane had been sitting on the beach for hours, staring out at the wondrous ocean that wasn't really an ocean, when suddenly the horizon jumped up and down. The water turned from blue to green to black, then froze into ice, crackling; then it was hot and boiling. A fish popped out of the shifting water and spread its fins like wings, hovering a few seconds before exploding into a spray of rainbow-colored sparkles. Lightning shot down from a cloudless sky and hit the water, creating huge splashes of something dark and thick, like oil. She looked down at the sand, and within a matter of seconds, it had changed color three times.

Par for the course in this place that seemed beyond the realm of the physics she understood so well.

She'd just lifted her gaze back to the ocean when a thump of sound shook the air and the ground, a thunderclap that made her bounce off the sand. She threw out her arms for balance and searched the beach for any sign of what had happened.

The sound thumped again. Then again. The land around her shook, but this time didn't stop. The trees behind her trembled; several were uprooted and fell, crashing against each other. Dots of light fell from the sky, vanishing before they hit the ground. Farther down the beach, pillars of stone shot through the sand, rising up until it looked like they had their very own Stonehenge to explore. The ocean froze, then cracked into a million icy pieces, exploding upward a hundred feet, then falling again like a rain of crystal. The sand nearby swirled in little tornadoes, the funnels spinning faster and faster.

Suddenly Chu was by her side, having sprinted in from the shifting woods. He collapsed next to her when another jolt of sound and quaking shook the world.

"This is madness!" he shouted at her. "Things are becoming more and more unstable!"

Jane wanted to argue with him—that was always her instinct—but she knew he was right. First, the strange gash in the air earlier, peeking into another Reality. And now this, a sudden uptick in the strangeness that was the Nonex. She nodded at Chu.

The thumps of noise stopped. The land grew still. The pillars that had risen on the beach slowly sank back underground. The ocean liquefied, glistening and smooth. The small funnels of spinning sand stopped, collapsing with a dusty poof. All seemed still and quiet.

Thoughts and plans were forming inside Jane's head, but they weren't solid enough to describe. Like an epiphany in another language, the ideas still needed to be translated, but they were there all the same.

Reginald Chu had a look in his eyes that made her think his mind had spun in the same direction as hers.

"Together," he whispered, his voice still loud in the sudden silence. "If we can work together, then I think there's a way for both of us to be happy in the end."

CHAPTER
3

ONE LAST TRY

I t's hot, Mom."

Lorena Higginbottom looked over at her daughter as they trampled through the woods. The girl did have a few strands of hair matted against her forehead, like squiggly little worms. "Well, the fall weather should be here soon."

"I'm so hot my *sweat* is sweating."

"That doesn't make sense, dear."

"I know."

They'd visited these woods in eastern Washington every day for the last week, stomping their way along the same path often enough that a solid trail was beginning to appear, making the journey a little easier. Lorena had the straps of a duffel bag looped over her shoulder, its contents consisting of a single item. An extremely important, rare, expensive, incredibly-difficult-to-create item that she'd guard with her life, if necessary.

The item was long, solid, and heavy, with a brass shell

lined with dials and switches. A Chi'karda Drive was housed inside it—a complex network of chips, wires, and nanotech that could literally alter reality itself.

It was a Barrier Wand.

And the only hope she had of finding her son.

"If it doesn't work today," Lisa said as she ducked under the low-hanging branch of an oak tree, "I think we should try something else."

"Can't argue with that," Lorena responded. "I wanted to do this without getting George and the others involved, but we might not have a choice."

The two of them stepped across the forest floor, *cricks* and *cracks* filling the air along with the pungent smells of pine needles and bark and something else that wavered between sweet and rotten. Sunlight broke through the canopy of leaves and sprinkled the ground with golden drops.

"What do you have against Master George anyway?" Lisa asked.

Lorena almost stopped walking, but she caught herself and kept going. Did she really want to talk about her feelings toward the leader of the Realitants right now? They were so complicated. "Nothing at all," she finally said, a simple enough response.

"Come on, Mom. I know there's something. I'm not quite as stupid as Tick always says I am."

"Tick says no such thing!"

"Mom, answer the question." Lisa pushed her way past a small branch and seemed to make no effort to keep it from swinging back and smacking Lorena in the face.

"Ouch!"

"Sorry."

Lorena heard the girl snicker. "I'll get you back for that, young lady." She was glad her daughter couldn't see the sudden smile that sprang up, but it couldn't be helped. Lisa's playfulness was a welcome thing indeed.

"So . . . answer the question."

Lorena had no choice but to address the touchy subject. "As I said, I have nothing against that man whatsoever. If I did, not in a million years would I have let Atticus continue working for him and his merry group of heroes. It's just complicated."

"Then why haven't we contacted him? Why aren't we working together with him? He knows a lot more than we do!"

Lorena kept her doubts about that to herself. "I may be out of practice, but I'm no dummy when it comes to the Realities, you know."

Lisa stopped and faced her mom. "I know, Mom, but don't you think we could figure this out a lot faster if we had their help?"

"Maybe." Lorena stepped closer to Lisa and reached out to grip the girl's shoulders. "But I have my reasons. Number one, George has a heart of gold, but he can be reckless when times get . . . tense. That's okay usually—but not when my son's life is on the line like this."

"And number two?"

Lorena gathered her thoughts for a second before answering. "The world's in shambles, Lisa. All the natural disasters, all the deaths, all the homeless and sick, all the damage. And who knows what kind of permanent damage the other Realities have experienced. George and the Realitants are going to have a lot on their plate, and to be honest, I wouldn't be able to blame them if Atticus wasn't their top priority."

"What? How can they—"

"He's one boy, Lisa! One life. The Realitants have to worry about billions of others."

"Then what are you saying?"

"I'm *saying* that even though George claims he's going to do whatever it takes to find out what happened to Atticus, I can't put my full trust and hope in that. We need to take it on ourselves to get this done. Do what *we* have to do, and let them do what *they* have to do."

Lisa pursed her lips, obviously considering it all for a long moment. "Maybe it helps that two groups are coming at it from different directions. Only one of us needs to find him."

"Bingo." Lorena did her best to smile, but for some reason, her heart couldn't make it feel genuine. Once again, speaking of the world and the trouble it was in had soured her mood; everything seemed worse since her son had vanished.

"So we go to the spot," Lisa said, "and we try again."

"Bingo times two."

"And if it doesn't work today, then we try something else."

"Bingo times three."

"Okay." Lisa turned around and started walking again.

As Lorena followed, she thought for the millionth time that she was crazy to involve Lisa in this quest. Yes, she was endangering yet another of her children, but she couldn't help it. Lisa was bright, and upbeat, and funny. Brave. And the girl loved her family as powerfully as Lorena did. She needed Lisa. Edgar—bless his heart—wasn't the right person to help her now. And someone had to be with little Kayla.

Lorena *needed* Lisa. Desperately. She couldn't do this alone. Lorena would just have to do whatever it took to keep the girl safe until they figured things out. Until Atticus was back together with them all.

~~~

They reached a clearing about twenty feet wide, their recent visits and footsteps and sit-downs having flattened the grass considerably. A circle of thick pines bordered the spot, the tree branches stretching to the sky far above. Lorena saw a squirrel scurry its way up one of the trees, dropping an acorn in its haste.

Lisa slipped off her backpack; she'd been in charge of the food because Lorena had to carry the heavy load of the Barrier Wand. They'd done this every day, and sharing a nice lunch put some cracks in the heavy dome of doom and gloom that hung over their mission. The two of them sat down in the middle of the clearing, facing each other.

"You want the turkey or the ham?" Lisa asked as she pulled out the sandwiches.

"Turkey. That ham's been doing something awful to my stomach."

"Thanks for sharing, Mom. My hunger just doubled."

"Sorry, dear."

They chomped through the meal, and then it was time to get down to business. Lorena unzipped the duffel bag and pulled out the hefty shaft of the Barrier Wand. The scant drifts of sunlight that filtered through the leaves glinted and winked off the shiny golden surface as she maneuvered the thing until she held it directly in front of her folded legs, its bottom end sunk into the debris of the forest floor. She looked past the Wand at Lisa.

"It's a thing of beauty, don't you think?"

Lisa shrugged. "Maybe the *first* time I saw it."

"Oh, I never tire of it. Maybe it's knowing the unimaginable power that's coiled up inside of it. I'm a scientist, and yet it still feels like magic to me."

"A cell phone would be magic if you showed it to somebody a hundred years ago."

Lorena felt a burst of pride at the statement. "Well said, Lisa, well said. Just like Arthur C. Clarke."

"Who?"

The pride bubble burst a bit. "Never mind."

"Let's do this thing."

"Yes. Let's do. I'm going to crank up the Chi'karda Drive to its highest level. We've got nothing to lose."

Lisa didn't answer right away, and Lorena saw a flicker of deep concern in the girl's eyes.

"Don't worry, Lisa. I don't think it can hurt us. I'm more worried about it doing damage to the Wand itself." Lorena didn't know if that was the total truth, but it was close enough without planting even more worry inside her daughter.

"Go for it, then."

Lorena spent a minute or two moving the dials and switches of the Wand, adjusting and flipping and turning each one until she was satisfied that its power was at maximum and that it was locked onto Atticus's last known nano-locator readings.

She eyed Lisa. "This is it. If it doesn't pull in that boy now, it never will. If you hear a loud buzz in your head or feel like your fingers might fall off, don't be alarmed."

"Of course not." The slightest roll of Lisa's eyes made her look half bored and half amused, but Lorena knew that fear still lurked behind it all.

"Want a countdown?"

"Mom!"

"Okay, okay. Here we go." She reached for the button on the top of the Wand and pushed. The click was surprisingly loud, as if the entire forest and all its creatures had quieted at the same moment.

Nothing happened. At first. Then a low hum seemed to rise up out of the ground, along with a vibration that tickled Lorena's legs, made her shift and scratch at the underside of her thighs. The noise rose in volume and depth, like giant tuning forks and gongs had been struck, the sound ringing all around them. Lorena's eardrums rattled, and a pain cinched its way down her spine.

The world around them exploded into a swirl of gray mist and terrible, thunderous noise.

CHAPTER
4

CONCERNS

Master George stood at the head of the table. He and the other Realitants were in the conference room of the Grand Canyon complex. George hadn't sat down since the meeting began, and he didn't know if he could. Sitting seemed like such a casual gesture, something done for rest and relaxation. How could he do that when the world—the *worlds*—were in such utter chaos?

"Been runnin' our lips for thirty minutes, we 'ave," Mothball was saying. Her stern expression made George incredibly sad. She hadn't smiled since Master Atticus had winked from existence. "And still not a flamin' thing done. Need to make some decisions, we do."

"Darn tootin' right," Sally added, the burly lumberjack of a man also looking gruffer than usual. "Get dem plans a'yorn hoppin' so we can quit gabbin' at each other. I'm downright sick of these here chat-and-chews."

Now it was Rutger's turn to speak up. "Look, you bunch of grumpy fusses—"

"That's enough," George interrupted. He hadn't needed to say it loudly or harshly. His little friend of so many years cut off and didn't argue. "Thank you. Just let me *think* for a second."

He looked around the room at Sato, Paul, and Sofia—the only other Realitants in attendance. Those three looked like youngsters who'd been thrown into the horrors of life far too early. And like people who'd lost a dear friend. Both of which were true. They sat slumped over, staring at the table, their faces turned toward the ground.

The other Realitants—people he'd worked with for countless years—couldn't afford to come to the meeting. They had too many problems to deal with in their own areas of responsibility. For now, this small group was all George had.

"Listen to me," George finally said. "I know that Master Atticus is on all of our minds. His . . . loss has put us on edge, and I don't believe we've said one nice thing to each other since he disappeared. But the world is in crisis, and we *must* meet our responsibilities. There are things we can do to help."

To say the world was in crisis was the understatement of the year. When Mistress Jane tried to sever the Fifth Reality with her new tool of dark matter, it had sent ripples of destruction throughout the universe, almost destroying it. Atticus seemed to have saved the day—or at least delayed the ultimate end—but the aftershocks were devastating.

Tornadoes, earthquakes, fires. Everywhere. Millions of people dead. The governments of the world were desperately trying to keep things under control and reach out to the hungry and wounded scattered all over.

Paul cleared his throat, and everyone looked at him. But before he spoke, his expression melted into something full of misery, and he sank back into his seat. Sofia reached out and squeezed his shoulder.

"Master Paul," George began, but he found himself empty of words. He suddenly lost every ounce of leadership he'd ever had in his bones. Despair threatened to swallow him whole.

Sato—who was usually rather quiet—suddenly shot to his feet and slammed a fist down on the table. "Snap out of it!" he yelled. "We all need to snap out of it! Quit moping around like babies and start acting like Realitants. If Tick were here, he'd be ashamed of us." He sat down, but his eyes burned as he gazed at each Realitant around him in turn. "I've got an army. The Fifth will do whatever they're asked. Just say the word, and we can get started."

George realized he was staring at the boy, transfixed. A spring of encouragement welled up inside him. "Thank you, Master Sato. I think we'd all agree that we needed that."

"Just make a decision. Do something. Or we'll go crazy."

George nodded then straightened his posture, his strength returning. "You're quite right, Sato. Quite right. Enough of our talk. Let's go around the room and make assignments. It is indeed time to get to work. If something comes up that seems more important, then we'll change those plans, but getting to work is our number one priority. Mothball, you first."

The giant of a lady looked as if a little bit of life had been breathed back into her as well. "Alright, then. I'll start winkin' me way from one end to the other—not just in Reality Prime but all of 'em. Start makin' reports and such. We don't know much, now do we? Not with the communications so bloomin' shot."

"Excellent idea," George said. "We need to determine exactly what's happening or we'll never know what direction to take in the long run."

"Your middle name Danger all a sudden?" Sally cut in with his booming voice. "You plan to hightail it this way and that all by your lonesome, do ya? Not on my tickety-tock watch, you ain't. I'll go with Mothball."

George loved the idea. "Perfect. Plans settled for two of us. Rutger, I think we both know what you need to do."

The fat little ball of a man shifted in his seat. "Um, well, I'd be happy to go on an adventure with my fine two friends, but . . . I seemed to have sprained my . . . elbow. Yes, yes, it's giving me quite the fits lately . . ."

"Master Rutger, please." George struggled to keep from laughing. "We all know very well that we need you here. Our instruments that survived the disasters have been reporting strange anomalies across the Realities. We need your keen researching mind devoted to solving that puzzle."

Visible relief washed over Rutger's features, but he tried to hide it with his words. "Oh, well, I guess you're right, then. Pity. I would've gladly risked further injury to my elbow to help Mothball and Sally."

"I have no doubt of it."

"Didn't know you could even see your elbow," Mothball muttered. "What with all that natural padding."

"Well, at least mine don't jut out like pelican beaks!" Rutger countered. "Try gaining a pound or two so we quit thinking a skeleton rose up from the dead to scare the willies out of us."

"Well, I would, now wouldn't I, if you bloody let us have a bite or two at supper before you gobbled it all down that fat neck of yours."

"Ah," George said through a sigh. "This is more like it. If you two are going at it with each other, then at least *something* is right in the world."

"What about us?" Sofia asked. It was the first time she'd spoken since the meeting began, and her soft voice was sad but strong. These new Realitants had life in them yet. "Our families are fine—we've checked on them, visited them—so we can do whatever you need us to do now."

"Yeah," Paul added, a little more spirit in his face too. "I can't sit around this place one more second, listening to Rutger brag about his cooking and telling stupid jokes."

George looked at Sato. "And you?"

The boy folded his arms across his chest. "I said I'm ready. And my army is too."

"Okay, then." George thought a moment. There were countless things that needed to be done throughout the Realities. Where to start? "Sato, I want you to go back to the

Thirteenth Reality and destroy the remaining creatures that Jane manufactured at the Factory. We need to make sure that world is safe and back to the way it was meant to be."

"Done," Sato said immediately, without the slightest hint of fear.

"And . . . us?" Paul asked.

George put his hands on the table and leaned forward. "You two are going to pay a visit to a very old friend of mine. She lives in the Third Reality, and we can only hope that she doesn't eat you for supper when you arrive."

CHAPTER
5

SQUISHY GRASS

Lisa screamed when it happened, but she couldn't hear her voice over the terrible sounds of thunder that pounded the air like detonating bombs. One second she'd been sitting in the forest, looking at her mom and the Barrier Wand, hearing a hum and feeling vibrations in her legs. The next, she'd been whipped into a tornado of swirling gray air, spinning, the world tilting all around her. The noises pounding her skull. She tried to find her mom—at least *see* her—but there was nothing. Only a gray whirlpool of smoke.

And then it ended. Abruptly.

Lisa's body slammed onto soft, squishy ground. She immediately felt moisture seeping through her clothes and jumped to her feet—which was a bad idea. Her mind was still recovering from whatever she'd just been through and dizziness twirled inside of her until she fell right back down. She was lying on a huge field of grass, saturated with rain.

Heavy clouds hung in the sky above her, making the day seem dark.

Her mom was close, the Barrier Wand in her lap. She sat up and stared at Lisa, dazed.

"What . . . ?" Lisa began.

"I have no idea," her mom replied. "All I did was try to latch on to Atticus's nanolocator and pull him in. It shouldn't have sent *us* somewhere else."

"Well, unless we went back in time to before trees grew in Deer Park, it sent us *somewhere.* We were sitting in the woods about three minutes ago."

Lisa hated the feeling of the wet grass soaking her pants, so she tried standing again, this time much slower. Her legs wobbled a bit, and the endless sea of grass tilted a few times, but soon she was steady.

She turned in a slow circle, taking in the view of the place to which they'd been winked. Super green grass stretched in every direction, running down a slope toward a stream that splashed and sparkled as it cut across a rocky bed. On the other side of the stream, trees dotted the land, growing thicker and taller until they became a huge forest. There was no sign of civilization anywhere.

"Mom?"

"Yeah?"

"Where in the world are we?"

⁓

Three hours of searching didn't answer that question.

They walked together to the stream, crossed over at a

narrow spot where large rocks jutted out of the rushing waters, then explored the other side. They eventually made their way to where the trees thickened into a dark, ominous forest. They'd found no clues or signs of life—human, anyway—and when they stood at the wall of pines and oaks, it was almost as if they were stopped by an invisible barrier.

"Why can't I get myself to go any farther?" Lisa asked.

Her mom's answer didn't help. "Because we're in a strange land, and there might be hideous monsters in there."

"Good point. Let's just walk around the edge of it; maybe we'll stumble across something eventually."

"As good a plan as any."

They set off, Lisa right behind her mom, who still hefted the golden rod of the Barrier Wand in her hands.

"Tell me more about the old days," Lisa said. The clouds still churned above, dark and heavy, but it had yet to rain again. At least the air was nice and cool.

"The old days?" her mom repeated.

"Yeah. You used to be a Realitant. How'd you go from that to being a stay-at-home mom? Seems kind of lame."

"Lame? You wish you had a different woman stomping around the house telling you what to do?"

Lisa snickered at the image. "No, you're way too good at it. It's just . . . being a Realitant seems so cool and adventurous. What happened to make you give it up?"

The land started to rise up, and the walk was getting a little harder. Lisa saw the crest of the rise a few hundred feet ahead. She hoped they'd see something there. Something helpful. Her mom still hadn't answered.

"You awake up there?" she asked her.

"Oh, I'm awake. I'm just thinking about your question. It's more complicated than you know. It's making me remember a lot of things, and I'm not even sure where to start explaining."

"How'd you join them? How'd they recruit you?"

Her mom laughed softly. "It wasn't much different from how they recruited Atticus. Some letters, clues, and riddles. It was kind of easy, actually."

"How long were you a member?"

"About four years, maybe a little longer. It wasn't all the exciting adventure you think it was—and nothing like what our poor boy has gone through—except for . . ." She trailed off, and there was something dark in her words, like the storm that brewed far above them.

Lisa pushed her. "Except for what?"

"I wasn't actually there, but I was still technically a Realitant when . . . when Sato's parents were killed. Mistress Jane had been getting more and more suspicious. Acting weird. And it all came to a head that night, when she started using the powers she'd stolen from the Thirteenth. She crossed a line, and Sato's mom and dad paid the price for standing up to it. Nearly all of them there that night did."

"What happened?"

"Jane burned that poor boy's parents to death." She said it so simply, but the words were horrible enough. "I didn't know the world could be so evil. I wanted out. I'm ashamed in many ways—for abandoning the Realitants, abandoning my friends—but I don't regret it. There's a difference, you know. I chose my family, and I've never once regretted that."

Lisa felt guilty, like she'd stirred up feelings her mom didn't deserve to have. "Well, Tick and I are glad you did. And think about it—if you hadn't done such a good job of raising him, he would've been a stinky Realitant instead of a *good* Realitant, and he wouldn't have saved the world. See? Makes perfect sense."

"You're a sweet little thing," her mom replied.

"Yeah, I know. I've gotta have *some* way of making sure I stay your favorite."

They reached a sudden rise in the slope that was steeper than before, which made Lisa feel even stronger that some kind of revelation waited on the other side.

She trotted ahead to pull even with her mom, who hadn't slowed a bit. "We better be careful," she whispered. "There might be something over this hill that we don't want to see us."

Her mom nodded. "You've got the caution of a Realitant. Maybe old George will make you one after we save Atticus and bring him home."

"Maybe. Come on."

Lisa dropped to her knees and started crawling up the steep rise. Her mom crawled right next to her, holding the Barrier Wand awkwardly on her shoulder.

"You want me to take a turn with that?" Lisa asked.

"No, thanks. I made this one, and I want to keep it nice and close right now."

"When did you make it?"

"I'll tell you later."

They reached the top of the hill, where the land flattened for a couple of feet then dropped again, plummeting down another slope to the land beyond. When she saw what awaited them, Lisa forgot she was supposed to be careful, and she poked her head up, gawking so that anyone within miles could see her if they looked hard enough.

In the middle of a flat plain, there was a castle. Half of it had been destroyed, with stone and rock and wood collapsed in heaps around the edges of the destruction. Black figures crawled over the ruins like ants.

"What *are* those things?" Lisa whispered.

Her mom answered in a deadened voice. "Creatures of the Thirteenth Reality. Creatures of Mistress Jane. Just as Atticus described them." She turned to Lisa, her face pale. "How did we end up *here*?"

CHAPTER 6

POOR MR. CHU

Tick sat on a rock and stared at the ocean.

Though it wasn't any normal ocean. The color of it changed about every three minutes, going from blackish-blue to red to orange, morphing in waves as though someone flew along the surface, spilling huge buckets of food coloring. Fish leaped out of the waters, but sometimes land animals did as well. Deer. Lions. Elephants.

The Nonex made no sense whatsoever. And things seemed to be growing even more unstable lately, sharp up-ticks in the madness. Like the thumping sound and earthquake attack of the day before. It was all a mixed soup for the senses, and it was beginning to make Tick want to hit somebody. Namely a grumpy, arrogant man named Reginald Chu.

Tick hated the man. Far more than he hated Mistress Jane, for whom he still felt an enormous amount of guilt—he'd scarred the woman for life, after all. And despite her evil ways, she'd shown moments where she doubted the path she'd chosen. If anything, Tick had driven her more toward the darkness.

But Chu was different. The man seemed crazy, and crazy wasn't an excuse for being bad. Every single thing he said or did pointed to one thing for him—power. Dominating others. Ruling. Just the other night, the three of them had been sitting around a fire, talking about theories on how they could make it back to Reality Prime. The conversation hadn't lasted ten minutes before Chu went off about how they needed to hurry, take some risks, because he might be losing his stranglehold on the Fourth Reality. With all the destruction and chaos happening, he feared someone else might be trying to take over what had once been his.

Tick had stared him in the eyes and told him to shut up. And Chu did. Which made Tick feel like king of the world, at least for a little while.

Jane and Chu were scared of him; Tick had no doubt about that. He'd shown them that he had more control of his powers over Reality and quantum physics—lifting firewood, igniting fires, making the sand leap into the air and swirl into shapes—than ever before. One time, as a joke, he levitated Chu, spinning him in a circle a few times. Even Jane had laughed, and when Chu came crashing back to the ground with a loud flump and a grunt, Tick had expected the man to be enraged. But instead, he simply stood up, brushed himself off, and told Tick he hoped the boy would come work for him some day, that a boy with such power was destined to do great things.

That was Chu, though. Always thinking about power. Always planning his next step to world domination. What a big, fat jerk. Tick didn't like the feeling that such hatred gave him—like his insides were rotting—but he couldn't help it.

There was the crack of a broken twig in the woods behind Tick. He turned to see Chu leaning out from behind a tree, staring at him.

"That's kind of creepy," Tick said. "Spying on a little boy like that."

"Spying?" Chu replied. "What exactly am I spying on? You sitting like a frog on a log, staring at nothing? We're wasting time. Jane agrees with me."

Chu walked out of the woods and approached Tick, coming to stand next to him. Tick didn't bother standing up or offering to slide over for the man to sit down.

"What exactly would you want me to be doing right now?" Tick asked him, returning his gaze to the ocean, which had turned a pinkish color. "Building us a log cabin so we'll have a place to mope about while we're stuck here?"

"We need your power, and you know it. Jane is willing to take some risks. You should be too. We're all getting a little crazier with every passing day. We need to *do* something!" The man's voice had risen with each word until he was shouting.

Tick stood up and faced him. "I know. We'll do it when I'm ready. I trust my instincts a lot more than I do your mad desire to get back and stomp on people. *Chill.* Please."

Chu looked utterly stunned, and it was a beautiful thing

to see. Tick had to hold back the smile that wanted to leap across his face. He almost felt sorry for Chu, and decided to throw him a bone, out of guilt.

"Tomorrow," he said, sitting back down. "We'll try something tomorrow."

CHAPTER
7

TRICKS ON THE BEACH

Things had changed for Tick when he battled Mistress Jane outside the Factory in the Thirteenth Reality. They'd changed drastically.

He'd been driven by pure and absolute desperation. He'd done what he needed to do for the Haunce, healing the damage done by Jane that would've ended Reality and the universe. And when he'd had to fight Jane afterwards, he'd known more than ever that death was his reward if he messed up. Though maybe he'd learned some things from the Haunce that he hadn't realized.

When he and Mistress Jane were going at each other like two wizards settling a centuries-old spat, Tick's mind had been focused on his Chi'karda like never before, channeling it, funneling it, *understanding* it. He didn't really know how he knew—he could never sit down and write a book about it or explain it to someone—it was like walking or running or breathing. Things just clicked, and suddenly he *knew* how to do it. His body and instincts and mind all worked together to use the Chi'karda and manipulate the world of quantum physics. He felt like a magician. A magician of science.

And it was *fun*.

Now it was early the next day, when he'd promised Chu they'd try to get out of the Nonex, and Tick had spent the morning out on the beach, practicing his new abilities. He had stacked three logs vertically, end to end, pointing toward the sky. He used his mind and pushed out with his senses, touching the strings and pulleys of the unseen particles of science. Carefully, he moved one, and then another one. The tower stood thirty or forty feet in the air.

"Impressive," Chu said. "Really. Can we get on with it and do something that actually matters now?"

Tick suddenly had an image pop in his head of Chu's giant mountain palace, and how bad things had gone there. That was where Tick had hurt Jane, where he had almost died. Sofia had risked her life to save him. Remembering it again made Tick angry.

He shifted his thoughts and pushed his Chi'karda. The stacked logs flew through the air and shot toward Chu like spears. He cried out and started to run, but Tick was one step ahead of him, turning the logs vertical again and slamming them into the ground in a circle around Chu. He was in a prison, the logs thick enough and close enough together that he couldn't squeeze between them.

"Stop acting like a child!" Chu screamed, facing Tick with rage burned into his expression. "Take these things down! Now!"

Tick looked over at Jane, whose red mask had tilted up slightly in a smile. Her yellow robe and hood stirred in the slight breeze of the day, and images of her past deeds popped into Tick's mind as well. He almost used his Chi'karda to throw some things at her, too, but remembered that she could fight back.

Maybe it *was* time for Tick to quit acting like a brat. He didn't feel like himself lately. They needed to get out of the Nonex. Not just for his own life, but so he could see what was going on back at home. His family and friends could be in danger, maybe even dead. The thought made his heart sink. He'd already tried winking a message to them, but it didn't work.

"Atticus," Chu said, obviously trying to remain calm. "Please. I don't want to interfere with your powers. I'm not an idiot. But I know you want to get out of this place just as much as I do. I can't go back and change the past, but—"

"Shut up!" Tick yelled. He didn't know where all this anger was coming from. "I don't want to hear any lame apologies from you. We all know you're planning to go right back to doing what you do if we get back to the Realities. Well, guess what? I'm not going to let you. So keep that in mind."

Before Chu could respond, Tick exploded the logs, breaking down their substance into millions of tiny splinters and swirling them away in a cloud of wooden mist. He purposefully let a few splinters nick Chu in the face and arms. The man cried out again and gingerly touched the sore spots. Guilt immediately racked Tick, mixed with a little bit of satisfaction.

"Tick," Mistress Jane began in her scratchy, painful voice. "Preach all you want about what we've done in our past. But look at yourself. You're heading down the same road. Maybe you should have waited until you could control your power before you started judging others. Power is a . . . powerful thing. I don't know how else to put it."

Her words made Tick even angrier. "Don't you dare say that. I would never—never—use my power to hurt other people like you have."

Jane's mask smiled broadly. "Then what did you just do to Reginald?"

Tick looked sharply at the man, who had several spots of blood on his face and arms. He wanted to get defensive, explain that he was just giving Chu some of his own medicine, but a small part of him knew that Jane was right. No one was born thinking they'd rule the world someday. It developed in baby steps, a slippery slope. He had to be careful.

"He deserves every bad thing that could ever happen to him," Tick said, defiant. "But I won't do something like that again. I promise."

"Yeah, right," Chu responded, glaring at him. "You just wait, kid. Wait until you start to feel the joy of being stronger than someone else. You'll be working beside me before you turn twenty years old. That's a guarantee."

Tick looked at him without answering.

"Let's get to work," Jane said. "Nothing matters if we can't get back to the real world."

Tick felt a little lost right then. A little confused. And scared at what might happen when they started messing with Reality on a big scale. He decided to set everything aside and quit thinking for a while. They had nothing to lose, and he could deal with his feelings about what Jane had said later.

"Okay." Tick pointed down the beach at the campfire that had become their central meeting spot. "Let's go sit down."

"And we're not standing up again until we're in a different Reality," Chu said as he started walking that way. "I can't stand one more day in this place."

Tick and Jane exchanged a glance. She said nothing, her mask melting into a blank expression, and Tick wondered what was going on inside her head. He shrugged, and then the two of them followed Chu to the campfire.

They sat on the stumpy logs they'd brought out on the first day, circling the small flames that spit and hissed as they burned. The fire smelled good, and Tick remembered campouts with his family. The memory hurt his heart, and he swore to do just as Chu had said. They needed to get out of the Nonex.

"We've talked for hours about every theory in the book," Chu said. "Time to put up or shut up, as they say. What are we going to try?"

Tick had listened to every conversation they'd had in the Nonex, and he understood most of them. Master George had made him study pretty much every science book ever written. But none of it seemed to matter right then. The only thing he trusted was his instinct.

He realized Jane was talking, but he'd completely tuned out. Feeling a sudden boldness and certainty, he interrupted her.

"I know what we need to do."

CHAPTER
8

ONE QUESTION

Paul had been waiting for this day for a long time. A mission for the Realitants for which he was in charge. Of course, Sofia probably thought *she* was the boss, and he'd let her keep thinking that, but he knew the truth.

This was Paul's time.

Master George had ushered them into his little office, where they sat on a small couch, and he was perched on a wooden chair with his Barrier Wand balanced on top of his lap. He had a grave look on his face, which was business as usual since the whole world had fallen into chaos.

"Are you both ready?" the old man asked.

Paul nodded.

Sofia cleared her throat. "Of course we are. But you haven't really told us much about what we're supposed to do."

Their fearless leader pursed his lips, looking as if he had a whole bunch of nasty thoughts in his head that he didn't want to share. "The Third Reality is one we haven't charted very well, and, given recent events, we've lost all other means of communication with the Realitant we originally sent there. She can be quite . . . difficult, and she's made it clear that supervising the Third Reality is her job and her job alone. I need you to find her and ask her a very important question."

"You said something about her wanting to eat us," Paul said. "This chick a wolverine or something?"

"No, no, no," Master George grumbled. "And I highly suggest you not say such things to her when you meet. And most certainly, I recommend you not call her a . . . what did you say? A chick?"

Paul shrugged. He wasn't worried—he'd have this lady cooling her jets with some of his simple charm and good looks. No biggie.

"I think I'll do the talking," Sofia muttered. "Don't worry."

"Her name is Gretel," Master George continued. "The woman has a nasty temper, the worst I've ever seen. She makes Mistress Jane look like a princess on a pony. And she's been a bit . . . at odds with me for some time now. But she's brilliant, and I plan to send you with full means to communicate back to me through your nanolocators. Your first task is to reach her. Make sure she is calm. And then ask the question."

Paul thought the whole mission seemed a little strange. "What's this big question we're supposed to ask?"

Their leader hefted the Barrier Wand in his hands and

studied it, though his gaze was distant, as though he was trying to stall for time.

"Well?" Paul pushed.

"You may not understand it, but I need you to say these exact words to her. Are you ready? Though short, I've taken the liberty of writing it down on pieces of paper I've slipped into your packs."

"Sheesh," Paul said. "Just spill it already."

"Here it is," the man said, looking very serious indeed. "Six words: *May I please use your bathroom?*"

⌒⌒⌒

Paul was still snickering about the ridiculous question when the old man winked them to the Third Reality. Master George had refused to explain any further, saying that those six words were all they needed to know. They'd be sent to a place near a path. Follow the path. Find a house. Knock on the door. Ask the question: "May I please use your bathroom?"

Easy peasy.

Well, worst-case scenario, they'd be able to utilize the facilities before heading back.

Paul and Sofia stood on a soggy, muddy trail that cut ahead of them through marshland and swamp. The air was muggy and seemed to stick in Paul's lungs when he breathed, and the heat made it worse. They'd only been there for half a minute, and he was already sweating head to toe.

Trees rose up out of the black waters of the swamp, moss and vines hanging from their branches. There were the sounds of frogs and crickets and a million other bugs and creatures, and a fragrance that was an inch short of disgusting. Rotten eggs and burnt toast.

"Let me get this straight," Paul said. "This lady could live pretty much anywhere in the thirteen Realities, and she chose to live here?"

Sofia had her annoyed look set firmly on her face. "Do you even listen when Master George talks? He said that she was sent here to study this Reality. That's why she lives here."

"And this whole world is a swamp? I'm pretty sure they have a mountain or two somewhere. A sweet forest dig. A *desert* would be better than this."

"I just hope Master George didn't send us here so we'd be out of the way."

Paul snorted. "You kidding? He probably figured we'd drunk a ton of water, so here we are—waiting to ask if we can use this lady's bathroom."

"I wonder who died here, or how many," was Sofia's reply.

Sometimes she chose to ignore his comments as her best line of defense. Paul didn't mind. "Maybe there was a battle or something. It sure isn't a graveyard."

"It looks like the path starts here and goes in that direction." She pointed down the long trail, which wound its way through the nasty, steaming marshland.

"I bet we get bitten by mosquitos the size of my dad's truck."

"Probably."

"We'll get malaria and die."

"Probably."

"Okay. Let's go."

⁓

They reached Gretel's house about ten minutes later.

It was the exact kind of place Paul expected would be in the middle of a swamp. Old, moss-covered wood, the sideboards of the small cottage warped from too much moisture. Faded, worn paint that used to be white. A screen door that was half off its hinges. A porch that looked like it was about to collapse. The biggest trees they'd seen yet surrounded the place.

Paul had sworn to himself that he wouldn't make any Hansel and Gretel jokes since he'd first heard the woman's name from Master George, but he couldn't resist.

"We forgot to drop pieces of bread on our way here."

Sofia gave him a fake courtesy laugh. "I was waiting for that."

"Comedy never works when it's obvious."

Sofia flashed him a smile that *wasn't* fake, and Paul broke out in goose bumps. He hoped she couldn't tell. He started walking toward the porch to hide it.

When he reached the steps of the porch, he couldn't help but hesitate. It seemed as if their feet would crash right through if they dared take one step on the old, rotten boards. But before he could take that first step, the front door tore open with a bang. The screen that had barely been hanging on fell off completely. It clanged against the porch, bent and torn.

An old, old woman stood in the doorway, a huge knife in one hand and a pistol in the other. Paul yelped and backed away. He ran into Sofia, and they both collapsed to the soggy ground.

Gretel moved forward, the boards creaking under her feet. She had gray hair springing in all directions, a face as wrinkled as a newborn pup, and a tattered dress that looked as if it hadn't been washed in years. But her body seemed strong, solid. Especially the fingers gripped around those two weapons.

"How dare old Georgy Porgy send two *rats* here to nibble on my cheese," she said, her voice low but somehow full of venom. "I told him what would happen if he did that. I sure did. Death, true and true."

The old lady lifted her pistol and aimed it at Paul's face.

CHAPTER
9

A DUSTY ROAD

Whoa! Whoa! Whoa!" Paul shouted, holding his hands up as he got to his feet. Sofia did the same next to him. "You haven't heard why we came yet!"

Gretel cocked the old silver pistol and took a step forward. She kept the barrel pointed directly at Paul. "Don't need hearing your nonsense, boy. I'm here for a reason, and that reason is more important than two pipsqueak babies begging for their lives on my lawn."

Paul's immediate instinct was to tell her she was crazy for calling the mud and weeds on which they stood a *lawn*. Luckily, Sofia spoke up before he could, as calm and collected as a sheriff in an old Western movie.

"You want to shoot us, Gretel? Go right ahead. But you'll need to answer our question before you do."

Her words took the lady aback a little, as it did Paul. Was this really the time to ask if they could use her bathroom?

Then again, Paul thought it was the dumbest thing he'd ever heard come out of George's mouth anyway.

"A question, you say?" Gretel responded. "You say you have a question for me?"

"That's right," Sofia said. "Just one. May I please use your bathroom?"

The old woman swung her gun away from Paul and pointed it off somewhere in the distance. She pulled the trigger, and a boom rocked the air and smoke puffed up from the gun. Gretel spun the pistol on her finger like a cowboy and smiled, her teeth looking like they'd chewed one too many chicken bones throughout the years.

"Yes, you may, my darling," she said. "Yes, you may. Do come in."

Sofia glanced back at Paul, who shrugged. They both headed up the steps of the rickety old porch.

———

Mothball had always prided herself on being a nice, genuine person who could see the good in everyone. Yes, she loved to tease and rib, but deep down she had a heart of gold, soft and snuggly and warm. At least, that's what *she* liked to think.

But Sally irritated the living jeepers out of her. How in the bloody tarnations had she ended up with *him* on this mission? The man was like a walking bullhorn, he was.

"So, Miss Purty Legs," he said as they walked down a long country road in the Twelfth Reality. "Whatcha thinkin' this old bag of cornfeed's gonna help us with?"

"Don't know as yet," she replied. "Just hopin' I can hear a bloody word that comes out of his mouth over your yappin' tongue. No offense, of course."

Sally bellowed his deep, booming laugh. "None taken, missy. None taken. You should be used to yappin' after hanging out with that friend a'yorn. Rutger could talk the ear off an elephant."

Mothball couldn't help it—she laughed too. Sally always knew how to make her smile eventually. "The wee little fat man can talk, no doubt about it."

"Anyhoo, why we startin' with this farm boy again?"

Though she could swear she'd already explained this to him, Mothball did so again. "He's not really a Realitant, but he's a friend of ours. Lives out in the boonies so as he can keep tabs better without worryin' over communications and such. Watches over the world, he does. Has every satellite and radio and cell service you can dream up in this quaint little Reality. We pay him right nicely, too. He'll know what the goings-on are about."

"*Goings-on are about?*" Sally repeated. "What the heckamajibber does that mean?"

"We need to find what's the trouble here. We're on a research mission, silly bones. Clean out them bloody ears, would ya? Master George explained it all right nicely. Gathering information, we are."

"Well, I sho 'nuff knew that! I'm just tryin' to figger out how you people speak in them fancy lands a'yorn."

"I know the feeling," Mothball muttered under her breath.

They reached a dusty old mailbox on the side of the road

with the word "Tanner" printed on the side in faded black letters. A long, gravel driveway cut through a cornfield before disappearing into a grove of trees about a half a mile away.

"Here we are," Mothball said. "He's waiting for us I 'spect."

Thankfully Sally didn't say another word as they started walking down the long driveway.

~~~

Rutger sat in front of his huge screen, reviewing all the data he'd gathered from the instruments spread throughout the Realities. The ones that had survived the destruction, anyway.

He missed Mothball.

Yes, she was a tall sack of bones who took every chance she got to make fun of him. But she was also his best friend, and he hated thinking of her out there without him, especially considering how dangerous things had become. A world suffering from chaos that you *can't* help breeds chaos that you *can*. The thieves and looters and murderers would be out in full force now that the police, firemen, and other authorities were occupied with search and rescue.

Of course, Mothball was a tough old bear. She'd be fine.

He began scrolling through the data—everything from weather reports to measurements of quantum anomalies in atmosphere particle waves. The data was haywire, still settling from the massive disruptions caused by that red-faced Mistress Jane and her attempt to sever the Fifth Reality from existence. What a disaster that had been, saved only by the inexplicable powers of Master Tick. However, it seemed as if

54

saving the universe from one final and all-ending catastrophe had created lots of smaller ones.

Something caught his eye.

He zoomed in to take a look at one of the measuring stations located in an old forest in the Third Reality; a box of instruments had been left there almost a decade ago. There'd been an absolute *flurry* of activity there just a couple of days earlier, spiking the Chi'karda levels through the roof. And then it had ended abruptly, going from immeasurably high to zero in an instant. Rutger read through it all, trying his best to interpret what it could mean.

He noticed that the information had an attachment: a photograph. Many of the instrument boxes had cameras installed nearby, but Rutger was surprised to see that something had been taken and sent before whatever had happened to end the data flow. The box had to have been destroyed eventually.

He was so anxious that his fat fingers hit the wrong key twice, but he finally opened up the attached picture.

There were trees—lots of them. And down the middle of the photo, a gash, as if someone had painted over the forest scene with an image of a beach. And on that beach was Mistress Jane, looking toward the camera with her menacing red mask. Over her shoulder, standing a ways behind her in the sand, was another figure.

Rutger quickly zoomed in, leaning forward to get a better look. His gasp echoed throughout the entire Realitant headquarters.

It was Tick.

CHAPTER
10

PROBING

The air around Tick hummed.

He, Chu, and Mistress Jane had been holding hands for more than an hour, eyes closed, the campfire slowly dying. Tick could barely hear the last flickers of its flames over the thrumming sound that came from the Chi'karda that burned between the three linked humans. Anyone who might have observed the group from afar would have seen a massive cloud of tiny orange lights, a fiery mist that churned and boiled around them.

Chu, of course, had no power whatsoever over the realm of quantum physics. He had never known any kind of power unless it was manufactured with technology. But Tick and Jane were a different story. They both had control over the mysterious force that ruled all existence—Jane, because she'd been forever melded with the largest Barrier Wand ever created, and Tick, because of reasons no one had quite figured out yet. Master George had merely said he was on to something that might explain it and that it involved soulikens.

But they'd never really had a chance to talk about it, had they?

Tick couldn't allow his mind to wander. He pushed away the thoughts trying to barrel their way in and focused on the task at hand. Escaping the Nonex.

Jane and Chu had agreed to his plan without argument. It seemed they both had grown desperate to get out and were willing to rely on Tick's idea. He had, after all, worked directly with the Haunce and saved the entire universe.

And that's what Tick was banking on. Mistress Jane had channeled her Chi'karda—every last drop that she could muster—into Tick for him to use as he needed. Tick had gathered it in, mixing it with his own until he had more of the natural force around him—and within him—than any human should be able to endure. A few weeks ago it would've killed him instantly.

But he had learned so much.

The Chi'karda raged. It was pure power, collected into one place like a newborn star ready to explode with heat and energy. But Tick kept it at bay, probed it, felt it, soothed it in some way. The feel of it was pure and clean, like an inferno burning inside his chest.

He didn't know exactly what he was looking for, but he had a good idea. A sense more than anything. Tick felt like someone was standing right behind him, just inches away. His eyes couldn't see them, but he knew someone was there all the same.

The Haunce had taught him a valuable lesson. Reality spoke to you in interesting ways—not in the formulas and equations of mathematicians and scientists, nor in the dry, lengthy descriptions found in dusty old textbooks. Reality was on another level altogether, at one with our minds. It spoke to you in the best way your own self can speak back. And that's what Tick wanted as he probed things he didn't understand with the power of Chi'karda.

He was looking for a riddle.

Lorena Higginbottom knew her stuff.

She'd suspected from the very second they'd appeared on that rain-slicked grass that her Barrier Wand had winked her and Lisa into the Thirteenth Reality. Something about the smell and feel of the place had been her first clue. The big forest—with no signs of technology or civilization around—had been her next clue. And then, when they'd stumbled up to the top of that ridge and had seen Mistress Jane's ruined castle, any remaining doubt had vanished.

She knew that castle because she'd been there before. Just once. But that had been enough.

Now it was a collapsed shell of its former self, broken and crumbled. Fangen and other creatures swarmed what still stood, but they were too far away to know exactly what they were doing. But if she could help it, Lorena wouldn't take her daughter one step closer to find out.

They'd sneaked back down the hill until the castle was out of sight and entered the outskirts of the forest they'd been trying to avoid. They needed cover, and time to think. The dark depths of the woods chilled her, though, and she kept a wary eye out for intruders.

"So what are we going to do?" Lisa asked. They'd been whispering back and forth for a while now, but no solid plan had solidified yet.

"Well, like I said," Lorena answered, "my first instinct is to get ourselves back to that place we winked into and get out of this scary Reality."

"But?" Lisa prodded.

"But there has to be *some* reason we were pulled here. I was trying to isolate Atticus's nanolocator, pushing the Chi'karda levels to the extreme, and somehow, instead of bringing him to us, it brought us here."

"But why?"

Lorena had to refrain from giving her daughter an impatient look. "Well, dear, that's what I think we need to figure out. If we just wink back home, we'll never know."

Lisa opened her mouth to answer, but she didn't say anything as a sound came from deeper in the woods, like the whoosh of wind blowing through an open door.

Lorena searched the darkness between the trees but saw no sign of movement. The strange noise stopped after several seconds.

She and Lisa didn't say anything—they didn't need to. They were in the Thirteenth Reality, after all, a couple of miles from Mistress Jane's castle. Caution had already been strong, and now things were on full alert. They both stood up, slowly and quietly, reaching out to take each other's hand. Lorena held the Wand in her free hand, ready to club something if she had to. The Chi'karda levels weren't quite high enough to wink away from where they were.

Something crunched up ahead. Twigs cracked on the ground. Then again. And again. There was no sign of the source of the sound, but it was coming closer.

"Just step away," Lorena whispered. "Quickly now."

They faced the forest as they began to walk backwards, their footsteps also crunching through the underbrush. Lisa's hand was shaking, and sweat slicked her palm. The noises continued, but Lorena *still* couldn't see who was approaching. The mystery stranger picked up its pace, heading for them. The time for caution was gone.

"Run, Lisa!" she barked. "Run!"

She turned and yanked on Lisa's hand, pulling her along as she sprinted for the grassy hill outside the fringe of the woods.

Their pursuer picked up its pace to catch them, but then the sound of footsteps abruptly ceased, replaced by that whooshing sound again. A wind rose up into the air and over their heads, the noise of it making Lorena scream and look skyward.

When she saw what hovered above them, she cried out again and collapsed to the ground, pulling Lisa down with her. She rolled onto her back and stared at the thing that had come after them.

It was a creature with slanted, burning yellow eyes, its body made of what looked like ropes of gray smoke, coiled together to make a long body with arms and legs. It flew through the air, darting back and forth above them like a hawk examining its prey. Another smoky creature flew out of the forest to join its haunted companion. They circled, their yellow eyes leaving streaks of light in the air.

Lorena was frozen in place, squeezing her daughter's hand and holding the Wand to her chest.

The two wispy creatures abruptly flew down to the ground and grabbed Lorena and Lisa by their arms. Gripping them strongly, they lifted them to their feet with a painful jerk. And then they started marching the two terrified ladies back toward the slope of the hill.

Back toward the castle.

CHAPTER
11

A POND IN THE SNOW

The stairs hadn't broken when Paul walked up them, nor had the porch collapsed, potentially dropping them into a heap of spiders and snakes and rats. There'd been a lot of creaks and groans, but he and Sofia had made it to the front door and through it unscathed.

The inside of Gretel's home looked nothing like the outside. As soon as Paul stepped through the door, he knew that the dilapidated exterior of the shack was a disguise, something to make thieves and thugs figure they might as well not bother. He and Sofia stood in a lushly carpeted living room with fancy furniture—all leather and frilly carved wood—and portraits of grim-looking people on the walls. A fire crackled in a brick fireplace, and the air smelled of cinnamon.

"Nice place you got here," Paul said. "I'm glad you didn't shoot us or stab us before we got a chance to check it out."

Sofia elbowed Paul in the ribs. "Thank you for inviting us in. That's what my rude friend meant to say."

Gretel looked back and forth between her two visitors, her tongue cocked inside one of her cheeks as she examined them. "George and I've always had an arrangement. You kids understand? What I'm doing here is too important to let any jackawillie barge in here and mess with my stuff. He promised to never tell anyone that the password question was a test, and to never give it out unless it was serious business. Serious, serious business. I reckon we have things to talk about."

Sofia nodded. "Yes, we do."

"I don't think we know *what* we're supposed to talk about," Paul said. "Could you help us out with that?"

The old lady grinned again, showing her gnarly teeth. "George wouldn't have sent ya with that question unless it was something particular. The whole reason I'm here in the first place. And let me guess—*you're* here because of the earthquake I had."

"Yes!" Sofia answered.

Paul suspected that the lady didn't know the extent of the damage to all the Realities yet; she obviously wasn't communicating with anyone on a regular basis. "How bad was it?" he asked her.

"Shook me right out of my bed, I can tell you that. Ruined my dream about Clark Gable, too. I was half in a tizzy, grabbed my gun and shot a bullet straight through my roof. Thing *still* drips. Don't listen to that nonsense about how duct tape can fix anything and everything."

Paul was really starting to like this woman. "Who's Clark Gable?"

"Never you mind. Now have a seat, enjoy the flames. I'll be back with some warm milk and cookies." She started walking toward the kitchen.

"You *do* know it's really hot outside, right?" Paul asked as he and Sofia took a seat on a leather couch. They sank half a foot into the deep cushions.

Gretel turned to face them. "Yes, son. But I'm old, and old people get cold even if they're in a desert. Plus, the things we're going to talk about today are gonna chill us right to the bone. I think we both know that."

She slipped into the kitchen before they could respond.

~~~

Tick was in a trance.

He felt like an oracle from ancient times, going through a ritual to call down the rain. He still held hands with Chu and Jane, but he was barely aware of it. Eyes squeezed shut, he saw only a dark swirl of orange and black in his vision, and the air hummed heavily with the power of Chi'karda. His skin prickled with chills and sweat at the same time.

He'd been at it for hours, poking the depths of Reality with his senses, looking for something to represent a way out of the Nonex. He felt like an astronaut in deep space, slinging himself from one galaxy to the next, sending out probes to see if he might capture the right data he needed. He'd been on the verge of giving up—his muscles aching, his mind exhausted—when he finally found what he'd been searching for.

A doorway. A portal in the darkness, framed by that eerie orange light.

He mentally flew towards it. The opening expanded, growing larger and larger as he approached. Everything was symbolic now, and he went with what came. His body—his conscience, his imagination, his thoughts—catapulted through the portal, and suddenly the air exploded with light. He closed his eyes. He no longer felt the hands or presence of his two partners, even though he knew they were still there. Until this was over, Tick was on his own.

His feet touched a hard surface, and within his mind, he opened his eyes again.

He stood in a field of white snow. The sky above him was a piercingly clear blue, and the sun shone down with all its power, reflecting off the whiteness with a brilliant light that he'd first felt when entering the portal that had brought him here. He turned in a circle and saw that there was absolutely nothing in any direction. Just flat land and snow as far as he could see.

If anything could symbolize the Nonex, this was it.

There was one thing. Off in the distance, maybe fifty feet away, he thought he saw something blue—a bruise on the endless sea of white. He headed that way, his feet crunching and sinking slightly in the cold stuff below him with every step. There was no wind, but the coldness of the air bit into his skin, as if someone had just flicked on his senses with a switch. He looked down at his clothes and saw them magically transform from what he'd been wearing by the fire back on the beach to a huge parka and heavy pants and boots. Gloves and a thick wool hat on his head completed the transformation. Much better.

As he got closer to the spot of blue, it grew in size, but not just because he approached it. It literally *grew,* expanding outward like a drop of food coloring on a paper towel. Tick stopped and watched as its leading edge came toward him, then stopped at his feet. He could see that it was frozen water, but the icy lake seemed unnatural, as if it were made up of that nasty colored stuff used to create small ponds at the miniature golf place.

Tick dropped to his knees, knowing this was what he was supposed to do. Crystals of snow plumed out from behind him, dancing across the surface of the deep blue ice. Somehow they avoided a portion of the lake, forming a perfectly white rectangular frame. Tick knew what would happen before it did.

The rectangle flickered like a television coming to life, and then a moving image appeared on the ice, replacing the blue.

Tick leaned forward, placing his hands on the outer edge of the cold, frozen lake. What he saw stopped his heart for three full seconds. His mom and his sister, marching toward a huge wall of broken stone. They were led by two creatures that he'd run into before—long, gangly things that seemed to be made from coils of solid smoke.

Sleeks.

CHAPTER
12

CREATURES

Lisa had felt terror before. When she and Kayla had been taken to that strange house with those strange women and the earthquake had hit. The storm of lightning and thunder. That had been her first true taste of fear.

And now she was experiencing it again.

The creatures that had taken her and her mom were ruthless and brutal as they dragged the two of them down the slope and across the grass to the broken castle. Their grip was hard and their pace furious.

They walked along a stream, the rushing water sparkling and glinting in the sunlight, the sound not doing a thing to help soothe Lisa's nerves. She remembered Tick telling the story of his first visit to the Thirteenth Reality and the battle that had been fought here with the fangen. At the time, she could never have imagined that one day she'd be in the same place, in the same kind of trouble.

"What do you want with us?" Lisa's mom asked for the

twentieth time. And for the twentieth time, the creatures said nothing.

Lisa looked at the Barrier Wand that was still in her mom's clutches, surprised that one of the monsters hadn't taken it from her. If she remembered Tick's tale completely, the castle of Mistress Jane was another hotspot for Chi'karda, so her mom would need only a free minute to switch the dials and instruments and wink them out of there. They just needed the right opportunity.

Finally, they approached the ruins of the once-grand structure, the stream disappearing under a stone wall. Now that they were closer, Lisa could finally get a good look at the different types of creatures that had been crawling all over the crumpled and half-standing walls of the castle. Some matched Tick's description of the nasty fangen: blackish skin, splotchy green hair, giant mouths full of spiked teeth, thin membranes of wings stretching out from their backs. There were others. More of the smoky-rope kind that had captured Lisa and her mom. Some that were small and hunched and charcoal gray, like grotesque statues come to life. Some that looked like a cross between an alligator and a bull, with massively strong arms. They all blended together into one display of horror.

And their purpose was obvious. They were trying to rebuild the castle, stone by stone.

Their current captors stopped them by one of the more solid sections of the ruins, about thirty feet from where the stream slipped under the wall. A huge wooden door stood next to it—or what used to be a door. Now it was mostly shredded, chunks and splinters hanging off around the edges. Darkness lurked behind the opening.

The monstrous pair threw Lisa and her mom to the ground in front of the door. The two of them immediately crawled to each other and huddled together, the Barrier Wand snuggled between them, its surface hard and cold. Lisa's mom started slyly turning the dials and switches.

The creatures floated up into the air and flew over to the wall of the castle, their wispy figures like streams of smoke whipping through the wind. They landed on the hard stone and used their long arms and legs to crawl up its side, mixing in with the rest of the other dark and twisted creatures.

"Get us out of here," Lisa whispered to her mom.

"I'm working on it." Her hands slowly turned a dial until it clicked. "But I don't want them to notice. And I'm not even sure I want us to wink out of here just yet."

"What? Why?"

Her mom looked disappointed. "After all we went through to get here in the first place? There has to be a reason that Chi'karda and Reality pulled us here when we tried to grab Atticus. Maybe we're on his trail or something. Or maybe we're being guided to his nanolocator, and this is a stop along the way."

Lisa was a little ashamed for wanting to hightail it out of there, but being dead wouldn't help Tick much either. "Or maybe we're about to be eaten for dinner by all of these monsters."

"Maybe. Don't worry your little heart, girl. I have the Wand all set, and if worse comes to worst, I'll click the button and wink us away. We can start all over again. From the beginning. Without any hope."

Lisa groaned and rolled her eyes. "Okay, Mom. I got your point loud and clear."

There was movement in the darkness behind the shattered door, and a figure appeared, like a shrouded ghost. Lisa wanted to get up and run, but she kept her eyes focused on the person who approached. As the figure came into the light, Lisa could see a robe made of a coarse, off-white material, its hood pulled up and over the face, hiding it. Two hands emerged from the arms of the robe, the fingers folded together in front. Lisa had expected the hands to be gnarled and ancient, but the skin looked young and healthy.

A woman's hands.

The robed stranger walked to where Lisa and her mom sat. She was tall and thin, and the image of her hooded head gave her a commanding presence, like an ancient oracle or druid.

"You can wink away if you wish," the lady said, her voice a hollow ring. "But I ask only that you allow me to tell you one very important thing first."

"What is it?" Lisa's mom replied, cautious.

The woman reached up with those young hands of hers and pulled back the hood of her robe, revealing a homely, stoic face framed by short, black hair. She had a nose that pointed straight out like a carrot.

"We brought you here," she said, "because you're trying to find Atticus Higginbottom. And so are we."

CHAPTER
13

WORDS ON ICE

Tick's heart had dropped upon seeing his mom and sister captured by Sleeks, and he almost beat his fists on the ice where their images appeared, thinking he could break through, dive through, and save them somehow. He yelled to them as they were brought to the foot of Jane's now-broken castle and thrown to the ground, though he knew it was pointless. Full of desperation and rage, he could only sit there and shake. Helpless.

The screen—the rectangle of frozen pond—suddenly flickered, and the scene disappeared, replaced by a few lines of written words. Before he even read it, he knew it was some kind of riddle, and for some reason, it made him mad. He screamed and *did* hit the ice, cursing Reality for playing such ridiculous games with him. His family was in trouble, and here he was, forced to solve a silly puzzle again.

But on the other hand, he was good at it. The fabric of the universe understood his mind and was trying to help him. Was trying to form its complexities together and present to him a solution in a way he could best grasp it. Just like what had happened with the Haunce.

Tick gained control of his emotions and forced himself to read the words.

The smallest thing begins to grow
It needs no light, it needs no glow
This thing, it fears the weakest breath
And yet it cannot embrace death
The greatest man or bull or steed
Or queen or doe or stinging bee
Eats it, smells it, drinks it some
And one day it they will become

Tick sighed. He'd hoped the riddle would be easy, that the answer would jump out at him. But no. Of course not.

He started thinking.

⌒

"My name is Mordell," the woman said to Lisa and her mom. She sat on the grass next to them, her legs folded beneath her flowing robe, her back straight, and her hands settled on her knees. "I am a Lady of Blood and Sorrow, a new order started by our master, Mistress Jane, to serve her in the quest to create a Utopia for mankind. To bring eternal happiness to humans once and for all. We bear our name of despair to teach the world that we will do anything, make any sacrifice, to bring this Utopia to pass. We are servants only."

73

Lisa felt queasy as Mordell spoke. She seemed to have a blank stare as she recited her mantra, as if it had been beaten into her since she was a kid.

"Why are you looking for my son?" Lisa's mom asked. She had the Barrier Wand gripped in one hand, the other hovering above the button on top. Lisa also had a hand on the device. They could wink away with one click.

"Because we know he is with our master," Mordell replied. "We believe that they disrupted the fabric of Reality by using such astronomical levels of Chi'karda that they were ripped away into the Nonex."

Mom gasped, and one of her hands flew up to her mouth.

"The Nonex?" Lisa repeated. That didn't sound very good. "What's that?"

Her mom looked over at her, her face somehow showing even more worry than it had before. "We don't know much about it, but it's a place that both exists and doesn't exist, trapped somewhere between the dimensions of Reality. Sort of a no-man's-land, where your mind is the only thing keeping you alive. They say it's where you go if you ever meet one of your Alterants."

Lisa had the thought that her mom was a true scientist, unable to stop herself from breaking it down to textbook explanations despite knowing her own son might be trapped there. But her eyes held deep love and concern still.

Mordell continued. "Mistress Jane has been training us to understand the ways of Chi'karda. It flows here in ways it does not in the other Realities. We've brought every one of our kind from the stations we've established throughout the Thirteen Realities. Even as we speak, they are gathering inside the Great Hall of the castle behind me, which by fate, survived the destruction."

"What are they doing?" Lisa asked.

Mordell's eyes focused on hers for the first time. "We are meditating, probing the universe, seeking any sign of Atticus or Mistress Jane. We must find their nanolocators or sense their presence. We have to be ready to snatch them if they appear, as *soon* as they appear. Right now, it's as if they have been wiped from Reality."

Lisa's mom didn't seem surprised, as if she'd given up doubting anything anymore. "And how did you find us? Did you wink us here?"

"We have the data on your son's nanolocator. In our probing, we saw you looking for him. And then you were captured by the Great Disturbance that has plagued the Realities ever since our master disappeared. We rescued you from it and brought you here so that you could help us. We're no longer enemies; we have the same purpose."

Lisa's mind caught on those two words: *Great Disturbance*. The lady had said them as if they were the name of a place or a person. She asked what it meant.

Mordell looked into her eyes once again. "We call it the Void of Mist and Thunder, and if we don't find a way to stop it, the lives of our master and your brother, and the quest to build Utopia, won't matter. Because every last person in the Realities will be dead."

Lisa and her mom looked at each other, dread hanging

in the air like soaked curtains. How did you even follow up something like that with questions? There were too many to know where to start.

Mordell stood up in a move so graceful that Lisa didn't even notice until the woman was on her feet.

"Come," the Lady of Blood and Sorrow said. "There will be time for explanations later. Right now we need you to join us in our meditations and help us probe the universe until we find those we seek." She turned and started walking toward the broken door of the broken castle.

Lisa knew there'd be no discussing this with her mom. They both got up and followed the strange woman into the darkness.

CHAPTER
14

WATCHING TV

Mothball was thankful something had finally gone right in her life. Klint Tanner had given her a cup of hot tea as they sat down in his living room to talk about the world and its problems. The news was going to be rough and depressing, she knew it, but at least she had some tea to warm her bones and settle her nerves.

Sally had asked for chocolate milk, which embarrassed Mothball to no end. Especially when the buffoon asked if he could have a straw to "sip it up with." Oh, she liked the man well enough, she supposed, but how he'd become a Realitant, she'd never know.

Tanner sat down in a chair opposite them, a remote in his hands. There was a huge television on the wall, bigger than any Mothball had ever seen in her life. Of course, they didn't do a whole lot of that sort back in the Fifth Reality.

Tanner was a scrawny man with mussed-up hair and

whiskers on his chin. But he had sharp eyes, and he took his job seriously.

"I've put together a hodgepodge of what's been going on lately," the man said after everyone was settled. He clicked the remote, and the television buzzed to life. "I'd say sit back and enjoy the show, but I don't think you will very much. It's not pretty."

"Oh, doncha worry, son," Sally said, his straw pinched between his fingers as he slurped his chocolate milk. He looked like an overgrown two-year-old kid in overalls. "Back where we work, we sho 'nough used to things that ain't purty. Ain't that right, Mothball?" He laughed, a booming sound that could only be described as a guffaw.

Mothball wanted to slug him; she knew very well he was talking about *her*. But then again, Sally wasn't the handsomest cat in the litter, so maybe he was poking fun at himself as well. "Right as rain, you are," she said. "But I'm sure you were a cute wee one when you were born and all. Been downhill ever since, it 'as."

Sally laughed again.

"Shall we, um, get on with it?" Tanner asked.

"Yes, indeed," Mothball replied. "So sorry for my partner, here. A bit cracked in the skull, he is."

Tanner smiled, but it was a haunted one. "I'm afraid you're both going to lose your appetite for laughing soon. The whole world is in one big heap of a mess. Fires, riots, rebellions, anarchy. Looting and murders. Like I said, it's not pretty." He pointed his remote at the television and clicked it again.

A horror show came to life on the big screen.

⟋⟍⟋⟍⟋⟍⟋◦

Paul had never understood why people liked to drink warm milk. He'd heard of it before, but it always sounded nasty to him. Warm *chocolate* milk, maybe. But take out that brown stuff and he wanted no part of it. Milk was meant to be ice-cold, especially when washing down some cookies.

At least those were yummy. Oatmeal and raisin.

Gretel was sitting in her chair, eating and sipping along with Paul and Sofia, but she'd yet to say anything about . . . well, anything. Paul still had no idea why they were there, which was why all he could think about was how much he didn't like warm milk.

Sofia cleared her throat. "We really appreciate you letting us in, but I don't think we have a lot of spare time on our hands. I'm sure Master George wants us to learn what it is you have to tell us, and then get back to him."

Paul felt like he needed to add something. "Yeah, let's get on with it." He winced on the inside. That had come out a little harsher than he'd meant it. "I'm dying of curiosity here. Ma'am." He threw that in there to sound polite.

Gretel took the last bite of her cookie then drained her cup of milk. She placed her dishes on a small table beside her. "I understand your impatience, but you're going to have to bear with me a few moments longer before we get to *my* part of this story. First, I need to hear yours."

Paul wanted to groan and kick something, but he kept himself still and quiet.

"What do you mean?" Sofia asked.

Gretel shrugged as if it were obvious. "I haven't had one squirt of communication with the Realitants—or civilization at all, for that matter—in more than a year. I'm no longer what you'd consider 'active,' and informing me of the latest has to be on the bottom of George's to-do list. So I need to get caught up on everything that's been going on."

"Everything that's been going on?" Paul repeated. "That's like asking us to give you a quick wrap-up of the Civil War. You have any idea how much has happened in the last *year*?"

"Well, actually, no, I don't. Which is why I need you to tell me about it." She folded her hands in her lap and raised her eyebrows.

Paul looked over at Sofia. "You tell her."

Sofia had impatience stamped all over her face, and she started speaking immediately, as if she didn't want to waste one more second. She began in the only place that made sense—how she, Paul, Tick, and Sato got recruited by the Realitants—and then she flowed into the problems they'd had with Reginald Chu and Mistress Jane. On and on and on she went, speaking so fast it gave Paul a headache trying to keep up, but eventually she got to the part about Jane trying to sever the Fifth Reality from existence and almost destroying the entire universe instead. She sounded like she was telling someone how to make breakfast.

Finally, she finished.

Gretel didn't say anything at first; she just kept looking at Sofia as if she needed some time to absorb all the things she'd been told.

"Well?" Paul asked to break the awkward silence. "What do you think? Things as rosy as you pictured, living out here in your swamp palace?"

The old woman looked sharply at him, her expression turning grave. "Son, what you've just described to me is far, far worse than I imagined, even in my worst nightmares after the earthquake that hit this place. I think I finally understand why George sent you to me. Come, we need to enter my safe haven."

She stood up, her eyes distant, and gestured for the young Realitants to follow. Paul and Sofia exchanged uneasy glances then joined Gretel, leaving the comfy living room with the warm fire and entering a cold, uninviting room with shiny steel walls. There was a bare light in the ceiling that flickered and a large safe in one corner of the room. Gretel shut the door behind them with a heavy, ringing thud; Paul spun around to see that it was also made of steel like the inside of a bank vault.

Gretel spun a wheel-handle and clicked a big lock. Then she walked over to the safe in the corner—a big, black square—and started turning the large combination dial. Paul stared, wondering what in the world they were about to see.

As Gretel continued to work at the safe's mechanism, she spoke over her shoulder. "I don't call it the *safe haven* for nothing. It's a haven for my safes. A safe within a safe. What I'm protecting here is very important."

Paul asked the obvious question. "What is it?"

There was a loud click, and then the door of the safe swung open. Paul and Sofia stepped forward to see what was inside. It was an old, tattered, dusty shoebox. Gretel pulled it out and set it on the floor. Carefully. Then she sat right beside it, folding her legs underneath her like a teenager. Paul and Sofia sat next to her on the ground. Paul's eyes stayed glued to the box. He was so curious he almost reached out and opened the lid himself.

Gretel flicked both of them a knowing look. Then she lifted the warped lid and flipped it over. Inside the box lay a small cube of gray metal with a green button on top. The old woman lifted up the cube and held it out for everyone to see.

"Push this button," she said in a mesmerized voice, almost like a chant, "and the Realities will change forever. For good. Or for evil."

CHAPTER
15

THE LADIES OF BLOOD AND SORROW

T ick sat in the snow in the meditative pose of a Buddhist he'd seen once on TV—his legs crossed under him, his arms resting on top of them with his fingers pushed together and pointing upward, and his eyes closed. Couldn't hurt, he'd thought.

He'd been trying for at least a half hour to push all other thoughts from his mind and focus on the riddle he'd seen written on the ice. But he was having a hard time concentrating. The words floated in the darkness of his thoughts, visible in his mind's eye as white letters on a black background. He ran through the lines, letting the skills he'd developed for this sort of thing take their natural course as his brain digested and regurgitated the riddle again and again:

> *The smallest thing begins to grow*
> *It needs no light, it needs no glow*

This thing, it fears the weakest breath
And yet it cannot embrace death
The greatest man or bull or steed
Or queen or doe or stinging bee
Eats it, smells it, drinks it some
And one day it they will become

Tick sat in the wind and the cold and relaxed, doing what he did best.

Thinking.

Lisa and her mom followed Mordell down a long, cold passage under the hard stone of the castle, walking along the dark waters of the stream that rushed by. Lisa knew this was the place Tick and his Realitant friends had barely escaped from during their first harrowing trip to the Thirteenth Reality. Imagining them at that time—Tick and the others desperately waiting for the Barrier Wand to kick in and wink them out, while hordes of bloodthirsty fangen beat down the walls and came after them—sent chills across her skin. It made her feel incredibly sorry for her lost brother, and made her love him more than ever before. Tears welled up in her eyes.

She knew what had happened next. The Barrier Wand didn't even have a Chi'karda Drive inside its golden case at the time—Mistress Jane had secretly removed it—but Tick had displayed his unbelievable power over Chi'karda, using his powers to wink everyone to safety on his own. There had been signs and hints his whole life that there was something special about him, but after that day, the Realitants knew it for sure.

Tick was a wizard. A silly word, but that's how Lisa saw him. Sure, Master George claimed Tick's power could be scientifically explained—or someday would be—but Lisa didn't care about the specifics, the nitty-gritty details. Her brother was magic, he was special, and they needed to find him so he could do great things for the world. For *all* the worlds.

The passageway led through an arch to the right and into a small chamber carved out of black rock. Mordell silently led them through the opening and into the room that had absolutely no decoration or furniture of any kind. The only light came from a single torch that burned and hissed in a sconce on the wall. About twenty other women sat upon the hard ground in a circle. One break in the ring was vacant, and it was just big enough for the three newcomers to sit down.

"Even though its size is humble," Mordell said in a solemn voice, "we call this the Great Hall because its purpose is grand. This hallowed place is where the Ladies of Blood and Sorrow come to show our respect and devotion to Chi'karda and to renew our commitment to seek a Utopia for all mankind." She looked at Lisa and her mom. "Your presence here is allowed by my invitation only. Please, sit."

She motioned toward the empty spot in the circle. Lisa and her mom, holding hands, went over and sat down on the smooth surface of the black rock floor. Her mom cradled the Barrier Wand in her lap, and Lisa noticed that her finger hovered over the trigger button at the top.

Lisa took a moment to study the circle of women, all of whom were dressed in the same off-white, coarse robes that Mordell wore. The Ladies each had a meditative, almost blank look on their hooded faces. It was creepy in the scant light.

Mordell sat down next to Lisa. "We all know of the nature of this room in which we have gathered," she began. "The Great Hall, birthed by the will of our master, Mistress Jane herself. For reasons we may never learn, the Thirteenth Reality is more focused with Chi'karda's might, more concentrated, more plentiful in its power than any other world. And this hallowed place is the heart of that power, which is why our master built her castle on this land and carved the Great Hall in this rock. Using the methods taught to us by She Who Tamed the Fire, we will now join hands and probe the universe together. And when we find our master—and her companions, if possible—we must unite to bring them back here."

"'If possible?'" Lisa asked, not liking the sound of that one bit. Maybe they were using Tick as a means to an end and were planning to dump him as soon as they found Jane. And what was with all the fancy mumbo-jumbo talk?

Mordell turned to her, not looking pleased by the interruption. "You've spoken out of turn, girl. This is not allowed in the Great Hall."

Lisa refused to be intimidated by this servant of the

woman who'd tried to kill Tick. "I just want my brother to come back safely too. Make sure he does."

Mordell considered her for a moment then finally nodded. "I give you my word that if it's possible in any way to do so, we will. But understand that our master is our first priority, for the sake of you, and your children, and your children's children."

Lisa thought of a million nasty things that she wanted to say, but she kept her mouth shut. She could only hope now. She squeezed her mom's arm, who gave her a nod and a look as if to say, *Don't worry. Tick can fend for himself.*

Mordell returned her attention to her counterparts sitting in the circle. "We have with us today the mother of Atticus Higginbottom—yes, we know who you are—with a Barrier Wand constructed by her own hand. She has locked onto the nanolocator of her son, which will serve to benefit us in our search. The Wand's presence alone will aid us. Now, we must all take hands, including our visitors'."

Lisa had no problem grabbing her mom's hand, but she was a little wary of taking one of Mordell's. She clasped her fingers around those of the woman, which were icy cold and felt brittle, as if they'd collapse into a heap of powder if Lisa squeezed. So she didn't.

"Let us begin," Mordell announced. "Close your eyes. Grasp the Chi'karda that flows within this room. Reach into the Realities—reach into the universe."

The Ladies of Blood and Sorrow began to hum. Lisa was the last to close her eyes, but before she did, a spray of orange light started to glow within the center of their circle.

Tick didn't know how long he'd been sitting in the icy snow, next to the icy pond, feeling the icy wind. But he felt it all the way to the core of his bones, and *icy* was the only word to describe it.

He didn't let it faze him. He thought, concentrated, and focused on the riddle. He knew the fabric of Reality was at his fingertips, waiting for his mind to organize a solution in the way he best understood. The complexities of the universe had been laid at his feet in the form of a riddle.

When the pieces of the puzzle finally clicked into place, the answer hovered within his thoughts, a word as clear as if it were written on a sign hung in front of his face.

Dust.

He opened his eyes and whispered the word to the biting wind, which whisked it away and carried it to whatever ears needed to hear it.

A few seconds later, the world around him was ripped apart, exploding into a horrifying display of noise and light. Tick screamed, but no one heard the sound. Not even him.

CHAPTER
16

A RUSH OF VIOLENCE

Lisa was beginning to feel uncomfortable.

The rattling buzz in the room had grown to an unbearable pitch, vibrating her skull and shaking the walls and floor of the Great Hall. The rock creaked and groaned, as if the walls might burst apart and spray them with tiny fragments. It took all of Lisa's willpower not to open her eyes or scream or run away. Even through her closed eyelids, she could sense the bright orangeness of what she knew was the power of Chi'karda.

The Ladies of Blood and Sorrow continued to hum, and Lisa heard a slight rustling, as if the women were swaying back and forth in their trancelike state. What they were doing, she had no idea, and she certainly didn't know what she could do to help. But she felt the vibration of power inside her body, and there was definitely something big happening.

She squeezed her mom's hand, and her mom squeezed back. Something hard and warm—almost hot—touched

Lisa's forearm. She opened her eyelids to the slightest, smallest crack to see what it was. Her mom had moved the Barrier Wand closer, wanting to show her that it was heating up for some reason.

Yes, something big was definitely going on.

⁓

Tick's body was flying through a fog.

Lightning and thunder flashed and boomed all around him, streaks of white fire crossing the gray, misty air, barely missing his body. The horrible sounds rattled his head, pierced his ears painfully. He felt the sense of flying in his stomach and head, but there wasn't a great rushing of wind blowing at him. His skin was cold one second and hot the next. Even his vision would go haywire—everything turning into a grayish blur then coming into focus again, the edges of the lightning bolts sharp and clear and brilliant. It was as if his senses had a loose connection to his brain.

He tried to quell the rising fear and panic that threatened to consume him. He had no idea what was happening or where he was, much less how he could use his newfound powers to help the situation. He was hurtling through a void of nothing, surrounded by an angry, powerful storm of energy.

He twisted his head left and right, trying to see any sign of Chu or Mistress Jane. They were nowhere near him, according to what his eyes told his brain, but on some deep, deep level, he felt as though he were still holding their hands.

That maybe the storm was simply an illusion and nothing more.

He continued his flight. Nausea filled his belly. He tried to speak, but his voice was lost in the noise of the chaos around him. He had the horrible thought that maybe this was how he'd spend the rest of eternity—that maybe the Nonex, in the end, was nothing more than this.

Tick flew through a void of mist and thunder.

Mistress Jane didn't understand what was going on, and nothing on earth caused her more distress than *uncertainty*. She was a scientist, blood and bone, to the very core of her soul and mind. A scientist. And being here, surrounded by a world of mist and lightning and sound, she didn't have the slightest guess of what was going on. It made no logical sense. And that made her angry.

She looked to her left, though all movement was strange in this inexplicable void. Her senses told her she was moving at great speed, yet she felt no rush of wind. And her surroundings didn't seem to shift at a pace that made sense with the movement of her head.

Reginald Chu was a few feet away from her, keeping an even pace. His eyes were still closed, and he held his hands out before him like Superman. But he didn't look peaceful or asleep. His face was pinched, like someone waiting to jump off a bridge with a bungee cord. Sweat trickled down his brow, giving Jane even more evidence that their motion through this fog didn't match the physical effects on their body.

Jane knew Tick had done this somehow. He had vaulted them from the Nonex and thrown them into a place that was obviously even worse. Maybe she'd made a huge mistake trusting him to help her.

She closed her eyes and reached into the void with her senses, reaching to take back her Chi'karda from Tick's control. Surprisingly, it was there, waiting. She filled her body with the power, sucking it in, keeping it at bay until she needed it. Kept it there like a bomb waiting for a lit fuse.

The Great Hall had continued to buzz and vibrate, the Ladies humming, the orange power of Chi'karda burning the air with energy. Lisa could only sit and wait, though it was agonizing.

Mordell suddenly spoke up beside her with a voice that easily cut through the other noise in the room.

"We've found her! We've reconnected with her nanolocator! Reginald Chu is there as well. We need everyone to focus. Begin to pull them back."

The woman paused, and Lisa didn't dare ask the obvious question. Not because it had been forbidden, but because she was terrified of the answer. Mordell answered her anyway.

"There is, unfortunately, no sign of the boy, Atticus Higginbottom."

CHAPTER
17

FINDING TICK

Lorena knew something was happening with her Barrier Wand, and it wasn't just that the Drive within it was helping pool the power of Chi'karda for the Ladies of Blood and Sorrow. Something else was at play. The metal surface was hot, almost too much to touch now, and the Wand had a hum of its own.

Mordell's words had been like a death sentence. Lorena had suspected the truth from the start, and the people here obviously had different priorities than she did. They wanted Jane back, at any cost. Even if the cost was the life of Lorena's son. And she didn't plan to let that happen.

Breaking her handhold with both Lisa and the stranger to her left, Lorena opened her eyes and straightened the Barrier Wand in her lap. She quickly ran through the dials and switches, adjusting and evaluating, making educated guesses since she was in such an unprecedented situation. Sweat poured down her face.

"What are you doing?" Mordell shouted, the echo ringing along the walls and ceiling of the black, rocky room. "Rejoin hands this instant!"

Lorena gave the woman a nasty glare. "Back off, lady, or you'll be seeing and feeling a lot of blood and sorrow today."

A quick glance at Lisa showed that her daughter was smiling.

~

Tick felt something tugging on his heart.

Not like despair, or love, or missing someone. It was a literal tug, as if someone had sunk a hook into his heart and cinched it tight with a strong rope. And then the rope started pulling.

He cried out, feeling a fire ignite within him that scorched his insides with pain. He clutched his chest with both hands, gripping his shirt and pulling his fingers into tight fists, pressing on his sternum. It did no good. The pull on the rope was getting stronger.

It hurt so bad. The gray mist swirled around him; lightning bolts exploded through the air as the thunder thumped and boomed. His body continued to fly through it all.

And his insides screamed with pain.

~

Mistress Jane knew something had changed. She felt a presence within her, as if some other soul had joined with hers, trying to fight her for occupancy. She looked at Chu, who was still close to her, just as his eyes opened. He'd felt it, too.

He yelled something at her. His words were utterly lost in the deafening noise of the storm around them, but she could read his lips: *Save me.*

Jane thought of the Ladies of Blood and Sorrow and the things she'd trained them for. The endless possibilities they could accomplish within the Great Hall of her castle, where Chi'karda gathered so powerfully. And finally, something logical clicked into place for her. The Ladies had combined their efforts, pooled all their power, and had reached out for her nanolocator. Tick had pulled them out of the Nonex into some no-man's-land barrier between it and the rest of Reality. Just close enough to reestablish contact.

Jane smiled, knowing exactly what expression was on her red mask: joy.

Chu reached out a hand to her, his mouth still moving with unheard words. Fear enveloped him, and sweat covered his face even more than before.

Jane felt ashamed for him. Embarrassed by his weakness. But she knew what the man was capable of. And they'd come so close to partnering before. So close. Until the boy Tick ruined everything, including Jane's body.

Chu—her partner. Utopia—her mission. She twisted her body, straining to reach out with her arm.

Mistress Jane took Reginald Chu's hand.

⁓

Lisa watched as her mom worked furiously over the Barrier Wand, adjusting the instruments, fine-tuning them with the slightest of movements. The Ladies around the circle had continued their efforts, ignoring the mutiny of Lisa and her mom. Mordell and the woman who'd been sitting next to Lisa's mom had simply moved closer until they could reseal the ring of held hands in their magic circle. Maybe they figured they could deal with the turncoats later.

"Mom, what are you doing?" Lisa asked. She'd been scared to interrupt her mom's concentration, but she couldn't wait one more second.

"I've almost got it." She had her tongue pinched between her lips, and sweat trickled down both sides of her face. "I can't believe it, but his signal is there. Before it wasn't *missing* so much as showing that he didn't exist anymore. But he's there, no doubt about it."

"Really?" Lisa tried not to let her hopes leap to the sky.

"But it's so weak. So weak. I'm trying to latch on, trying to pull him closer. But I don't dare try to fully wink him in yet. His body could literally tear apart and turn into an atom soup."

Lisa's heart dropped. "Mom, please get him. Mom, please." She'd never realized until that moment how much she loved that stupid brother of hers.

"We will, baby," her mom said. "I swear it."

The buzz and hum and orange light of Chi'karda filled the room like a nebula.

～ つ

Things started to change around Tick, even as the pain inside his chest grew worse, like needles piercing his heart. His shoulders shook from the ache of trying to muffle the sobs that wanted to escape him, but he tried to push aside all the pain and focus on his surroundings.

The gray mist had thinned out, allowing his vision to reach much farther away. The bolts of white fire shooting through the air had not ceased at all, and he saw more of them than ever—a rain of lightning that continued for miles and miles. Violent sounds shook the gaseous world and continued to hurt his ears and splinter his brain with the worst headache he'd ever experienced.

And in the distance, coming straight toward him, were . . . *things.*

Dark objects. Huge objects. They looked like bulky chunks of broken spaceships, destroyed and shredded, hurling through empty space. There were dozens of them, flying through the gray air, rushing in. As they got closer, Tick could no longer tell if that was true or if he was actually hurtling toward *them.* But then he saw that they were less like spaceships, and more like floating mountains torn from their foundations—the edges rocky and broken, the centers filled with vegetation and trees.

He didn't understand why, but he felt a weighty sense of dread, and not just from the prospect of smashing into the stony chunks of land. There was something ominous about those massive rocks, like they were alive and wanted him dead.

The nearest one was only a few hundred feet away when hundreds of vines shot out from the nooks and crannies of the rock's craggy surface, like an army of snakes striking out at a predator. Their tips tapered to a point. The vines coiled in the air then came for Tick.

———✐———

Lisa jumped when her mom suddenly cried out, a sound that was impossible to tell whether it was good or bad. She was tight-faced and sweating as she ran her hands up and down the Barrier Wand like it was some kind of musical instrument.

"What's going on?" Lisa asked.

"I'm latched to him," her mom responded. "I just can't seem to wink the boy in."

CHAPTER
18

CORDS OF LIGHT

The vines flew through the air, coming at Tick as if they were magnetized ropes and he was a big piece of metal. He'd been sort of complacent since being pulled into the massive gray void, watching and observing, wondering what Reality was going to do to him now that he'd solved the riddle his consciousness had presented in his mind.

But the vines looked deadly, the massive structures of rock and vegetation were hurtling toward his body, and he had no more time to sit back. He'd mastered his control over Chi'karda. It was time to use it.

The ends of the first vines reached him and quickly coiled around his arms and legs. They cinched tight and jerked him forward even faster, throwing his body at the rock from which they'd emerged.

Tick struggled against the strength of the ropy chains, looked at the jagged granite chunk rushing up at him, and tried not to panic. He relaxed his arms and legs, letting his body go limp. Reaching down, deep inside his heart, he found the spark that had become so familiar to him, that burning flicker of flame that he knew he could ignite into an inferno.

Pure power exploded away from him, streaks of orange light and fire. The surge of Chi'karda slammed into the massive rock, detonating it into a million splinters of stone, which Tick whisked away with a single thought. Like a flinty cloud of smoke caught in a gust of wind, it flew to the right, gone from his vision. The vines that had imprisoned him were incinerated; not a single trace was left.

But there were dozens more of the floating mountains, and each one had more of the vines popping out of their surfaces, pointy ends focused on Tick. He took hold of his power, pulled it all back within his chest, sucking it in like a great vacuum. Then he used his eyes and mind to start destroying.

Looking this way and that, he hurled streaks of Chi'karda outward with each glance. They shot forward like streams of fire, arrows of might, smashing into each of the massive hunks of stone, dirt, and vegetation. The flying structures exploded, obliterated into dusty clouds that whipped away like the first one had. Tick barely had time to make sure he'd succeeded in destroying one before he had to look at the next threat.

Explosion after explosion, he destroyed them. Reaching with all his strength, he was able to send the Chi'karda beams farther and farther out, killing the vines as soon as they came into view.

Without warning, and just as he began to feel like he might get out of the mess, everything changed as quickly as one wink of his eye.

The endless gray sky disappeared, along with the fog of debris from the countless erupted balls of rock. Blackness replaced it, a sea of stars in the background, as if he floated in the deepest realm of outer space. His sense of movement also stopped, jarring him at first. Pulling in a deep breath, he heard the sound of his own gasp and felt his insides twist until he regained his equilibrium. All was silent as he hung there in the empty void.

Several seconds passed. Then each one of those pinpoints of light around him stretched out into a long beam of brightness, all of them pointed at Tick and moving at a blistering speed.

Lorena stood up, her mind so focused on the Barrier Wand that it felt as though she'd become one with it. The orange light of Chi'karda filled the room, blinding her vision. She couldn't separate what the Ladies of Blood and Sorrow were doing from the power generated by her own efforts with the Wand. She'd never experienced anything like it. She wondered if this was how Tick felt when he was controlling the Chi'karda directly. She'd quit adjusting the dials and switches without even realizing it.

And then she remembered. She was in the Thirteenth Reality. Things were different here.

Lisa was at her side, keeping quiet—bless her heart—but

a quick glance showed that the poor girl desperately wanted to know what was going on. Lorena went back to the business at hand, knowing she couldn't risk breaking her concentration. She couldn't put it into words or offer up a scientific explanation, but she had control over Chi'karda like never before, a link to Tick that she wasn't going to let go of. She was going to bring him home.

Even if she had to die doing it.

⌒

At first the arrows of light made Tick feel as if he were in a spaceship that had shifted into warp speed, about to blast to another part of the galaxy. But he felt no sense of motion, and the angles were wrong. As he twisted and turned in the void, he saw long lines of pure whiteness stretching toward him from every direction, like strings of perfectly straight lightning. And he didn't need a manual to know that their purpose was not to brighten his world so he could read a book.

The beams kept coming.

He could easily shift his body, even move away if he wanted to, but there was no point. The things were heading for him no matter where he looked. Unless he winked to another place, those long strings of white were going to reach him. Besides, where would he wink? *Could* he even wink out of the void? He felt surprisingly calm, confident he could deal with the problem.

The first needles of light reached his body.

Just like the vines, they wrapped around his arms and

legs; some slipped across his chest, others slithered along his ribs and side and along his back. He fought at them by flailing and kicking out, but it did no good. The Chi'karda he'd gathered before still swelled inside of him. He lashed out with the power, but *that* did no good either. It was as if the ropes of light were without substance until they needed it to serve their purpose, gripping tightly to his body.

There were dozens of the ropes, then hundreds, thousands. They bled together into a brilliant display of pure white light, covering every inch of his body. Only his head remained free, and he twisted his neck to see what was happening, trying to squirm out of it.

The bindings tightened, squeezing the air out of his lungs, but curiously, Tick felt no panic. His breathing remained even. The white ropes kept coming, flying in like eels until they hit his body and wrapped around the other coils of light. He'd become nothing but a head, sticking out of a blinding ball of brilliance with tendrils of light leading away from him in every direction.

Tick knew he couldn't let it keep going. He closed his eyes, pulled in more and more Chi'karda, filling his body and soul. He felt as if his insides were on fire. Still he kept at it, the power rushing into him like a falling deluge of scorching lava. He found himself liking it, loving the burn and surge of adrenaline, the power that filled him. He let it build, knowing he needed to unleash it but not wanting to. The earlier sensation of being tugged by a strong cable was still there, but it didn't hurt anymore.

The beams of light quit coming, but it didn't matter. He

was wrapped neck to toe, unable to move a single muscle. The trailing ends of the ropes stretched out from his body in every direction, as if he were stuck in the middle of a giant spider web. All was silent and still, the light blinding.

The cords around him suddenly grew taut, then began to pull at his limbs and torso. Trying to rip his body into pieces.

CHAPTER
19

FIGHTING THE VOID

At first Tick didn't feel the pain.

The power of Chi'karda within him burned so hot, so fierce, that he was unaware of all else except for a distant tugging sensation. Like he'd been thrown into a crowd and they were using his arms and legs as a wishbone. But the pain intensified, began to hurt. Bad. The pulling on his heart came back, too, as if two separate forces wanted to completely obliterate his body.

He screamed and released the power that had been building within, unleashing the Chi'karda with a mental burst of a detonation.

The bright whiteness of the ropes that had captured him was dimmed by the brilliance of orange light as Chi'karda erupted out of him. Streams of it shot from his body in arrows, and a cloud swelled from his skin, bulging underneath the cords like a burrowing animal.

The ropes held, pulling at him and continuing to jerk at

his limbs and squeeze his middle. Pain stabbed at his joints and muscles. The pleasurable burn of power had been replaced by a different kind of fire, an agony that hurt worse than anything he'd ever experienced.

He screamed again and sent waves of Chi'karda crashing out of him, focusing on the strings of frozen lightning as if the whole thing were a video game, his mind the joystick. Orange flames struck at them, disintegrating half of them in one swoop of power. Tick's body snapped to the left, flying through the air as the severed ropes found life again, coming back at him and trying to reattach their ends to his arms and legs. He held his breath and continued the onslaught of Chi'karda, firing away at everything in sight.

Sprays of pure whiteness erupted in tiny explosions like bursts of electricity out of a live wire as his power severed more of the cords. More and more and more of them. His mind worked relentlessly as he tried to destroy the things attached to him while at the same time keeping the others at bay. He floated in that strange outer space, throwing flares of energy at anything that moved. The mix of white and orange was brilliant and blinding, almost making him lose his focus.

His body ripped free from the bindings.

Tick quit aiming then and simply threw all his power out in wave after wave, destroying whatever dared come at him. Explosions of light and sound. The black air trembled; his skull rattled; his skin seemed to vibrate on his bones like they might slip free of his body. He was completely blind; the whole world had gone white and hot. There was wind and thunder and the smell of ozone and burning charcoal. It all added together into a chaotic jumble of anarchy, driving Tick insane as he continued to thrust outward with the power of Chi'karda as fast as he could gather it. He didn't know what else to do, and he was scared to stop.

Something tugged at his heart again. He felt it despite the madness all around him—that sensation of strings being pulled, of being yanked from the inside.

His body suddenly jerked away from the explosions of energy and flying white cords of lightning. He flew through the blackness of that place that had seemed like outer space, the raging battle he'd been fighting gone in a flash. Things changed around him. Instead of darkness, there was a blue haze, splotches of green and brown and red flying past him. Chunks of gray rock appeared, coming at him like a rain of meteors.

Tick used his mind to control his flight, dodging and flipping and accelerating to avoid the rocks. As he approached the biggest one, a jagged stone the size of a bus, he had to slam on his mental brakes, coming to a stop right before he smashed into the thing. This caused the tugging inside him to intensify, sending shocks of pain throughout his nerves.

He reached out and felt the hard surface of the rock. He crawled along it to the other side, then jumped off it by pushing with his legs. His body once again catapulted through the strange-colored air, and the hurtful tug on his heart lessened enough that he could bear it.

Things changed once again.

He dove into a thick liquid, almost like a gel. Cold wetness soaked his hair and clothes and skin as his perception changed. He could sense up and down, everything shifting around him until it felt as if he were near the bottom of a deep ocean, swimming upward even though his arms and legs did nothing to make it so. He tore through the dark waters.

There was just enough light raining down in wavering rays that he could see creatures coming toward him. Long, powerful leviathans that swam with their back fins beating against the current like the tail of a dolphin. But these monsters had arms and burning red eyes, and Tick knew they wanted to grab him and stop him from reaching whatever was tugging him forward.

The monsters reached out, swimming in all at once. Clawed hands reached viciously for his body, snatching and scratching as their fingers tried to gain purchase. Tick lashed at them, swinging sluggishly through the thick liquid as he continued his ascent. The creatures kept pace with him, trying their best to grab hold of his limbs or clothes. Kicking and squirming, he spun his body to make it harder to catch, and when one of the creatures latched on, he fought it off. He couldn't see much of their faces—they were all shadows and angles—but their red eyes burned like rocks of lava.

Two of them grabbed his legs, wrapping their arms tightly around one each. They squeezed, and their claws dug into his skin. The unseen forces still pulled him toward some unknown destination through a place he didn't even understand.

He burst through the surface, the two creatures still holding onto his legs as he rocketed toward a bright blue sky. The jellied water cascaded off them in blubbery droplets, and Tick looked down to see the faces of the monsters clearly for the first time. They weren't human at all: their bodies looked like sharks with arms, and their heads were smooth and glistening. Their eyes seemed to glow even brighter.

They flew toward the sapphire sky far above, but the weight of the two creatures and the pain of their claws and desperate clutches were making the journey unbearable. Tick punched down, smashing his fists into those odd faces. There was a piercing, awful screaming sound, but they held on. Tick punched again and again, those horrific cries ripping through the air, louder each time. He slammed down his fists once more, and they finally let go, dropping to the swiftly receding waters below them. He watched as they fell, listening as their screams slowly faded.

Tick continued launching toward the sky.

He looked up, a prickling sensation covering every inch of his body now, not just his insides. Forces pulled at him, like a magnet pulling a chunk of metal or Earth's gravity pulling a skydiver. Except he was flying up, heading toward a dome of brilliant, blinding blue.

Tick hurt. He'd been hurting for what seemed like days. But the closer he got to the blue wall of the sky, the more pain ripped through his body. He screamed like he'd never screamed before, the wind ripping at his face.

And then he hit the sea of blue, and it all went away.

PART
2

THE VOID

CHAPTER
20

HUGS AND KISSES

Tick's eyes were closed.

He opened them up and blinked a few times. He lay on a hard surface, and above him he could see the grooves and lines of a ceiling carved from black rock. Faces peered down at him, women in robes with the hoods pulled up over their heads. The women were old, and several of them made a circle around his spot as they looked at him with both wonder and fear.

"Hey," Tick said. His body ached from what he'd just been through—the flying and Chi'karda-laced battles, the plunge through liquid, the sharklike creatures, the lightning ropes, all of it—but not nearly as bad as it *should* have hurt. He felt almost at peace, though more confused than he'd been in a long time.

And then there were the sounds of commotion, people being pushed out of the way, calls of his name from two female voices that he recognized. *More* than recognized. Voices he knew as well as the sound of his own.

Lisa's face appeared above him first, then his mom's. Tears streamed down their faces as they came at him, pulling his body into hugs. Stunned, he hugged back, both of them in his arms, *their* arms wrapped around his shoulders and neck, his mom kissing him over and over on both cheeks. Somehow he managed to sit up, and they huddled for a long, long moment before anybody even spoke. Tick was overwhelmed, a part of him thinking it was all an illusion, terrified it might be and that he'd wake up any second. But sobs shook him as he fiercely hugged his mom and sister, a reunion that he'd begun to think might never happen.

Finally, his mom pulled back, as did Lisa. They both wiped tears from their eyes and cheeks.

"What . . ." Tick began, but his words were choked up in more sobs. Embarrassed, he wiped his own tears from his face.

"Happened?" his mom finished for him. "You're wondering what happened?"

"Uh, yeah," Lisa replied. "I think we'd all kinda like to know that."

Tick had begun to compose himself, and he suddenly felt like he needed to stand, get some fresh air, breathe. He got to his feet and looked around. The old women in their robes and hoods had backed away, gathering into groups of two or three and staring at him with questioning faces. They all stood in a small chamber carved from black rock, a place Tick had never seen before. He noticed a Barrier Wand lying on the floor by one of the slightly curved walls.

Looking at his mom, he said, "I think I could write down a million guesses of how I got here and be wrong every time. Where *are* we?"

She smiled in response. "There's a lot to tell. But that's an easy question to answer. We're in the Thirteenth Reality, in Mistress Jane's castle, in a room she calls the Great Hall."

Tick almost fell down. "The Thirteenth? Mistress Jane's castle?"

"Or what's left of it," Lisa said.

One of the strangers walked over to stand next to Tick and his little group. She had a long face and seemed to have an air of authority about her. "I'm happy to see that you've been pulled back from the Nonex, Atticus Higginbottom. I assure you that we tried as hard as we could to do so our-selves. You have my apologies. I'm sure our master will want to meet with you as soon as she's recovered."

Tick listened to the words coming out of the woman's mouth, getting more confused with each one. Finally, he just said, "Huh?"

She eyed Tick's mom, an eyebrow raised. "We will take our leave. You can do all the explaining you'd like to the young man. I haven't the time. But I'm sorry to say we'll be taking your Barrier Wand until further notice. Mistress Jane would not be happy if we allowed you to leave before she's spoken with you."

"Now just wait one minute, Mordell," Tick's mom re-plied. He was still wondering what the lady had meant by "your Barrier Wand." And why they were in Jane's castle. And how he'd gotten there. And lots of other stuff. "You have no right to do that after we helped you!"

Two of the other women grabbed the Wand that had been lying on the ground. It was slipped under a robe and gone from sight just like that.

"Hey!" Lisa shouted. "Give that back!"

Mordell spoke in a calm voice. "You're no longer considered enemies of our master. That's your reward for helping us. But we have plenty of creatures outside these doors that will ensure you do as we ask. Please don't push our hospitality. Wait here, and we'll return for you shortly. We'll also have food and drink brought to you."

Tick didn't feel like he knew enough about the situation to argue or help, but his mom was fuming, and Lisa had her arms folded and a red face.

"Mom," Tick said, "I'm not sure what's going on, but if we really are in Jane's castle, we better do what they say until we figure things out. Plus, I'm dying to hear how we all got here. Just let them go for now."

His mom visibly relaxed, as if she was relieved to have the burden of the decision taken from her shoulders. "Okay." She turned to Mordell. "Leave us alone and let us talk. And bring us that food." The hint of command in her voice made Tick want to hoot and holler like he was at a football game. This was his *mom*.

A smile crept up Mordell's face. "I've already said we would do the two things you ask. All things are done under the will and might of our master. Your food will be here within the half hour."

After a slight bow of her head, she and the other women shuffled out of the room.

They sat in a small circle as they spoke, sharing each other's tales. When they were finished, Tick knew *what* had happened, but not how or why. It was all crazy.

"So that bunch of old ladies winked in Jane and Chu, but were going to let me die out there?" he asked. "I can't believe I actually helped us get close enough to be saved, but then would've floated around in the outskirts of the Nonex for the rest of my life. That place wasn't fun, let me tell ya."

Tick's mom shook her head, looking half sad, half angry. "Jane and Chu appeared at the same time, lying on the same spot you did. The women didn't know that *you* were the one who'd opened up a doorway so they could reach them in the first place. Not that they would've done anything to return the favor—who knows?—but as soon as those two appeared, the almighty Ladies of Blood and Sorrow were done, totally ignoring our pleas to keep helping us so we could pull you in."

"Where did they go?" Tick asked. "Jane and Chu."

Lisa spoke up. "Mistress Jane marched off, her fancy red mask all scrunched up in anger. You'd think she'd have been happy after all that."

"And Chu?"

Lisa glanced at their mom, who provided the answer.

117

"He had a crazy look in his eyes. He said he finally knew how to 'finish his plans.' I think that's how he put it. Then he disappeared, winked away before the Ladies could stop him. Maybe he had people waiting for his signal to reappear back in the Realities."

Tick swallowed, realizing with a lump in his throat that *he'd* been the one who'd provided the opportunity for Reginald Chu—one of the most dangerous men in the Realities, who'd proven he wanted nothing but power at any cost—to come back from a prison he could've never escaped alone.

"Maybe I shouldn't have done that," Tick whispered.

CHAPTER
21

RAPPING AT THE DOOR

Master George lay his head back on the pillow, almost ashamed at how good it felt. He and Rutger had been working tirelessly for hours and hours, searching through all the data and reports from Mothball and Sally. Things were looking grim. Everywhere.

But the worst of it was what they *didn't* know. The disastrous results of Jane's meddling with dark matter had done something to the Realities. Something terrible. A lasting, lingering effect that they didn't quite understand yet. It had to do with links between the dimensions that weren't supposed to be there—rifts in the fabric of Reality appearing out of nowhere and killing people. Reports of gray fog and lightning and terrible thunder. George could scarcely hope they'd be able to *understand* it, much less do anything about it.

But even the greatest minds needed rest. Even his. The lights were off, the bed soft, the pillow even softer.

Muffintops—the best cat ever—was snuggled against his chest. If he could just sleep for one solid hour. That would do wonders for his—

Someone started pounding on his door, solid thumps with a squeezed fist, by the sound of it. George yelped, and Muffintops screeched, clawing him as she dug in her claws then jumped onto the ground. George's heart was practically lodged in his throat. The knocking continued without stopping.

Of course, it could only be Rutger.

"What *is* it?" George yelled from his bed. "Rutger, stop that incessant pounding! This instant!"

Rutger didn't stop, and was, in fact, saying some muffled words that George couldn't hear over the knocking. Sighing, he flipped off his covers and headed for the door, his disappointment at missing a nap overshadowed by dread. As excitable as Rutger was, he wouldn't be making this much fuss unless something bad had happened.

When George ripped open the door, Rutger almost fell down as his arm swung forward for another rap on the wooden door that was no longer there. He righted himself and looked up at his boss. George's heart lifted when he saw the huge smile on the little man's face.

"What *is* it?" George asked. "Goodness gracious me, you just about gave this old bear a heart attack!"

Rutger was breathing heavily, and he fought to control it. After starting and stopping several times, he finally got the words out, "Master Atticus is back! Tick is back! I've spotted him in the Thirteenth Reality, safe and whole and sound!"

George sucked in a gulp of air. "You're certain? No doubt?"

"Really? You really have to ask that?" Rutger's round face showed mock offense at first, but then he grinned.

"No, my good man, no, I don't. So, where is he then? Why haven't you winked him here straightaway? I want to see the boy!"

Rutger's smile vanished. "I tried. Something's blocking me. I think Jane must be keeping him in the Thirteenth Reality as a prisoner."

Master George's hands squeezed into fists at his sides. "Not this time. Jane is *not* going to interfere with us this time. Contact Sato. He and his army are already in that Reality."

Rutger turned to move, but George stopped him with his hand. "And get the others, too. We *need* to be together. Master Atticus could provide us just the lift we need. Finally, things are looking up."

Rutger smiled, then hurried off to follow his orders, his frantic waddle down the hall making Master George very proud indeed.

～～⌒

Tick, his mom, and Lisa had grown quiet, all talked out about the craziness of pulling Tick back from the Nonex. Now they sat with their backs against the black rock of the wall, the Great Hall empty and dark. A tray of dirty dishes and crumpled napkins sat on the floor next to the wall. Mordell had kept her promise to bring them something to eat. As well as her promise to keep them prisoner. Occasionally a fangen or another creature would pass by the opening to the chamber, just to make sure they knew leaving wasn't an option unless they wanted to be ripped to shreds or eaten.

Tick had been feeling guiltier by the minute. What had he done? How could he have been so selfish? He knew he needed all the Chi'karda he could summon to break free from the Nonex, so he'd used Chu and Jane. But he hadn't thought ahead to the fact that he'd be bringing the two worst enemies of the Realities back to their realms and giving them the opportunity to wreak havoc once again.

How could he be so stupid! He should have sacrificed himself and stayed in the Nonex, knowing those two monsters would be prisoners for the rest of their existence. He'd broken them free—or, at least helped it get started—just so he could come back, live his life, see his family again. The guilt ate away at his insides and made his stomach feel full of acid. And, of course, his mom could tell. She was a mom, after all.

"Atticus Higginbottom," she said, breaking the silence that had grown like a living entity, filling the room with something even darker than the air. "I know what you're thinking over there, and I want you to stop immediately. Do you understand me?"

Tick looked at her and tried to hide the despair that crawled inside of him. "What? I'm fine."

"You're fine, huh? And I've got bananas growing out of my ears. Nonsense, son. I know it's hitting you that Jane and Chu are freed from the Nonex. But it's not your fault. Who knows? Maybe they would've figured out a way to escape on their own eventually. It's what they do, how they got to where they are. They are masterminds, deceivers, manipulators, schemers. And *they* would've left *you* behind. The choices they make in life are not yours to bear. You did the right thing saving them. Maybe . . . maybe they'll change. Realize their mistakes and make them right."

Tick laughed, shocking himself just as much as the others. "Mom, now I *know* you're just trying to make me feel better. You heard for yourself what Chu said before they winked his power-hungry behind out of here. And Jane *had* her chance to become good. I ruined *that* when I melded her body to several pounds of metal. For somebody who was recruited to help the Realitants, I've sure done a great job of messing it all up."

His mom's eyes had welled up with tears, and she came over to sit next to him. She tried to pull him into her arms, and at first he resisted, but then he figured he could use some good old-fashioned mom-love and hugged her back. Fiercely.

"Listen to me," she whispered to him. "I'm your mom. I love you more than any human has ever loved a child before. Do you understand that?"

Tick nodded but didn't say anything. He was trying to hold back the tears.

Lisa was a few feet away, looking down as if she didn't feel like she had a right to hear this conversation.

"You did the right thing, Atticus," his mom continued. "Can you imagine—keeping a boy away from his mom? From his dad? From his sweet sisters? You did what you had to do to come back here, because you felt our love pulling you. You felt it across the universe and all the Realities and the barriers of the Nonex, because it's that powerful. You had no choice, son. Love is more powerful than Chi'karda, and you had to obey its call. We need you. Your family needs you. Nothing could keep us apart. Nothing will."

"Okay, Mom." Tick didn't really know what to say, but he squeezed his mom even tighter, not caring if he seemed like a two-year-old kid. "Thanks."

"And one more thing," she said. "You didn't just bring back two bad guys. You brought back *you*. Someone who has more power over Chi'karda than anyone in history. Even Mistress Jane. The Realities need you, Atticus. They need *you* more than they *don't* need them. Clear?"

"Clear."

Her words really affected him. Lying around feeling sorry for himself wasn't going to be the answer. He needed to be ready to take action. He swore to himself that he'd be prepared. He'd study and learn and practice. And if the day came that either one of his enemies tried to hurt the worlds again, he would stop them. He swore it.

"I love you," he whispered to his mom.

The shuffle of feet drew their attention to the entrance

of the chamber. Mordell, the long and lanky Lady of Blood and Sorrow, stood with her hands folded in front of her.

"I supposed you've had your time to rest and eat," the woman said. "But it's over now. At least for Atticus. Mistress Jane would like to see you, boy. She says it's high time you two spoke about the Fourth Dimension."

CHAPTER
22

A RIBBON OF SHINY SILVER

Sato stood atop the rock that jutted from the hilltop, allowing himself to finally enjoy a moment to himself. The land fell away in all directions, flowing with green grasses and thorny shrubs and leafless trees. Autumn had come to this area of the Thirteenth Reality, and there was a bite to the air that made Sato shiver. Far below him was a river that cut through the valley like a shiny silver ribbon, disappearing into a forest and the mountains beyond.

Somewhere along that river was the castle of Mistress Jane.

It had taken only a couple of days for his army to clean up the few scattered creatures left behind at the evil lady's Factory, otherwise known as the house of horrors. It was where Jane had used her frightening mix of science and magic to create mixed breeds of animals. Humans had been next on the list for her experiments, until the ones she was holding prisoner had been rescued by Sato and the Fifth Army.

All of them but ten.

Sato would never know the faces of the ten people he'd had to leave behind when the destruction became too much. Ten people left to die, crushed by stone and earth. He couldn't blame Master George and Rutger—they'd done what needed to be done. If Sato and Mothball had stayed to rescue those last few people, there would have been twelve dead bodies instead of ten. But that didn't change the fact that their loss haunted him day and night. If only he had been a little faster . . .

But here he was. Back in the Thirteenth again. They had hunted down any creatures of Jane's they could find around the ruins of the Factory, and something told him that any that were left were heading for the castle. He knew he was right after having received word from headquarters that Tick was now imprisoned there, along with his mom and sister.

Tick's sister—Lisa. Sato kind of liked that girl.

He shook his head, ashamed of himself. What a stupid thing to think at the moment. First of all, he couldn't believe that Tick was back, safe. *There* was a story he was dying to hear. And second, he hated to hear the words *Mistress Jane* again. Hated it. She'd killed his parents, burned them alive, right in front of his young eyes. He dreamed of it every night. The only silver lining was that maybe he'd finally get his chance for payback—at *his* hand, not Tick's.

A voice behind him interrupted his thoughts. "Master Sato, we're waiting for word on what we do next."

Sato turned to see an enormously tall man with thin features, his black hair hanging in straggles, his face gaunt, his clothes raggedy. But Sato knew that no one should ever make assumptions based on the appearance of these warriors from the Fifth Reality. They could break a man in half with two fingers.

He especially liked this one, Mothball's very own dad. "Gather them up, Tollaseat. We're marching for the castle. For Tick. For *Mistress Jane*."

Tick didn't put up much of a fight. With Jane's monsters hovering around outside the Great Hall, Mordell looking as if she'd bite anyone who gave her any trouble, and—most of all—out of pure curiosity, he decided to calmly walk with the old woman to where Jane waited for him.

They'd come out into the long underground passage that went along the river, the same place where Tick had used his own power to wink himself and his friends away from the fangen attack during their first visit to the Thirteenth Reality. More of those creatures lined the wall now as he and Mordell walked past them, their thin wings folded in, their fang-filled mouths closed, their yellow eyes glaring at him. Tick felt a nauseous chill in his gut.

It wasn't long before he began to see the extent of the castle's destruction. Walls had caved in. Huge chunks of rock had been torn loose from the ceiling and crashed to the ground, breaking the stone floor and creating spider webs of cracks everywhere. It got worse the farther they went; soon they were walking through a maze of debris. Tick looked in horror at some spots that appeared as if one puff of breath would cause the whole structure to come tumbling down on top of them.

They eventually reached an arch that exited into a dark staircase, narrow steps spiraling up to heights Tick couldn't see. Dust covered the steps, but the walls seemed solid enough. Mordell didn't say a word the entire time, just led him toward the upper reaches of the castle.

Tick was out of breath when they finally came to a wooden door.

Mordell stopped and looked at him with a grave face. "These are not the usual quarters of our master. The destruction caused by"—her eyes narrowed, and Tick knew she'd been about to say that it was all his fault—"the Great Disturbance made quite an impact on our grand castle. Mistress Jane takes her place here until all can be repaired. Wait until I beckon you to enter."

She rapped lightly on the wooden door three times. A few seconds later, it opened, and another woman in a hooded robe stared out at them. She nodded then allowed Mordell to step inside, shutting the door in Tick's face.

Tick was tempted to knock on the door himself—or better yet, just open it up and waltz inside. He wasn't nearly as scared of seeing Jane as he'd been in the past; his progress in the powers of Chi'karda had given him more confidence than ever before in his life. Forcing patience on himself, he stood and waited, knowing that Jane would probably make him wait awhile just to anger him.

He was right. At least fifteen minutes went by while he stood and stared at the walls and steps of the staircase. But just in case Jane was spying on him somehow, he refused to show his frustration or annoyance. He merely waited.

Finally, the door swung open. Mordell was standing there.

"In normal days, our master would disintegrate the wood, inspect you with snooper bugs, make a show of her great powers. But she says she is tired and weak, and that she expects understanding from you. Times are not as they once were."

Tick was surprised by the woman's words and shocked that Jane would dare show weakness, much less admit it outright. Not sure what to say, he shrugged, doing his best to act like it meant nothing to him either way.

"Then come." Mordell swung the door wide, and Tick stepped into a small chamber that led to another opening. Beyond that was a sparsely furnished room with a couch and a few chairs, a small window looking out on the fading light of day.

Jane was lying on the couch, the hood of her yellow robe pulled up over her head, her red mask set in a blank expression. With one of her scarred, withered hands, she motioned for Tick to sit down on a chair near her. He did so, wondering anxiously what she wanted to talk to him about.

"The Fourth Dimension," he said first, skipping the formalities. "This lady says you want to talk to me about the Fourth Dimension. Why?" His voice was naturally curt and devoid of feeling when he was around this woman. What kind of a person had he become to feel such things?

Jane sat up straighter and looked at him through the eyeholes of her mask. "You did something terrible, Atticus. Something really, really terrible."

CHAPTER
23

JANE'S TALK

Tick didn't need one more thing to feel guilty about, and for once he'd been taken by surprise. Here he was, in the castle of Mistress Jane, the woman who had planned to suck the life out of human children and use it to create monstrous creatures, and she was telling *him* that he'd done something terrible.

"And what exactly is it that I've done?" Tick asked.

Jane grunted as she swung her legs around off the couch and placed her feet on the floor, sitting upright. Her artificial face still had no expression. "My castle, Atticus. It's not a pretty sight. My beautiful room atop the palace is now nothing more than a pile of rocks crushed on top of other rocks. My castle—other than a few spots like this one and the Great Hall—lies in ruins. Most of my servants were killed. My most faithful and trusted servant, Frazier Gunn, is nowhere to be found. My body is weak, and my mind is tired. And here I sit before you now."

Tick didn't see where this was going at all. "What does that have to do with me?"

"My point, Atticus Higginbottom, is that I'm not in any mood to fix the problems you've created for the Realities. Not in a mood at all."

"Tell me, what horrible thing did I do again?" Tick was surprisingly curious.

Her mask melted into a frown. "When I used the Blade of Shattered Hope, Atticus, I was trying to do something that would benefit humanity in the long run. You saw only the short-term point of view—the destruction of an alternate reality—but it was a vital step forward on a journey toward a final and perfect Utopia. Eternal happiness for the rest of mankind's existence. You did *not* understand!"

Tick's anger flared. "Don't sit there and preach to me! There's not a rational person alive who would call anything you've done *good*. You'd have to be totally insane, which I think you *are*. So I guess it makes sense."

"Insolent boy," Jane muttered harshly, like an expelled breath of frustration.

"And you still haven't told me what I did that was so terrible."

"You cracked open the Fourth Dimension!" Jane yelled, standing on her feet as she did so. "You've unleashed a force that we hardly understand! And for all your noble talk about saving people, you've done the worst thing possible! The very energy that created the universe is now on the verge of exploding outward to do it all over again."

Her red mask was pinched in vicious anger, her eyebrows

slanted like crossed swords. And her scarred hands were squeezed into fists as she breathed in and out heavily. "I knew it as soon as I got back. I've always known there was a link between the Chi'karda here and the mysteries of the Fourth Dimension. Your battle with me, and the unprecedented amounts of Chi'karda we unleashed, broke that link, Atticus. Every single one of the Realities is in an enormous amount of trouble. All the earthquakes and tornadoes and destruction will seem like the good old days soon enough."

Tick realized with a sinking stomach that Jane was telling him the truth.

"Look, I have no idea what you're talking about," he said. "Just sit down and relax. Neither one of us is going anywhere."

"Sit down and relax?" Jane repeated, as if he'd told her to eat a live rat. But she sat down anyway, folding back into the soft cushions of her couch. "There's no time for relaxation, boy. I first suspected something was wrong when we were in the Nonex and I saw the rift in the air that led to another world. Another Reality. For that rift to reach the Nonex, I knew it wasn't as simple as a pathway between worlds. It had to be something much deeper. And then there was the incident with the earthquake and the subsequent uptick of craziness."

Tick knew that the Nonex was a place where a gorilla could suddenly erupt out of the sand, then turn into a moth and fly away. All kinds of unexplainable stuff happened all the time, but Jane was right. The craziness had ratcheted up considerably right before they escaped.

"You do remember the rip in the air I saw?" Jane asked.

"Huh? Oh. Yeah. I do."

"There was a boy and his father, or perhaps his grandfather, in a forest, looking back at me. And I knew something was off about it, something dangerous. I backed away, and just in time, too. A terrible storm of gray mist and thunderous lightning exploded within that rift, destroying whatever was close by on both sides of the rift. You saw what the area looked like afterwards."

Tick remembered. It had reminded him of TV footage of a tornado's aftermath. "So you're saying that what you saw was the Fourth Dimension?"

"A better way to put it is that I saw what comes *out* of the Fourth Dimension. The Void of Mist and Thunder. It's always been a rumor, a myth—pure speculation. Until now. I believe the Void is a living thing, but without conscience. The complete and pure power of creation. All it wants is to escape its prison and consume everything in its path. It's mindless and hungry."

"How do you even know about it? You already have a name for it, but you never told anyone about it. Why not?" Tick felt sick inside. Here was yet another thing that had gone wrong. And somehow it linked back to being *his* fault.

"I'm old," Jane said. Her red mask had returned to a blank expression, but Tick knew anything could set her off. "I've researched the origins of our universe in hopes of making it better. That crotchety old George and I worked on this project together, years ago. Trust me, I'm sure he's figured out what's going on by now and is sweating a river."

"What *is* the Fourth Dimension?" Tick asked. "I still don't really get it." He hated admitting that to her, but he had no choice.

"Well, you know what 3-D is, correct? Three dimensions?"

"Yeah."

"Well, the Fourth is named that because it's a step beyond anything we understand in terms of vision and . . . placement. Three-D is exponentially greater than 2-D. And the Fourth is infinitely greater than 3-D. The power of the Void is much, much greater than any kind of energy we know in our own dimension. If unleashed, it will consume this world like food and use it to recreate another. And all of us will die along the way."

Tick almost wanted to laugh. "You're really clearing things up."

The mask flashed to anger. "Stop it. Now. None of your childish sarcasm, do you understand me? What I'm talking about is very serious. More deadly than even my Blade of Shattered Hope. *Do you understand?*" She shouted the last question, making Tick lean back in his chair. "It was your meddling with that Blade that ripped open the Fourth Dimension in the first place!"

"Okay, I get it." Tick was scared, but he didn't want to show it. "But this isn't the first time you've tried to work with me. The last time ended with you trying to choke me to death. Remember?"

"Oh, Atticus." The anger and spirit seemed to drain straight out of Jane, her shoulders slumping and her mask melting into another frown. "Do you still really believe I was trying to kill you that day? We had to stop Chu, and at the time, hurting you was the only way to get you to release your Chi'karda. You couldn't do it at will like you can now."

Tick looked at the floor. Jane confused him so much. She seemed to have some good in her, but she'd also done some terrible, awful things. But could he really blame her completely after what *he'd* done to *her*?

"I don't know what to do," he said quietly. He was tired of thinking. "I just don't."

"Atticus," Jane said, her raspy voice quiet, like a small clearing of the throat. "I'm not going to sit here and pretend that you and I are best friends. I resent you for what you did to me, though I know it was partly out of your control. I *know* you hate me. And I'm not making any promises to stop fighting for a Utopia for mankind. When this issue is dealt with, I'll continue with my mission. I will do whatever it takes."

Tick looked up sharply. "You will, huh? You'll go right back to destroying entire worlds and throwing little kids into awful experiments? No skin off your back, right?"

Jane pounded a fist on her knee. "Yes! I will do whatever it—"

Her words were cut off by the door slamming open, the entire room seeming to tremble. Jane and Tick both shot to their feet to see who had come in.

It was Mordell, and her face was pale with fright.

"The Fourth Dimension has torn open outside the castle," she announced in a shaky voice, as if she had to avoid shouting to preserve the dignity of her order. "The Void is attacking our creatures."

CHAPTER
24

FOG AND THUNDER

Lorena had been holding Lisa in her arms—the girl had finally dozed off—when she heard the terrible sound in the distance. It was like a great, rushing wind, with cracks of thunder splintering it. And then she heard the screams. Unnatural screams that she knew came out of the mouths of Jane's creatures.

Lisa's head popped up immediately, her chance at slumber gone. "What *is* that?"

"I don't know, sweetie." Lorena's heart picked up its pace, and a swell of panic bulged in her chest, making it hard to breathe. If something was making those awful monsters scream, then what would it do to *them*?

She heard the scuffle of feet running along the passage outside the Great Hall. Grabbing Lisa's hand, she stood up, and the two of them went over to the arched exit to investigate. The two fangen that had been assigned to guard them were gone, and dozens of creatures were frantically scurrying past the opening, *away* from the shattered door that led outside to the castle grounds. Any noise of their passage was drowned out by the sounds of thunder crashing and booming, which were getting louder.

"What on *earth*?" Lorena whispered, barely hearing herself. She looked at Lisa, whose eyes were wide and scared.

"It sounds like a storm!" her daughter yelled to her. "But how could it be hurting all those people?"

"You mean *creatures*." Lorena shook her head. "It has to be something more than a storm."

"Let's go look!" Lisa shouted.

Lorena frowned at her, thinking her daughter had surely gone nuts. That, or she was still young enough to let curiosity overrule common sense.

Lisa pulled her mom closer and spoke into her ear. "If it's not just a storm, and if it's hurting the *bad* guys, then it must be on *our* side. We need to find out who or what it is and let them know that Mistress Jane has Tick!"

Lorena had started shaking her head before Lisa even finished. "No way!"

"But this is our chance! No one's guarding us!"

"No way," Lorena repeated. But then she peered into her daughter's eyes and saw that courage had replaced the fear to a degree. Motherly pride filled her chest and made her change her mind. "Okay, maybe just a peek. But we stop when I say so. Do you understand?"

Lisa smiled, a pathetic little effort. "Okay. I promise."

Like two spies, they slipped out of the Great Hall and

ran down the passage alongside the internal stream, toward the broken door and the gray wall behind it.

Sato pulled up short when he saw the strange anomaly appear right in front of the castle. They'd been marching for several hours, the sun sinking toward the forest on the horizon, the Fifth Army like a slow-moving tsunami behind their leader. Sato had promised them that one day soon, they'd return to the Fifth Reality and take back their world from the Bugaboo soldiers who'd gone insane and ruled with crazed minds.

But for now, the army was pledged to help the Realitants get things back in order. And before even that, Sato wanted to see his friend Tick again. See him safe and sound.

They were cresting the rise of a hill, the land sloping below them toward the castle, when Sato saw something that made no sense, made him doubt his own eyes. Made him wonder if they'd been working too hard and his mind was on the fritz.

Starting at a spot about fifty feet above the ground, close to the ruined castle itself, the air seemed to rip apart like a burst seam, the blues and whites and greens of the world replaced by a stark and empty grayness that spread in a line toward the grasses below. Lightning flickered behind the torn gash in reality, and even from where he stood a mile or so away, Sato could hear the rumbles of thunder. Not just hear it—the noise made the ground tremble and his head rattle.

Tollaseat stepped up beside him. "There's been rumors

of the like, there 'as. Fabric of the world rippin' apart and whatnot. Sendin' out destruction for the poor blokes who might be standin' nearby."

Sato nodded. He'd heard some of the soldiers whispering about it, but seeing it in person sent a wave of unease through his bones and joints. There was something terribly unnatural about it, and he knew it meant trouble.

"What should we do, sir?" Tollaseat asked. His voice revealed a trace of fear, but Sato knew the man and his fellow soldiers would storm the odd thing if he asked. Which he did.

"We need to know what that is," Sato said, hearing the strong command in his own speech. "And we need to save Tick. One mission has become two."

Tollaseat clapped him on the back. "We'll roll it up and bottle it, we will. Take it back to old Master George with a wink and a smile."

"That we will," Sato agreed. "Let's move out."

The Fifth Army started marching down the hill.

⌒

Tick felt weird following Mistress Jane down the long, winding staircase. He felt weird about being around her at all. He was pretty sure two mortal enemies had never acted like this before, trying to kill each other one week, then chit-chatting about the world's problems before scurrying down some steps to investigate a bunch of noise and fog the next.

He *was* curious. Was it a coincidence that the Void Jane had spoken of—this beast of the Fourth Dimension that represented some kind of pure and powerful energy—would attack her castle just as they had begun to scheme against it? Or did it have more of a mind than Jane thought?

They reached the bottom of the stairs and stumbled out into the main passageway, which was flanked by a narrow river on one side and the castle's interior stone wall on the other. It was a scene of chaos. Creepy chaos. Dozens of Jane's creatures, mostly fangen, were running pell-mell along the pathway, many of them wounded, some falling into the water. If the creatures started chasing him, he thought he'd die of fright before he could even think to use his newfound powers. But they all just kept fleeing, heading deeper into the castle.

Jane stopped to assess the situation, looking in the direction from which all of her creatures had fled. Tick did the same, but all he could see was a gray light. A rumble of something loud and booming came from there.

"Come!" Jane yelled, sprinting toward the odd light and the noise. Her robe billowed out as she ran, and her hood fell back, revealing the scarred horrors of her head, where her hair had once grown healthily. Feeling another pang of guilt, Tick followed her.

Lorena pulled up short about a hundred feet from the jagged edges of the broken door, stopping Lisa with an outstretched arm. No matter how much bravery they'd found, the loss of caution would be absurd. They could see better now, and Lorena wanted to understand what they were running toward.

A mass of churning gray air hovered behind the wide

opening of the doorway like clouds that boiled before unleashing torrents of rain. Streaks of lightning sliced through the grayness, illuminating the world in brilliant flashes of white fire. The thunder that pounded the air was deafening, making Lorena's ears feel as if they were bleeding. All the fangen and their cousins had either fled or lay on the ground around the door, battered and dead. Which made her wonder what she and Lisa thought they were doing coming this close to the danger.

The booming sounds stopped so suddenly that Lorena's ears popped, and the silence was like cotton that had been stuffed in her ears. There was the slightest buzz of electricity in the air, and the gray clouds behind the door were now full of tiny bolts of electricity, a web of white light. Lisa was about to ask something, but Lorena shushed her. Things were changing.

The churning, smoky cloud began to coalesce into sections, filtering and swirling, as if some unseen hand had begun to shape the substance like putty. Soon there were gaps in the mist, the green grass and blue sky shining through from beyond. The gray fog continued its shaping until several dozen oblong sections stood on end, scattered around like a crowd of ghosts. Then heads formed as the misty substance solidified into slick, gray skin. Arms. Legs. Eyes full of burning fire.

Oddly enough, they were roughly the shape of some of Mistress Jane's creatures that Lorena had seen fleeing. Though these were bigger and more crudely formed.

The one closest to Lorena started walking toward her.

CHAPTER
25

THE VOIDS

Sato was about a hundred yards away, Tollaseat and the rest of the Fifth Army right behind him, when the mass of fog and lightning in front of the castle started to shift and take shape. *Dozens* of shapes, bigger than most men, were continually refining themselves, their edges sharpening, until they looked like Mistress Jane's creatures. Arms, legs, wings, the whole bit.

Sato realized he'd stopped without meaning to.

"What bloody kind of business is that, ya reckon?" Tollaseat asked him from behind, a deadly whisper that fit the mood.

"I have no idea," Sato answered. "But there can't be anything good about it. We need to get there. Come on!"

Sato burst into a sprint, and his soldiers followed, their feet pounding on the grass like the hooves of a hundred horses.

Tick rounded a bend and finally came into view of the busted door through which he'd been before, a long time ago. Outside of it, dozens of gray shapes that roughly resembled Jane's creatures stood in the fields beyond the castle walls. He couldn't quite compute what was happening—they looked *similar* to what Jane had created, but they were also bigger, and . . . *different*. More humanoid.

The few figures in the front were walking forward, through the door. Their eyes shone with brilliant displays of fire, as if they were windows into a furnace. Tendrils of lightning shot across the surface of their slick, colorless skin.

Then Tick saw two people standing between him and the oncoming creatures.

"Mom!" he yelled, breaking into a run to reach her. "What in the world are you doing out here?"

She turned to face him, as did Lisa, and Tick's heart broke a little when he saw the fear in their eyes and expressions.

"We're trying to figure out . . ." his mom began to shout, but didn't finish. She pulled Lisa behind her and came toward Tick until they met. "It hardly matters. What are those things?" She gestured to the briskly walking gray people about fifty feet away.

Mistress Jane joined Tick, her red mask staring with a slight look of awe at the oncoming ghostly figures. The fire of their eyes reflected off the shiny, wet-looking surface of the red metal covering her hideous face.

Tick felt a shiver of panic, but he knew he had to put

146

on a brave front for his family. "It has something to do with the Fourth Dimension breaking into our Reality. It's pure energy, so maybe it can take things from our world and recreate them. Don't know, though. Come on."

He pointed down the passageway. The creatures were coming straight for them, marching with purpose. Their faces had no distinctive features—just eyes full of flame. Their arms and legs bulged with gray muscle, and their shoulders and chests were broad, but the wings—on those that had them—were misshapen and barely hanging on. Trickles of electricity continued to dance across the surface of their skin.

The Voids—that's how Tick thought of them, no other word coming to mind—had reached them and stopped. Now fully inside the castle, they lined up in several rows that reached back dozens of feet. There had to be at least fifty of the things. Eyes of fire, gray skin charged with lines of white lightning. But they were still now, staring at Tick and the others.

Mistress Jane spoke in a whisper. "The Fourth Dimension is even more powerful than I thought. What has it done to my sweet, sweet creations?"

~~~~~

When the gray creatures started entering the castle, Sato's urgency picked up even stronger. Tick was in there somewhere, and these things looked like nothing but trouble.

He sprinted harder, hearing the thumping of his soldiers

at his heels. They reached the torn land where the spinning mass of gray air had churned up the soil and ruined the grass. Sato ran across it, taking care not to trip over the divots and chunks of dirt. The inside of the castle was dark, but an eerie orange light shone from somewhere. Sato wondered if it might be coming from the faces of the creatures themselves, but they all had their backs to him at the moment.

Sato stopped at the threshold of the huge entrance and held up a hand. Tollaseat and the others stopped on a dime, and not a peep came from anyone.

The gray monsters had quit walking, and they huddled close together, watching something on the other side. Sato couldn't see over their heads.

"Come on," he whispered.

Trying his best to make no noise, skulking on the front pads of his feet, he moved forward, approaching the back of the pack. He was about ten feet away when one of the creatures turned around sharply to face them. Sato was shocked to see that the thing had two wide eye sockets filled with flickering, hot-burning flames. It was like the inside of its head was a forge, ready to heat up some iron for sword-making.

"What in the name of—" Tollaseat started, but further movement by the gray man cut him short.

A mouth was opening in the gray face, the gap also full of fiery flames, red and orange. It expanded until the upper edge almost touched the eyeholes, an entire face looking in on an inferno. The creature's long, thick arms ended in stumps that looked way too much like fists coiled in anger. But then the gray man stopped moving. He held that strange, menacing pose with its oven of a mouth stuck in a huge yawn.

Sato didn't know whether he should attack. He knew nothing about this enemy, or whether it really *was* an enemy. And if it was, he didn't know what kinds of power it had to fight them back. But he had to do *something*.

As he slowly took a few steps toward the creature, Sato's right hand reached down inside his own pocket and fingered one of the cool, round balls that were nestled in there. He pulled one into his grip, then out of his pocket. It was a Rager, its trapped static electricity bouncing to get out and destroy things.

The gray man started to growl, like a whoosh of air had ramped up the fire in his head.

〜⌒

Tick had been thrilled when he noticed Sato and his Fifth Army come marching through the broken door, many of the soldiers holding Shurrics, those deadly weapons of sound. Sato disappeared from sight—he was shorter than the Voids standing outside—but the heads of people of the Fifth Reality rose above the creatures, and their faces were mixed with awe and excitement. Not much fear.

All of the Voids had opened their mouths wide, fire raging within, their faces slightly angled toward the ceiling of the passage. Their arms were rigid at their sides, stumpy fists on the ends, wilted wings hanging off their backs. A low groaning sound came from the rear of the pack, like the roar of an airplane's engine as it started up.

The whole scene reminded Tick of a standoff in an old Western movie, and he didn't like it one bit.

"Mistress Jane," he said. "If you've got some advice, now would be a great time to share it."

The robed woman stepped forward, seemed to assess the situation for a few seconds, then turned to face Tick. Her mask had no expression, but the roaring, growling sounds were getting louder and louder.

"I don't know how to fight this kind of power," Jane said. "The Fourth Dimension has obviously taken my creations and turned them into a weapon of some sort."

She'd barely finished her sentence when one of the Voids in the front row ejected something from its mouth—a beam of pure flame, fiery and steaming, like a spout of lava shot from a hose. It flew up, then out, then came down and headed straight for Jane's head.

CHAPTER
26

RAGERS AND SQUEEZERS

As Tick dove forward, his shoulders smashing into the side of Jane and tackling her to the ground, somewhere in the back of his mind, he was aware that once again he was saving a person who'd devoted her life to doing evil things. No matter her intent. They crashed to the ground, and Tick felt a hot streak fly above him, almost enough to singe the hairs on the back of his neck.

He rolled off Jane in time to see the short stream of liquid fire sail past the rest of the crowd and hit the wall on the other side of the stream. Instead of splashing like lava, the fire sparked and burst into tiny explosions, crumbling some of the stone. Chips of rock rained into the water. But the weapon—or whatever it had been—left no trace, evaporating into the air with a puff of steam.

Jane and Tick jumped back to their feet, and everyone faced the Voids. Their mouths were still open in firing position, but none of them were doing anything just yet.

"Could it have been a warning?" Tick's mom asked. "Is there any way we can talk to them? If they're really from—"

"They *are* from the Fourth Dimension," Jane interrupted. "And talking to them would surely be a waste of time. I can't imagine they think like us, talk like us, see the universe like us. Our comprehensions of the Realities are probably as different as those of a spider and a redwood tree."

"Or more like a human and an ant," Tick murmured. "Maybe we're nothing more than something they need to step on."

Jane shook her head slowly back and forth. "We need to kill them, plain and simple. Atticus, prepare yourself. Pull in your Chi'karda, boy."

Tick felt a rushing behind his ears, his heart thumping. He turned to Mordell and made sure he avoided eye contact with his family. "Take . . . please take my mom and sister somewhere safe. Please."

"Atticus Higginbottom!" his mom said, planting her feet and propping her hands on her hips. "We can do just as much—"

Another one of the Voids shot a stream of flame and lava from its mouth. The fire sliced through the air toward the wall then curved, swinging around to head for Tick's group. Everyone collapsed to the ground—Tick yanking on his mom and sister's clothes—just as the deadly cylinder of bright red and orange flew over them and splashed into the wide stream next to the passage. Sparks and shoots of fire went everywhere as the water boiled and hissed for several seconds. Then it ended.

Tick grabbed his mom and looked her in the face. "Let me do this, Mom. You need to keep Lisa safe. Let me do this!"

Another burst of fire and lava came shooting through the air. This time it was Lisa who shoved Tick and his mom out of the way. The fiery stream slammed into the floor where they'd been lying. Sparks showered onto Tick; he swatted them off his shirt and stamped out the little fires around him.

"Mom!" he yelled. "You have to go! Jane and I can fight them off!"

There was no more argument. Mordell helped his mom and Lisa get to their feet, and then the three of them sprinted back down the passageway, heading for some place Tick hoped would protect them. Maybe the Great Hall. He turned back to the Voids in time to see another stream of fire erupting from a creature's mouth. The lava shot forward in a violent burst, as if the thing wanted it to reach the three fleeing women.

Tick acted without thinking. He triggered something in his heart, deep within his chest, and pulled something out with his mind and soul. A spinning cloud of orange sparkles ignited into existence around his body, and he threw some of it at the flying barrage of fire and lava. They met in mid-air and erupted into a fireworks show, sparks dropping and dancing on the ground. But it had worked, and Lisa and his mom disappeared around the bend, with Mordell on their heels.

It was Jane and Tick now. They exchanged a glance that somehow said, *Here we go again. Enemies working as allies.*

They stood side by side and faced the army of gray men, the Voids from another dimension. Tick wanted to say something but kept his mouth shut and waited for the battle to begin.

Sato had pulled back his men and women, funneling them through the broken door and onto the flattened grasses outside the castle. Three of the gray men had fired spouts of flame and lava at his army, and one of the attacks had hit home, enveloping a giant woman named Erthell in fire. Two of her companions had thrown her into the river to put out the flames, and then stayed to help her back onto the bank.

Sato wasn't running away either. Without any kind of shield to protect themselves, he wanted to fight back from cover. He and several other soldiers lined up against the wall outside the entrance to the castle, Shurrics at the ready. Even more soldiers stood right behind them, ready to jump out and throw Ragers and Squeezers—the nasty little grenades with metal hooks that contracted into whatever they hit—at the enemy to cause distraction and pain.

"Ready the volley!" Sato shouted. "As soon as they fly and ignite, we start pounding them with sound. Ready?"

"Ready!" came the roar of their reply. Tollaseat was on

the other side of the broken door, and he flashed Sato a wild grin.

"Now!" Sato commanded.

Little balls full of dancing electricity and dozens of Squeezer grenades flew out of his soldiers' hands, catapulting through the air toward the lines of gray men. At the sight of the volley, the creatures started shooting bursts of lava and fire from their mouths, squirting pure heat in all directions. Some of them hit home, incinerating the Realitant weapons on contact. But some of the weapons got through and exploded, working their magic.

A couple of Ragers hit the ground several feet in front of the first of the creatures, cracking into the rock and collecting debris like shavings to a magnet. It happened so fast, but the process never stopped wowing Sato. The little balls rolled forward in a burst until they weren't little anymore, becoming great mounds of earth and stone that crashed into the unsuspecting gray men, throwing several to the ground and rolling over them. The ones that died seemed to explode into gray mist and were whisked up into the air, forming a small cloud. Jagged bolts of lightning crackled through the gray masses.

A few of the Squeezers made it through as well, exploding when they hit anything solid, their little metal clips flying in all directions. When they made contact with the gray skin of the creatures, the grenades' sharp, needlelike ends contracted and squeezed. The monsters roared with pain, flames leaping out of their mouths. The entire castle rumbled from the awful sound of it. One of the creatures was hurt badly enough that it dissolved into mist and flew toward the circling cloud like its companions had done. Several clouds hovered above the castle now.

"Fire the Shurrics!" Sato yelled.

He and his fellow soldiers aimed and obeyed, shooting out blasts of pure sound waves at the creatures. The leading edges of the waves, heavy thumps that were felt instead of heard, flew forward until they slammed into a few bodies of the gray men. Most of them erupted into mist and rose to join the other lightning-laced clouds. But there were still plenty more creatures to fight, and Sato kept shooting.

He caught a glimpse of the battle raging on the other side. Streaks of sparkling orange and thick, gray bodies flew in all directions. Their screams were like the roars of a blacksmith's forge.

Sato fired his Shurric at the enemy.

CHAPTER
27

BEAMS OF FIRE

The battle had begun slowly once Tick's mom and the others were gone. The few shots of fire and lava from the mouths of the Voids were easily blocked by Jane or Tick, taking turns as if they'd done this for years. There seemed to be more action on the other side of the creatures, where Sato and his army had obviously started attacking with some of the Realitant weapons. Tick recognized the sounds of Ragers and Squeezers and that skull-rattling thump of a Shurric. And there were weird cloud shapes of gray mist hovering near the ceiling above—tiny bolts of lightning dancing within.

But then things close by changed.

The entire front row of Voids closest to Tick opened their glowing mouths even wider, and pure flame poured out, gushing with lava and brilliant yellow light. There were at least a dozen perfectly cylindrical geysers of fiery material coming at Tick and Jane like a mass of thick snakes.

Tick threw all his focus into the Chi'karda that burned within him and sent it out in waves to crash against the oncoming heat. There were spectacular explosions and sparks and hisses of flame raining to the ground, bouncing like yellow raindrops. He had to keep his eyes open against the blinding light in order to see what was coming and where to aim his powers. Spots swam in his vision, purple blotches and streaks of black.

He wiped his hands across his face and blinked hard several times. Still the streams of pure fire came at him, and he blocked them, destroyed them. Jane was doing the same, but it was taking every bit of their effort. The point at which Chi'karda and Void-fire met and exploded was getting closer and closer to where Tick stood. He needed to change tactics, shift the advantage.

With a scream and an almost violent push of Chi'karda from his body, he ran forward, blasting away at anything dangerous that came in sight. His sudden movement seemed to take the Voids by surprise; several of them quit shooting their deadly venom. Tick narrowed his eyes, focused all his energy on the bodies of the Voids, and threw his power at them. An almost solid wall of orange sparks erupted from him like a wave, flying forward until it crashed into several gray men. The orange power swarmed around the Voids, picking them up and tossing their strange forms into the air, sweeping them away like a giant with a broom. Those strange, furnacelike screams tore through the building; the ghostly sound gave Tick the creeps.

He turned to see Jane copying his method, running

forward and bringing the attack to the Voids. A wave of Chi'karda shot out from her and sent even more of the gray humanlike creatures toward the ceiling like tossed bags.

Several spouts of Void-fire suddenly came shooting at Tick from the untouched creatures next to the far wall. Without time to react, he dove for the ground and rolled, feeling the impact of the fire hitting the ground near his back. Sparks and chunks of rock sprayed into his skin, needles of pain that made him roll harder and faster. As he spun, there was suddenly a drop below him—the hard floor vanished, and he was in open air. It was like time had frozen just long enough for him to realize that strange fact.

He plunged into the ice-cold waters of the castle river. The freezing liquid bit at every one of his nerves. He gasped for air as he began to right himself and swim back to the stone edge.

Something grabbed him by the ankle and pulled him under.

~~~~~~

They were making progress.

Sato called on his soldiers to enter the castle proper, firing away with their weapons as they advanced. The enemy's numbers had been cut in half at least, the gray bodies collapsing into a mist of smoke before swirling up to the high ceiling to form yet another lightning-laced cloud. It was like a storm had gathered in a false sky and rain would fall at any second.

Gray creatures still catapulted up from the ground left

and right on the other side of the fray, and Sato began to feel confident they had turned the tide. He kept firing, slamming the sound power of his Shurric into one creature after another. Beams of molten fire continued to shoot all around him; one came straight at Sato, and he dove and rolled to avoid it. He jumped back to his feet and kept fighting, as did the rest of the Fifth.

He heard the sound of splashing to his left. He risked a quick look and saw that Tick was flailing in the water of the river, trying to make his way to the edge. He seemed disoriented, or like he'd forgotten how to swim.

"Cover me!" Sato shouted to his closest soldier.

Sweeping his weapon left and right as he ran, Sato booked it to the river's edge, wary of any arrows of fire that might come his way from the gray men. But the battle seemed almost over—he could see that witch, Mistress Jane, using her powers to destroy the same enemy he fought. That made a million questions tear through his mind—almost made him stop running. Mistress Jane. He couldn't possibly accept that she was on his side.

"Sato!"

He looked down to see Tick's face in the water, his hand reaching out for him. He was still thrashing as if he might drown.

"Tick!" Sato shouted as he got to his knees, leaning over to see if he could grab his friend's hand. Tick was about five feet from the river's edge. "Swim over here!" He looked behind him every couple of seconds to make sure nothing came at him that might dissolve his head in lava.

"Something's got my foot!" Tick yelled. "A tentacle, maybe! It's wrapped around my ankle!"

Sato leaned a little farther out and was almost able to grab Tick's hand. "Just . . . come a little closer!"

Tick didn't answer, just kept beating at the water with his arms. His body moved a couple of inches, but his hand was still out of reach.

Sato inched forward, his knees now extending past the edge, straining to clasp . . . those . . . fingers.

He made contact and squeezed his fist around Tick's and pulled, snapping his friend almost a foot closer. But then Tick jerked to a stop, almost causing Sato to tumble into the water. Something definitely had hold of Tick and wasn't letting go without a fight.

"Kick your body to the right!" Sato yelled as he pulled his Shurric around and took aim. The thing was heavy and hard to hold steady with one hand, but the noise and chaos of the battle still raged, and there was no one to help him. He risked another quick glance behind him and saw fire and gray bodies flying through the air.

Tick was doing his best to follow the order. Sato, with a shaking hand, pointed the Shurric at a spot that seemed clear of his friend and pulled the trigger. A soundless thump rocked the building, and water shot up in great spouts as if a meteor had just splash-landed. Tick suddenly tore loose and swam forward, almost leaping out of the river.

Sato dropped his weapon and grabbed Tick by the torso, pulling him the rest of the way. They collapsed on the ground, both of them soaking wet, sucking in and blowing out deep breaths.

Sato remembered that they could be incinerated at any second. He flopped over onto his stomach and surveyed the scene. Even in the last few seconds, everything had changed drastically.

There wasn't a gray creature in sight. To his left, Jane was standing stiffly with her arms held out in front of her, looking as haggard as any person Sato had ever seen. Her shoulders slumped, and she was struggling to breathe. Her mask was tilted on her exposed, scarred head, and its expression showed pure exhaustion. To his right, the Fifth Army appeared even more disheveled. Bodies lay scattered on the floor, many of them horribly injured or dead. Those standing seemed like wilted flowers, hoping for water and sun.

Sato's eyes wandered upward. Dozens of tightly wound clouds of gray mist hovered by the ceiling, lightning flicking and striking both within and between them. He was about to get to his knees, order everyone to flee the castle, when all the clouds suddenly collapsed into one, like some sort of separating membrane had been whipped free. The entire mass began to spin, a whirlpool of thick, gray mist churning in the air. A funnel formed in the middle and started lowering toward the ground. A breeze picked up, grew stronger, whipped at Sato's wet clothes.

Something terrible was about to happen.

"Run!" he screamed. "Everyone get out of here!"

CHAPTER
28

A MIGHTY WIND

Tick was sopping wet. And freezing cold. His ankle hurt from whatever weird creature had been gripping it, trying to pull him under to his death. He was exhausted from using Chi'karda to defend against those beams of fire and to fight back at the Voids.

But something odd was happening above him. His relief at seeing that the Voids were gone lasted all of two seconds. Looking up, he saw that the small, electricity-filled clouds from earlier had grown in number until they'd gotten too big, collapsing into one giant, churning mass of gray. As the funnel cloud began to lower to the ground, the wind picked up measurably, making his already wet skin grow even colder. When Sato screamed for everyone to run, Tick didn't waste any time pondering the command.

He jumped to his feet, feeling the sogginess of his clothes, the weariness of his bones and muscles. Sato grabbed him by the arm and pulled him along as they ran together toward the giant door with its frame of broken wood.

The wind was increasing in speed by the second, whipping the air in a frenzy. Tick's clothes flapped like flags on a speedboat, almost hurting his skin, and it felt as if every one of his hairs might rip out and fly away. The spinning funnel of the gray tornado descended rapidly as Tick and Sato ran, and Tick saw Mistress Jane standing on the other side of it all, motionless.

Her body disappeared behind the tornado as its leading point crashed into the stony floor. Lightning arced and arrowed through the cloud, the rattles of thunder sounding like detonations, deafening. The moment when storm met stone was violent, as if the cloud had been a giant fist of steel smashing down, shards of rock vaulting toward the ceiling from the shattered surface. The entire castle jolted, the floor jumping into the air and crashing back down again. Tick sprawled across the floor, still dozens of feet away from the exit. Others fell all around him, and tiny splinters of stone flew through the air, smashing into people.

Tick felt pinpricks of needles on his cheeks and threw his hands up to protect his face. Struggling against the wind and the still-shaking castle, he stumbled to his feet and leaned forward, making it several steps before he crashed to the ground again. He caught sight of the funnel that continued to twist like a giant drill digging into the hard earth below the layer of stones it had already destroyed. Rock chips flew in all directions, and with a broken heart, he realized that even more bodies littered the ground, many of them still moving, still trying to get up.

Like him.

He couldn't let this destruction continue. He had to *do* something. It had yet to become his instinct to use Chi'karda, to use his powers to fight instead of running away. But how? How could he fight a giant tornado filled with lightning?

His mind focused on the air around him, on the particles, molecules, atoms. Surrendering to his instincts, he created a wall, a shield from the countless chips of rock flying through the castle like tiny daggers. The wind suddenly decreased, and he saw the rocks bouncing off an invisible barrier inches in front of him. He stood up, his fists clenched, his brain working in overdrive. The exhaustion that had been consuming his body seemed like a distant memory as the pure fire of Chi'karda burned inside of him, raging as strongly as the winds that swirled around his shield did. Speckles of orange swam along his skin and thickened into a cloud, but it didn't obscure his vision. He was looking at the world through different eyes now.

The tornado of gray mist spun, churning like it was digging a hole to the other side of the earth, thickening at its core. Debris spun out from the ground and was caught in the mighty winds until everything was a fog of dust and stone.

Tick needed to help those who hadn't been able to escape. Sato was on his back, his face cut up, his eyes wide as he stared at Tick in disbelief as if he were a freak.

Tick's heart almost broke at the sight, but he knew what

he had to do. He threw his hands out, threw his thoughts as well. Sato's body suddenly leaped from the ground and flew like a tossed football, tumbling end over end and out the broken doorway. Tick swept his vision and his hands across the passageway, doing the same thing to each person he saw, whether alive or dead. Body after body catapulted into the air and went sailing through the exit, ripped from the ground as if a giant string had been attached to them, yanked by a puppet master. Tick didn't know how he was doing it, but he did it all the same. Instinct ruled his powers now.

He sent the last few people flying out of the castle. He didn't know if they'd land safely out there, or if they might break bones, or worse, but he knew they'd die if they didn't leave this place; that was all he could do.

When he was finally alone, he turned to face the massive cyclone of fog, its bolts of lightning flickering down the edges and smashing into the stone. It was almost like the energy from the bolts was trying to help dig the hole even wider. Thoughts rushed through his mind then, wondering if he should just turn and run. The people were safe; they could run or wink away and let this thing do whatever it wanted to do to Jane's precious castle.

She appeared to his right.

Wind tore at her robe as she inched along the far wall of the passageway, her back to the stone as she moved, her red mask tightening into an expression of fear as she stared at the tornado ripping apart the ground. Water had been sucked up into the churning funnel as well, sending a spray of mist in all directions and adding an odd blueness to the gray core. Jane was soaked.

A terrible thought hit Tick. What if this thing really didn't stop? What if the Fourth Dimension kept throwing all of its power into the Realities, growing and growing until it consumed everything? A spinning mass of material as big as the universe? He had to sever the link. Somehow he had to stop this; he knew it without any doubt.

He put out his hand toward Jane, manipulating the world with his thoughts. Her body jumped up into the air and flew toward him, landing right beside him. The look of shock on her mask gave him the smallest bit of satisfaction.

"What are you doing?" she yelled over the terrible noise.

"We have to stop this thing!" he shouted back. "We have to break the link!"

Jane's mask wilted at the suggestion. "I don't know if I can do it! I'm spent, Atticus! I have nothing left in me! I need to rest!"

Tick had to hide his shock. For her to admit to that . . .

"We have to try!"

Jane stared back at him through the eyeholes of her mask. Then she gave him a reluctant nod.

The two of them turned toward the tornado and held out their hands as if they were going to walk in and embrace the spinning thing.

"Try to collapse it!" Jane yelled. "Throw all your Chi'karda into collapsing its mass then we'll blow it apart! We have to hope that ends it and seals the breach into the Fourth!"

"Okay!" Tick screamed, his heart pumping. The power was an inferno inside his chest, and he was ready to unleash it. "Let's do it!"

He pushed his hands toward the spinning beast and released the Chi'karda that had been building and building. Streams of orange fire exploded from his fingertips and into the tornado, getting caught in the spin. Jane was doing the same. Soon the gray funnel was colorful and bright; the lightning was more brilliant and sharp, the thunder louder.

Tick screamed with the effort as he pushed more and more of his powers at the Fourth Dimension, trying to envision what he wanted, trying to make it happen. His body began to shake, his muscles weak. Chi'karda poured from him and Jane in spouts; the streams were almost the same color as what had come from the mouths of the Voids.

Now everything was shaking—the ground, the castle, his skull. The funnel of the tornado was white-hot, blinding. Impossible noises erupted from its form, and the wind was torrential, ripping away the shield Tick had built around himself.

He screamed again and threw all of his strength into the storm.

There was a sudden concussion of pure energy that ripped away from the tornado like the blast of a nuclear bomb. Tick felt his body be jerked into the air, and then he was flying. What remained of the castle exploded, every last brick of it cracking apart and flying right along with him.

He didn't hit the ground until he'd been thrown a thousand yards. A chunk of rock landed on his head, and all he knew was pain.

CHAPTER
29

JOINTS AND EARDRUMS

Lorena held Lisa close, and it broke her heart to feel the trembling of her daughter's bones. The girl had always been strong-spirited and tough, but no one could be expected to hide their fear after the last few days of their lives.

Mordell had brought them back to the Great Hall, whispering something about its natural powers and it being the best place to protect them. They found the farthest corner of the chamber carved from black stone and huddled together while Mordell sat nearby; she had a look on her face as if she wanted to be closer but had to maintain her dignity as a Lady of Blood and Sorrow. There wasn't much for the three of them to do except be scared and listen to the sounds of battle.

They were distant, but terrible: the swooshing of fire, screams of pain, shouts of command. Soon it all changed to a great, rushing noise, like wind passing through a narrow canyon, or a tornado. The screams intensified. And then the worst sound—breaking rock. It wasn't the loudest noise, but it made the entire castle quake and tremble. Lorena felt the vibration in her joints and eardrums.

She'd never felt so helpless. Her only son was out there, fighting something that seemed impossible. Something that shouldn't exist. And to add to it, he was fighting alongside the woman who'd tried to kill him and countless others. Atticus was putting his faith in a madwoman. It took every ounce of Lorena's willpower to not run back out that door and try to help her boy—she almost itched from the desire. But she had Lisa to think about. And Edgar and Kayla back home. Atticus could take care of himself—he'd proven it over and over.

And so the battle raged on, the sounds of fire and wind increasing in volume. Lorena could do nothing but sit and hold her daughter and imagine all the awful things that might have happened, or might be happening, to her sweet, sweet son.

Everything changed again in a moment. An instant so terrible and horrifying that Lorena knew she'd never sleep again without it haunting her nightmares.

It was an eruption. A detonation. A thunderclap of sound and movement that shook the Great Hall as if it were nothing but an empty cardboard box. Lorena and Lisa both screamed as they flew across the room, smacking into Mordell and rolling another few feet before coming to a stop. The air was filled with the noise of cracks and booms, as if the entire castle had exploded and collapsed in on itself.

Lorena threw away her caution and scrambled to her

feet, trying to set aside the panic that thrust itself through her nerves. She grabbed Lisa by the hand, lifted her to her feet, and ran to the exit of the Great Hall, swaying back and forth as the floor continued to tilt and pitch. She'd just stepped in front of the doorway when she stopped, her heart plummeting. Rock and stone and brick had collapsed into a heap, blocking the arched opening completely. Dust choked the air.

Mordell's voice from behind Lorena made her jump and spin around to see the woman standing there, impossibly looking even more grave than before.

"The Great Hall has survived," the Lady of Blood and Sorrow said. "But I'd guess nothing else has. We're trapped."

Sato was lying on his stomach, his hands held over his head to protect himself from the debris that had been raining down for several minutes. Every inch of his body had been battered and bruised by falling rocks, but luckily, his skull had been spared for the most part. It'd been rough going since everything went haywire inside the castle.

Not to mention the fact that he'd been thrown through the air. Twice.

First when Tick used his powers to pick him up and whip his body out of the castle. Saving him. And second when the castle suddenly exploded, a wave of pure energy erupting from its core and tossing him and the rest of his army hundreds of feet away like they were nothing but dried leaves. That had saved him again, because if he'd been any closer, he probably would've been crushed by larger chunks of stone from the destroyed castle.

And so, he was alive.

He pushed himself to his knees, groaning from the aches and pains that riddled his body. He was woozy too, the dusty grass beneath his knees seeming to bob up and down like the surface of the ocean. What little energy he had, drained right out of him, and he collapsed again, but at least he was able to spin himself a bit and land on his rear end. He could see the rubble that had once been the great castle of Mistress Jane, the woman who had killed his parents.

What had been half-destroyed before now lay in utter ruins. A giant heap of crumbled stone and wood and plaster. Pieces of the castle lay scattered outward from the main body all the way to where Sato sat and beyond, reaching the forest that wasn't too far behind him. But as satisfying as it was to see the carnage, he felt a tremor in his heart for what still pulsed and throbbed in the middle of the destruction like a beating heart.

The tornado of mist still churned where it had been, with nothing but open sky above it. Except it wasn't much of a tornado anymore.

It was a seething, roiling mass of gray, its billowing surface frothing and foaming before turning back in on itself, leaving little wisps of fog streaming out like some kind of dreary decoration. Lightning continued to flash and strike in huge bolts of brilliant white, the thunder rumbling across the ground and echoing off the wall of trees behind Sato. The mass was probably fifty feet wide and a hundred feet tall. It was still moving in a circular motion, but not as intensely as a tornado anymore. It was like a living thing, devouring the air around it and ever growing, slowly.

Members of the Fifth Army were scattered all over the field, groaning and rubbing their eyes and stiffly testing their joints, looking for injuries. Sadly, some *weren't* moving, and Sato felt the heavy weight of leadership once again. He'd led people to their death.

Something caught his eye as he scanned the area—a body that lay lifeless but wasn't as big as the others. A boy.

Tick.

A blister of alarm popped in Sato's heart as he leaped to his feet and started running, finding strength from some hidden part of his soul. He dodged and maneuvered around soldiers, his eyes focused on his friend, who wasn't moving a muscle, not even a twitch. Sato didn't know if he could take another death of someone so close to him. He was ashamed that he didn't feel quite the same about his army fighters, but this was different. Tick had become not just one of his closest friends, but a symbol of everything the Realitants stood for.

Sato jumped over a prostrate woman of the Fifth then slid onto the grass like a baseball player, coming to a stop right at Tick's head. The first thing he noticed was that his back was rising and falling, ever so slightly. Tick lay on his stomach, his arms spread out awkwardly, as if he'd landed and conked out immediately. But he wasn't dead. Thank the Realities, he wasn't dead.

Sato reached out and gently shook his friend's shoulders. No response.

He grabbed him by the arm and carefully rolled him over onto his back so he could get a good look at him. His eyes were closed, his clothes ripped and filthy, his skin covered in dirt and soot. But most troubling was a huge gash on the side of his head, blood matting the hair down like dark red gel.

"Tick," Sato whispered, trying to fight back the tears that wanted to pour out. Why? Why did everything in their lives always have to be so terrible?

"Tick," he repeated. Then he picked him up and slung him over his shoulders, grunting under the weight. He began to walk, though he had no idea where he was going.

CHAPTER
30

COMING TOGETHER

Paul walked through the twilit forest of the Thirteenth Reality, Sofia and Rutger to his right, Mothball, Sally, and Master George—using his Barrier Wand like a cane—to his left. No one said a word as they picked their way through the bush and bramble. The massive concussion of sound they'd heard a few minutes earlier was enough to silence anyone for a week. Paul forced his thoughts away from the terrible possible explanations for that sound and concentrated on moving forward.

Ever since he'd returned to the Realitant headquarters, he'd been dying to know what in the world the little button in the box Gretel had given them was for. Old George had sent them to Gretel for a reason, had given them a secret password for a reason, had wanted that box with nothing in it but a plastic green button for a reason. But neither he nor Gretel would tell him what it was supposed to be used for. Phrases like "a need-to-know basis" and "you'll find out soon enough" were thrown around. But that didn't satisfy Paul.

Not one bit.

Oh, well. They had much bigger problems on their hands. There was trouble here in the Thirteenth Reality, and any notion they'd had of getting rest and relaxation was out the window. Master George hadn't needed to tell them that when he said they'd all be winking there to regroup with Sato and find Tick. The situation was surely dangerous.

Paul smiled. It was as if his brain was so used to bad stuff that it wasn't allowing him to focus on the best piece of news he'd ever received in his life. Tick was alive. Tick was back. Now they just had to figure out this mess and get him home safe and sound.

The woods had slowly thinned over the last hundred yards or so, though the air up ahead seemed slightly murky, like a dust storm had passed through recently, which seemed impossible for a place so green and vibrant with life.

"Shouldn't we pick up the pace a little?" he asked the small crowd of Realitants.

"No need for haste, my good man," came the not-surprising reply from Master George. "Our old friend Jane might have placed a few traps along the edge of the forest. Won't do us much good to run willy-nilly right into them and spring the things."

Paul was annoyed. "Won't do us much good if we show up and everyone's dead, either."

"Don't talk like that," Sofia said. "He's going to be fine."

Paul heard a deadness in her voice that scared him. He

realized that she had already begun the process of accepting that just because Tick was back and alive didn't mean he was okay or safe. Paul didn't look at it that way. If their friend was back, he'd figure out a way to get out of any mess thrown his way. The guy was a freak of nature—in a good way.

"I mean it," Sofia added.

"Sorry," Paul muttered. "I'm just anxious to see him. Help him if he needs it."

She nodded but didn't say anything.

They finally reached a point where the end of the woods was visible, and all of them saw it at once. A person with a body slung over his or her shoulders, stumbling at the last line of trees. Even as Paul watched, whoever it was fell down and out of his view. For the first time, he could focus on the scene beyond. And it was like a scene out of an old war movie.

Dust-choked air. Bodies littering the ground, many moving sluggishly to get up, some not moving at all. Countless chunks of rock and wood strewn about the grassy fields. And past all of that, the closest edge barely in sight, was a big pile of ruins and rubble. Paul had been here before so he knew what it was—Mistress Jane's castle, completely destroyed.

Sofia broke into a run, her feet crashing through the weeds and twigs of the forest floor. Before Paul could follow her, she stopped like she'd seen a big snake. Then she was yelling.

"It's Tick and Sato!"

Tick's head felt like the end of a stubborn nail that refused to go into the wood straight. Like a hammer had pounded on it, bent it, yanked it straight, then pounded it all over again. He was barely aware of someone picking him up, then later falling again. He tried opening his eyes, but the light was like a sunburst right in front of him, stabbing and making the ache in his skull even worse.

Now he lay face-first on a ground that was prickly with twigs and pine straw. He groaned a couple of times to make sure whoever had tried to help him knew he wasn't dead, but even the sound of that went off in his head like clanging church bells. A sudden burst of nausea filled his gut.

Please don't throw up, he thought to himself. *Oh, please don't throw up.*

He heard noises then, shouts and the cricking and cracking of footsteps. It all became a painful blur to him, and he figured it didn't matter much anymore. He hurt, and that was that.

Someone rolled him onto his back, and that was the last straw. He jolted to his elbows and threw up to the side. When he finished, he flopped back flat to the ground and grimaced as a fresh wave of agony punched its way through his skull and down his spine.

"Tick?" said a soft voice. A girl. It took him a few seconds to recognize Sofia's voice, and his heart lifted. "Tick, are you okay?"

He wanted to tease her that she'd just asked him the dumbest question in history, but he figured that raising his voice—even talking at all—would hurt too much. So instead he mumbled something. Not even a real word, just an acknowledgment that he'd heard her. He still refused to open his eyes, terrified of the light.

He heard a crunch of ground covering right next to him and figured someone had knelt there.

"Master Atticus?" That was definitely George, and his heart lifted a little more. "Goodness gracious me, boy. What on earth has happened here?"

"Yeah, man. Quit napping down there and talk to us."

Paul. The relief inside Tick was swelling more by the second. At least his friends were safe, and he wasn't dead. Things could've been a lot worse.

"Really, Paul?" Sofia said. "Even now you have to be sarcastic? Look at that nasty gash on his head. We're lucky he didn't bleed out."

"I'm sure he wanted to hear that," Paul muttered back.

"Sato, what happened?" Master George asked.

Sato too? Tick thought. This was too good to be true. Maybe he was having one of those dreams where you see all your friends and loved ones before you died. That thought jolted him back to reality.

He sat up, the pain like strikes of lightning in his head. "My family. My mom. Lisa. Where . . ."

The pain and nausea were too much. He passed out again.

Lisa was starting to accept the fact that she was about to die.

It surprised her how easily the realization came. Although she felt a terrible sadness, it wasn't really about death itself. It was more about not seeing her dad and Kayla and Tick before she went. At least she had her mom.

They'd been silent for so long now. After a couple hours of trying to move the rocks and debris that blocked their exit from the Great Hall, they'd finally given up. Almost nothing would budge, and the one chunk of stone they were able to move was instantly replaced by several more from above. There was no sign of daylight in any of the cracks. What an awful way to die. They'd either starve or suffocate.

With cheerful thoughts like those, she'd resigned herself to sit with her mom, holding each other as they waited for the inevitable.

She was just thinking how stuffy the air had become when she heard a scrabbling sound near the exit, as though an animal was trying to burrow its way through the stack of debris. Then there was a crunching, some cracks, and the hollow scrape of stone against stone. Dust billowed out from the mess as rocks began to shift and collapse. Lisa didn't know what to think, but refused to let herself feel any hope as she waited to see what was happening.

Finally a huge section of the rubble shifted and slid away, leaving a huge gap, choked with dust. A robed figure appeared, hunched over and filthy. Mistress Jane stepped into the room, the light from the lone torch barely reflecting off her dirty red mask.

Mordell lost every ounce of her usual reserved demeanor. "Master!" she yelled. "Master, you're alive!"

"For now," she said in her raw, scratchy voice—it sounded weaker than ever. "Come. We have a lot of work to do."

CHAPTER
31

FROM HEAD TO TOE

When Tick came to his senses again, the pain in his head had lessened a bit. The tiniest, tiniest bit. But the nausea was gone, and it didn't seem like the whole world would swim away from him at any second.

Someone—he didn't know who—helped him sit up. Groggy and dazed, he waited a few seconds before opening his eyes. The light had faded considerably, the orange glow of sunset settling somewhere to the west beyond the trees. The others were sitting around him on the edge of the forest; they could see the long fields of grass, littered with rubble and debris, that led to the utter ruin of what had once been the mighty castle of Mistress Jane. He could just barely see the slowly spinning mass of gray mist that still churned within it. He looked away. He didn't want to look at it or think about it.

He couldn't believe all the people sitting around him. It was like a reunion too good to be true. Mothball, with her scraggly hair and her clothes hanging off her skin-and-bones body, her face lit up by a smile that seemed almost out of place in the gloom of their situation. Rutger, his round body nestled next to her like a fat penguin. Master George, dressed up as always, though his suit was wrinkled and dirty, with a Barrier Wand laid across his lap. Sally, sitting cross-legged in his plaid shirt and overalls like a lumberjack waiting for an order to start cutting down the trees around them.

And then Tick's three best friends, sitting in a row, staring at him like they expected him to give a speech. Sato. Sofia. Paul. They were dressed as if they'd just gotten home from school, but worry etched lines on their faces. Tick didn't know if it was the fading light, but they looked older. They definitely looked older.

And then an emptiness hit him again, hard. It was like he was looking at a portrait of his life, and a big chunk had been ripped out. His family.

A wave of despair almost made him pass out again. "My mom and sister," he said, hearing the panic in his own voice. "I told Mordell to take them somewhere safe. Any idea what happened to them?"

Everyone in the group looked at one another; they didn't need to say anything.

"We have to go look for them," Tick said, starting to get up.

Master George reached out and put a hand on Tick's shoulder, gently making him sit back down. "Atticus, none of us even know what *happened*. The castle is completely destroyed, and Sato's army is just now recovering and counting up their losses. Before we can help you or find your family, we need to know *what* we're dealing with. A few minutes more won't change their plight. In fact, the more informed we are, the more we can help them. Do you understand?"

Tick didn't. For some reason, he was angry. "I'll go sift through every one of those stones by myself if I have to."

"You mean they were *inside* the building when it collapsed?" Master George's face paled.

Tick stood up. "*Yes,* they were inside. And if you haven't noticed, there's a big tornado right in the middle of all that mess. Maybe growing closer to my mom and sister right now."

"Which is exactly why we need—"

"No!" Tick yelled. "No."

He was lost and confused by the worry that ate away inside of him, but he didn't care. He got to his feet and started marching toward the ruined castle, ignoring the pain that lanced through his body from his skull to the bottoms of his feet.

⁓

Lisa didn't like what Jane had gone on to say about the Fourth Dimension and the all-consuming Void it had unleashed. She assumed that it would consume *her* too. But Mistress Jane had said little else—including whether or not Tick was safe. Instead she had rested for a time, eyes closed, until she was ready. Then she started using her fancy powers to move and shift more of the rubble so they could get out of the destroyed castle. Lisa watched, fascinated.

The woman's robe was a mess, caked with grime and dust, ripped in countless places. Her hood hung off her head like a discarded flag, revealing a scarred mass where her hair should've been, the skin red and raw. Lisa knew she was supposed to hate Mistress Jane—the crazy lady who'd killed people and done evil, evil things—but how could you not feel sorry for someone who looked so miserable and probably felt even worse?

But nothing seemed to faze Jane. She held up her wounded hands like Moses parting the Red Sea, and sparkles of orange flew from her body in sprays of bright mist. Grinding sounds filled the air as rock and stone moved at her will, shifting and flying and breaking apart. Dust clogged the air, but she used her power to whisk that away as well, obviously needing to see what she was doing.

After several minutes of this show, Lisa was expecting to see daylight spill into the room, but it never happened. She had no clue what time it was, and her heart dropped a little to think it might be in the middle of the night. She'd never wanted to see sunshine so desperately, and she was dying to get out there and see if her brother was okay. To see if he'd survived whatever force was trying to "eat this world," as Jane had put it.

Her mom reached out and squeezed her hand as if she'd sensed the thought. "I'm sure he's okay. He has to be. If this witchy woman made it through, I'm sure our boy did too. Don't you worry."

Lisa looked at her mom and forced a smile. "Yeah, I'm sure you're not worrying one bit. Are you?"

"Of course not." She grinned back. "Okay, maybe a teensy tiny bit."

Mistress Jane stopped what she was doing. The fiery orange cloud sucked back into her like something shown in reverse on video, and she lowered her hands. The woman's shoulders slumped as if she'd used every last ounce of her energy. Now that the rock and stone had quit grinding and cracking, Lisa heard another odd sound. Like a rushing wind, with a hum and bulge of power behind it. It reminded her of the heavy thrum of machinery, as if somewhere around the corner was a manufacturing plant still trying to work its way through the landfall of a hurricane.

Mordell had stayed very quiet through the whole ordeal, but now she walked up to Mistress Jane and gently put her hands on her boss's shoulders.

"Are you alright, Master?" she asked in a voice Lisa barely heard over the noise coming from outside. "May I help you sit down?"

Jane turned around, and her mask showed no emotion at all. "My friends. My creatures. I . . . What did the Void do to them?"

Lisa thought that was a strange thing to say and exchanged a confused look with her mom, who shrugged her shoulders slightly then spoke. "What do you mean, Jane? After everything that has happened, the abominations you created are the only thing you're worried about? Do you even care in the slightest that my son could be out there, hurt or dead? *Do you?*"

Lisa's mom had grown angrier with every word and had shouted the last question. She visibly huffed like a bullied kid on the playground.

But Jane seemed to have no reaction. Maybe she was just too weary. "I fear for your son, too, Lorena. I do. But you could never know what it's like to stand here and not sense the presence of hundreds of your own children. The Void took them . . . transformed them somehow."

Lisa's mom took a furious step forward and stopped, as if she realized how crazy it would be to threaten this woman who'd done the magical things they'd just witnessed. "I could never know? You stand there and say I could never *know*? I have an actual child out there, and you're talking about things that were created only to hurt and kill others."

Lisa had never seen her mom so mad.

Unfortunately, so was Jane. Her red mask pulled back into a fierce expression. "How dare you speak about them that way! You have no inkling what you're talking about! I won't stand for this disrespect!"

Lisa knew her mom was about to do something stupid. She quickly grabbed her arm and pulled her back. "Who cares what she thinks, Mom? Let's just get out of here and—"

There were several soft thuds of something landing on the ground nearby, and Lisa heard her mom gasp. She quickly turned around. Several people had jumped down from the piles of rubble to join them, and the one standing

closest sent a wave of something indescribable through Lisa's body, filling her heart and making it beat rapidly.

She and her mom ran to Tick and pulled him into a hug so tight she might have feared for his life if they all weren't laughing and crying so hard.

CHAPTER
32

TALKING ALL AT ONCE

Tick didn't know if he'd ever felt such a burst of pure emotion. As he hugged his mom and sister—both of them seeming to have a contest on who could squeeze him the hardest—he was crying one second then laughing the next. It was as if he'd lost his mind and all the control that went with it. But the feelings surging through his body were so strong, he didn't quite know how to handle it.

All the things he'd been through recently flashed across his mind: being taken by the Sleeks, the ordeal with the Blade of Shattered Hope, the terrible battle with Mistress Jane at the Factory, and then the short time he'd been in the Nonex, wondering if he'd ever see his family again. When they'd first been reunited in the Great Hall, he'd been too dazed to fully appreciate what it meant to be back together again. But now—especially after thinking they might have been crushed by the collapsing castle—it had hit him all at once.

Finally, reluctantly, he pulled away and took a step back. And the first thought he had when he looked at the tear-lined faces of his mom and Lisa was that they were still missing two important pieces.

"Dad," he said. "Kayla. I wish we were all together. Do you think they are okay?"

His mom nodded. "We left them at home, and I'm pretty sure Edgar wouldn't dare venture out with all the problems going on. They've got plenty of food, and the house wasn't hurt in the earthquakes."

"We need to hurry and get back to them," Tick said. "Make sure they're okay and let them know we're all safe."

His mom simply nodded and smiled, fresh tears squeezing out of her eyes.

Lisa reached out and patted him on the shoulder. "Good thing you had such an awesome big sister all those years, huh? Or you'd probably still be bawling your eyes out somewhere, too chicken to save the universe."

"Yeah, something like that." Tick rolled his eyes, then remembered with embarrassment that there were people standing around gawking at them. Master George, Mothball, Sally, Rutger, Sato, Paul, and Sofia. Mistress Jane, her robe in terrible shape, her exposed head as bad as ever. And Mordell, who looked like she'd just drowned her own puppies in a bathtub.

George was leaning on his Barrier Wand.

"Can you wink us back to my house?" Tick asked the Realitant boss. "I could do it myself, but I'm a little spent." He smiled wearily.

His mom spoke up. "We've got our own." She stared sternly at Mordell. "What did you do with it?"

The woman shook her head.

"Lost in the rubble, I take it?" his mom responded. "Do you have any idea how long it took me to build that Wand? How much it means to me?" Her voice rose, and her face reddened.

"I'm terribly sorry," Mordell replied.

Tick felt he should ask when and where and how his own mom had created a Barrier Wand, but nothing surprised him anymore. She could tell him all about it once they were home. He decided he had the strength after all. "It's okay, Mom. I can wink us back. I've done it before, but now I know how to actually use the stuff that makes me a freak."

"Hey," Paul chimed in, "I'm the only one here allowed to call you that."

"He's not a freak," Sofia said. "You're just jealous."

Everyone started talking at once, then, as if a cork had been popped off and permission had been given to converse freely. Mothball and Rutger were next to Tick, speaking over each other to say how happy they were that everyone was safe. Tick's mom was arguing with Mordell about the lost Wand. Lisa was trying to calm their mom down. Master George and Sally were discussing their options, and Paul and Sofia wanted to butt in and have Tick to themselves, but Mothball and Rutger would have none of it. Even Sato seemed to be talking to someone, but Tick couldn't tell what was being said or *who* it was.

"Silence!"

Mistress Jane's voice boomed throughout the room, echoing back and forth unnaturally off the carved black walls as if she'd used Chi'karda to make it happen. It sliced through everyone's conversation instantly. The Great Hall fell quiet, the only sound that of the churning, rushing noises caused by the spinning mass of whatever had come out of the Fourth Dimension.

Tick stared at her, ashamed that he was too scared to disobey and curious about what she was going to say. He readied himself, pooling the Chi'karda within him in case the woman tried to do anything questionable.

"How can you all stand here like all is well in the world?" Mistress Jane asked, her mask covered by disappointment and disbelief. "Kissing and hugging and crying with joy? Making jokes and making plans for reunions? Am I the only one in this room who is aware of what's happening just a few hundred feet from here? Do any of you have even the slightest inkling of what's at stake?"

"We need no lectures from you," Master George said. "Nor your hypocrisy. You're the only one in this room who deliberately and maliciously tried to destroy an entire Reality—and almost destroyed all else in the process. The entire universe, according to the Haunce."

Jane waited with a condescending look of patience on her mask until Master George was finished. "Don't blame me, George. If you and your so-called Realitants hadn't interfered, my Blade would've done its job, and we'd be on our way to creating the Utopia we so desperately need. But instead, we were put on a course that led to *this*. To rips in the fabric of Reality. A breach to the Fourth Dimension. Say all you want that Atticus and the Haunce saved us, but I say that all they've done is make things worse."

Hearing that made Tick blister inside with anger. "Oh, really? What could possibly be *worse* than destroying the entire universe? Care to explain that, *Jane*?" He stressed her name, spitefully refusing to include her title.

She stared at him. "The universe would not have needed saving if you hadn't tried to stop me in your arrogance, boy. And now what we have is an entity that no one truly understands—not even the Haunce. The Void will grow and strengthen. It will spread throughout my world and then the rest of the Realities. It will inflict pain and suffering the likes of which you couldn't comprehend. Better that we had all ceased to exist at the hands of the Blade of Shattered Hope."

Now it was Tick's turn to stare back. If she was telling the truth, what did the past matter anyway? What did their terrible history with each other matter? He felt a sinking in his gut that almost made him sit on the black stone floor.

"I want everyone to listen to me," Master George said. "And I want you all to listen very carefully. There's quite a bit of anger in this room. And we stand on the ruined grounds of a castle that represents the bitterest of enemies to me and my organization."

Mistress Jane's mask shifted, suddenly and violently, to a look of outrage. But George held up a hand and, miraculously, Jane didn't say anything.

"But," the old man continued, "I'm asking each one of us to put all of that aside. Including—perhaps especially—myself. Jane, you know very well that you and I have countless reasons to despise each other. But this threat you've spoken of . . . I believe it's real, and my good associates here have gathered numerous pieces of evidence. We all knew there'd be terrible destruction as a consequence of . . . recent events. But there's something much deeper going on. And animosity toward each other will only increase our speed along this path to eternal death."

Tick became aware that his mouth was hanging open. It'd been awhile since he'd seen Master George like this—so formal and full of speeches—but there was so much to process in the few sentences he'd spoken that Tick's reactions couldn't keep up with it.

The old man continued. "Jane, I don't even need to ask my fellow Realitants this question, but I must ask you. Are you willing to put aside your grievances—and your personal aspirations—to work with us until we can solve this problem?"

Jane's mask had smoothed back out to a neutral expression. "You insult me with every word that comes out of your mouth, George. Implying that I could actually say no to such a request. Implying that I could be so selfish as to—"

"Answer the question!" Sato suddenly screamed. He'd been still and quiet before, but now his face burned with hatred. "It was a simple yes or no question!"

Mistress Jane slowly nodded her head, and a little smile broke out on her mask as if she wanted to wound Sato by showing that she wasn't fazed by his outburst. But when she spoke, her response was the last thing Tick had expected to hear.

"It's not *me* you should all be worried about. We're going to have a major obstacle to any plans we might have to stop this thing."

"What are you talking about?" Master George asked.

Jane's smile vanished completely. "Reginald Chu."

CHAPTER
33

A CROSSROADS

hu? What does he have to do with this Fourth Dimension problem?" Tick asked.

Mistress Jane sighed, a croak of a sound that reminded Tick of what he'd done to her throat and the rest of her body when he'd thrown the Dark Infinity substance at her in Chu's palace. It seemed so long ago, and he never would've guessed that all of their lives would stay so intricately connected.

"I know him," she said. "I know the way he thinks, and the way he lusts for power. I also know he's a very, very smart man. I'm sure he's back in the Fourth Reality, studying and watching and gathering data just like George has been. He'll know about the breaches in Reality, and eventually he'll come to the same conclusion we have made about the Fourth Dimension—that *it's* been breached, unleashing the Void. And then there's the final thing I know all too well about him: his arrogance. All of these together will spell our

197

doom as surely as the mass of gray fog that churns atop my once-great home."

"What do you mean?" Tick asked at the same time as at least three of the others. He exchanged quick glances with Paul and Sofia, both of whom looked as worried and as curious as he felt. Sato kept his angry gaze focused on Jane.

"You've witnessed yourself what Chu will want," Jane said. "The power of the Void is massive, and Chu will see it as nothing but an opportunity. A chance to harness a new source of energy that could be the last piece to his puzzle that will allow him to rule us all. I won't waste our time with defending *my* actions anymore, as noble as they are and as beyond comprehension for you as they may be, but we can all agree on Chu's motives. He wants power, and he wants all of it. He wants to rule the rest of the Realities along with the Fourth. I find it ironic that his world is numbered the same as this . . . thing that threatens all of us. Chu will not *fear* it. He'll embrace it until he figures out how to control its energy for his own use."

For some reason, Tick thought back to one of his first experiences with the strangeness of his new life. The Gnat Rat that had been hidden in his closet. That creepy mechanical thing full of robotic gnats that had stung him and sent him to the hospital. Even though Master George had sent the robot as a test for Realitant recruits, Reginald Chu had invented the device. The man had been a thorn in Tick's side ever since.

"I agree that we have many problems, indeed," Master George concluded. "Jane, I won't stand here another minute and debate morals with you. The Realitants have a job to do, and you can either work with us or against us. Make your choice."

Jane shook her head. "I most definitely do *not* have a choice, and you know it. It's *my* world where this entity has begun its massacre, and it'll be my world that gets consumed *first*. I'll work with whomever I need to in order to stop it. Not to mention the fact that you need me and my knowledge. You could have asked a little more humbly, but yes, I will help you."

"More *humbly*?" George repeated. "Your *world*? The very fact that you . . . oh, goodness gracious me. Never mind. We are all in agreement then?" He looked around the room, gathering nods from his Realitants. Tick gave his when the glance came his way.

Their leader nodded. "Good. Each one of us will put our animosities aside, our grievances, our petty wishes for revenge, and work together. Though none of us truly understand what this new threat is"—he held up a hand when Jane began to protest—"some know more about it than others. And we all know it's very, very grave. We'll begin work immediately. No rest, I'm afraid. No vacation, no relaxation. The world leaders will have to deal with the aftershocks from our . . . most recent troubles on their own." His eyes darted to Jane for the briefest of moments.

Tick could think only of his family. "Okay, then. I'll take my mom and sister back home, and then I'll meet you at the headquarters. The Grand Canyon one, I guess?"

Master George looked hesitant for some reason,

fumbling with his words a bit before simply giving a quick nod of his head.

"Sounds good," Tick replied, wondering what that had been all about. "We better leave before that tornado starts making creatures again."

"First smart thing I've heard yet," Paul agreed. "Let's get out of this stink hole."

Tick turned to face his mom and sister, sweating from the thought of winking them all back home. He was pretty sure he could do it, but there was always a risk. He thought about asking Master George, but the man only had Tick's nanolocator reading, so they'd have to take the actual Wand with them when they winked. That wasn't going to work.

"Alright," he said, pushing everyone else and their problems out of his mind. "Let's hold hands while we do this."

His mom didn't budge. "Atticus, we're not going back home."

"What do you mean?"

She looked annoyed, like the answer should have been obvious. "We played a big part in bringing you back from the Nonex. Am I right or wrong on that?"

Tick knew where she was going and hated it. "Definitely right."

"I was a Realitant once. I built my own Barrier Wand. I just risked my life—and the life of my daughter—to bring you home safely. And if you think I'm going to let you out of my sight again, you're sadly mistaken. Not to mention the fact that Lisa and I are both capable of helping out. You're going to need every single body working on this that you can get."

Tick looked at her for a long time. He knew he couldn't let this happen. He couldn't. He'd never be able to focus on what needed to be done—and *not* focus on how dangerous it might be—if he had his family around. He'd be able to think only of them, saving them, protecting them. He could *not* let them stay.

"But what about Kayla? She's what matters most right now. I—*we*—need you to go back and make sure she and Dad are okay."

His mom folded her arms together in a defiant gesture. "Your *father* is perfectly capable of taking care of our sweet little princess. Don't insult him like that. Lisa and I are staying, and that's that."

"Mom, you—" He stopped. There was no arguing with that look in her eyes. But he also knew what needed to be done. He was racking his brain for the words to say when someone tapped him on the shoulder. He looked to see the weathered, reddened face of Master George.

"Yeah?" Tick asked.

"I, er, wondered if I might have a moment with you."

Tick wanted to leave so badly. "Can I figure this out first?"

"Only a moment," the old man interrupted. "I need just a few seconds of your time. Please." He held out a hand and raised his eyebrows. "Please." The windy, rushing sound of the Fourth Dimension cyclone was like the pulse of a rising tide on the beach.

"Okay." He gave a look to his mom and then joined Master George over by the wall farthest from the entrance to the Great Hall.

"What's going on?" Tick asked him. "I need to get them back safely before I can do anything else."

The Realitant leader's voice dropped to a whisper. "There are urgent matters at stake here, Master Atticus. Quite honestly, we don't have the time for you to go home right now. I need you, and I need you immediately."

"Just let me get them—"

"No." His face was tight, his voice curt. Tick had never seen him so insistent. "There are times when you must remember that your power doesn't put you in charge. Do you understand? You've sworn your services to the Realitants, and I'm giving you an order."

Tick sighed, feeling lower than low. "Okay, then. Yes, sir."

He turned away from his boss and looked squarely at his mom and sister, both of whom stared right back. Tick's mind spun, calculating. He felt the gathering force within his chest.

"I'm really sorry, Mom," he said.

Then he winked her and Lisa back to Reality Prime.

Chapter 34

Diabolical Plans Again

Reginald Chu sat in a chair, looking out a window that had no glass.

The chair was inside a structure that could barely be called that—it was nothing more than a few panels of wood nailed together with a makeshift roof of plastic thrown on top. The floor was nothing but the sodden rot of an old forest floor. And the single window existed because one of the stray pieces of wood used for the hut just so happened to have a hole in it. The air was hot and steamy, seeming to rise from the moist earth as if a pool of ancient lava rested somewhere beneath the ground.

It was a far cry from the offices he had enjoyed the last time he'd been to the Fourth Reality. This had been his home, the world he had ruled singlehandedly. Until the Realitants came. Until Mistress Jane betrayed him and helped push the Higginbottom boy to the madness that had demolished his entire headquarters, which had been shaped by the most advanced technology possible into a literal mountain of glass and steel. But Chu Industries was like the great phoenix of legend. Its shell had been destroyed, but the spirit was about to rise again from the ashes.

A surprisingly low number of people had been killed that day. Many of his top executives survived. And since that fateful day when he was catapulted to the Nonex by the unfortunate meeting with his Alterant—that slimy, weakling of a science teacher—the cogs and wheels of his great empire had been turning. Planning for his return. Putting the pieces of the puzzle back into place. Watching for the first sign of his nanolocator.

And now he was back.

But he didn't want anyone besides his closest staff to know about it. Not yet. That was the reason he was in the middle of a forest, miles from the temporary location of Chu Industries, in a hut cobbled together by two idiots on the bottom of the payroll. Two idiots who had been taken care of as soon as their work was done. He relished the discomfort of the pitiful makeshift office they'd created for him. He needed the shack. It reminded him of how great his power had once been, and it motivated him to find that power once again.

There was a tapping—three hits—at the ugly slab of wood that served as his door. Reginald waited. Another three. Then two. Ten seconds passed. Five taps. Chu reached below his chair and pushed the button on the tiny device that had been taped there. The shack may have looked harmless, but if anyone tried to enter without his permission, they would've been completely incinerated by the automated lazbots hidden in the trees.

"Come in, Benson." He knew who it was because only one person had been taught the code that had been used on the door. There was something incredibly dopey about the man, but Benson was faithful beyond anything Chu had ever witnessed. So faithful he'd almost died on several occasions.

Just as he'd been instructed, he waited until Chu repeated the command—"Come in, Benson"—before finally slipping inside the small hut of discarded wood.

"I'm ready to give you a full report," the man said nervously, which pleased Chu. At Chu Industries, there was no room for error.

"What did you find out." Reginald always spoke his questions as statements. They were commands for information, not requests.

"I spoke with every department head," Benson began, his eyes cast to the floor and his hands folded before him. A servant, through and through. "In almost every way, we're back to full strength. Everything from personnel levels to supplies to research and development. Most importantly, the underground facility is only a few weeks from completion. This time your mountain will be a real one, boss."

"Benson."

"Yes, boss?"

"Don't ever call me 'boss' again."

"I'm sorry, sir. I just wanted to show some respect—show who's the, um, boss."

Reginald stood up. He figured there was time for one more lesson before the real data started pouring out. "Benson. I think you would agree with me that neither I, nor you, need any reminder whatsoever that I am your boss."

"Yes, sir. Of course, sir."

Chu sat back down. "Good. I won't interrupt you again. Tell me everything. Especially about the findings concerning the Fourth Dimension."

Benson started talking, and as more time went by, the more quickly he spoke.

True to his word, Chu didn't say one thing or present one inquiry. A half hour later, he knew exactly what he needed to do and how to do it.

Within six months, Chu Industries would no longer be a company. Or an empire.

It would be Reality itself.

CHAPTER
35

A SIGHT OF GRAY

We should never have let her go," Rutger said. "Someone a lot bigger than me and a lot stronger should have stopped her."

"Maybe someone a little less roly-poly, I'd say," Mothball quipped.

They all stood on the hill that led to the forest, looking down in the early-morning light upon the ruins of the castle and the great, slowly churning mass of gray air that still raged in the middle of it all. Sato's army was assembled nearby, observing as well. The invading, mysterious entity below hummed and buzzed and growled as it spun, crackling when tendrils of bright lightning shot through its surface. Tick watched in awe, knowing the thing had almost doubled in size since he last looked at it from a safe distance.

The Void of Mist and Thunder. Pure power, according to Mistress Jane. How could they rely on her information about what was happening? Well, that was an easy answer—they *couldn't.* They needed to get back to headquarters and begin their own research.

"I'm just saying," Rutger continued, "never in a billion years should we have trusted that woman. Not in a trillion."

No one really argued with the butterball of a man because what he kept insisting was so obviously true. Soon after Tick had used his own hold on Chi'karda to wink away his mom and Lisa—something he'd hear about for sure in the future—Jane had used hers to wink the rest of them to this spot of temporary safety. The rumbling, machinery-like noises of the Void had grown louder and louder; the ground had begun to shake as its mass crept closer to the Great Hall. They'd needed to get away.

But then she'd gone on about how she needed to do her own part in all of this, and that she'd meet up with them soon enough, when both sides had made some progress. Master George had been furious, his usually red face growing closer to pure scarlet as he lectured her on how this problem needed all of their heads together, and then . . . she was gone. Without a word, she winked away, one second there—disheveled and scarred and exhausted—the next second, gone.

And so, a smaller group of Realitants stood in the chilly air of dawn, watching with empty bellies as an unknown force of gray fog began devouring the universe.

Typical stuff for people like us, Tick thought. Simple job. Hopefully they'd be done in time to beat rush hour tonight and get home for an early supper.

He snickered at his own lame joke.

"Telling jokes in your head over there, sport?" Paul asked him. He stood next to Sofia, and neither one of them seemed to think anything was even remotely funny about their current situation.

"No. It wasn't that kind of laugh. It was more like the we're-definitely-going-to-die-so-why-even-bother laugh. You know."

Paul actually broke a smile, a genuine one, even. "Oh, yeah. Like in the movies. The bad guy always giggles before he gets pushed out a plane or something. Or right as the axe starts swinging down."

"Uh . . . yeah," Tick said with a sarcastic nod. "Something like that."

"Rutger's right," Sato cut in, curt and abrupt. "Every single one of us was stupid to let Jane leave. We should've shackled her to a tree—something. Now we have three enemies to worry about—Jane, Chu, and that . . . thing down there."

Master George sighed, looking about as weary as Tick had ever seen him. "Sato. Rutger. My good men. I understand your concern, but I assure you, there's no way we could have stopped her. Like Master Atticus, she has herself become a Barrier Wand and has power beyond what we even think. I believe there was honor in her once, and I know she couldn't possibly want the end of her own world—as she puts it—to come about. We'll have to trust that she is off doing something that will truly help the cause."

Sally suddenly spoke up. He'd been so quiet, it seemed as if he wasn't even around, despite his huge stature and ridiculous clothes. "I trust that snicker doodle of a woman 'bout as much as a hen can toss a rooster barn. Cain't believe she was ever one a-yorn, ole George. Just cain't believe it nohow."

"She was," their leader said through another heavy sigh. "She most definitely was. And, sadly, one of the best we ever had. Who knows what might have been if she hadn't been assigned to the Thirteenth Reality? Power corrupted her like mold condemns a building. Slowly, but certainly. As it grew inside of her."

"So?" Sofia asked. "What do we do now? What's first?"

Master George pulled in a deep breath, sticking his chest way out and adjusting his filthy suit. "Some of us are going back to the Grand Canyon in Prime. We need to put our thoughts together and make sure we understand everything we can. We need to *understand* before we can do anything to stop this madness."

"Some of us?" Tick asked. "Who *isn't* going, and what are they doing instead?"

George gave a tired look to Sato, and Tick knew he was about to ask his friend to do something dangerous. "Sato, my good man. I want you and your army to stay here. I need you to research this business about the creatures of Mistress Jane being transformed by the Void somehow. I believe there may be something extremely important to learn there. We also need someone close by to observe this . . . monstrosity and report back regularly on its progress."

Tick expected to see a flash of disappointment in Sato's features—he was missing out on a chance to go back to safety, shower and eat, rest up—but instead, he stood a little straighter and gave a stiff nod.

"Okay," he said simply. "That's what the Fifth and I will do, then."

Tick was filled with an unexpected sadness. They'd all *just been* reunited. He walked over to Sato and held out a hand, fighting to make sure he didn't let a stray tear leak out somehow.

Sato took his hand and shook it, squeezing it hard. "Glad to have you back, Tick."

"Yeah. Good to be back. Glad to see you alive. I know you saved a lot of kids that day at the Factory."

Sato's hand dropped to his side; Tick felt the blood rush back in his own. "We had to leave a few behind."

Tick didn't know what to say to that.

"But . . . it's good we could save the ones we did," Sato added. He looked at Master George knowingly, as if they'd had a conversation about it countless times.

"Yeah," Tick responded lamely. "Well, looks like there's gonna be a lot more to save. You think we're up for it?"

Sato smiled, something so rare that Tick almost took a step backward. "My Fifth Army will save so many people that the Realities will get sick of us. Jealous they couldn't have done it themselves."

Tick forced out a laugh. "I doubt that. Well, good luck, man. I'm sure we'll all be back together soon enough, fighting this Void thing somehow. Sound good?"

"Yeah. Sounds good."

Tick was pretty sure he'd just had the lamest conversation of his life, but he hoped that Sato knew how he felt in his heart. The others came over and said their good-byes, including a very long one between Mothball and her parents that included some very disturbing wailing along with the tears.

When everyone was done, Tick gathered with Master George, Sally, Mothball, Rutger, Paul, and Sofia. The Realitants. They used George's Wand this time, winking away from the cyclone of the hungry Void from the Fourth Dimension.

Tick knew they'd be back.

PART
3

THE BLUE
RIVER

CHAPTER
36

A NAP ON THE COUCH

Mistress Jane was beyond exhausted. She felt a deep, aching weariness like nothing she'd ever felt before in her life. Her arms, her legs, her chest, her bones, her nerves, her veins. Her brain and head and skull. She was just so tired. And it seemed as if every last souliken she'd ever owned had drained out of her over the last couple of days. She needed rest. Desperately. Food and sleep.

Which was exactly why she couldn't handle another single minute with those buffoons who called themselves Realitants. She'd fed them what they wanted to hear about helping them against the Void and Chu, but she had her own ulterior motives. If it weren't for Atticus Higginbottom, the Realitants would have absolutely no reason to even stay on her radar. But that insolent boy changed so many things. Everything.

She was in a place no one would have ever guessed. In an apartment—an ordinary, drab, dusty old thing that hadn't been lived in for years—located in the middle of New York City, Reality Prime. It had been the first place she'd ever rented on her own, and where she'd fallen in love so long ago. Where she'd completed her studies and first dared wink herself to other realities with the Barrier Wand she'd made with her own hands. It was here, sitting on this same frumpy couch, where she'd first had the thought that the Thirteenth Reality might change her life and, eventually, all of Reality itself.

The place had been rented and paid for ever since. Cleaned every so often by a maid. Jane couldn't bear to get rid of it, not after all the memories born within its humble walls. And, with her castle destroyed, her body depleted, and her future in doubt, she didn't know where else to go except to this place that had once been home.

She lay back on the couch, pulling her tattered robe around her body like a blanket. As horrible as she felt, being here brought her the smallest bit of comfort.

Her life was at a crossroads. The plan she'd had to essentially destroy and rebuild the Realities from the ground up had been foiled. She'd accepted that. Perhaps it was a little easier to take since immediately afterward, there'd been the threat of spending the rest of eternity in that awful, awful Nonex. Making it back safely had been a breath of fresh air that took the stink off the failure that had led to it.

But life could be so ironic sometimes. Now there was something beyond her control that threatened to annihilate the Realities. If the Void succeeded, that may be that. Destruction with no hope of rebuilding. Although, deep down, she didn't believe it. There was always a solution. Always a way. *Everything* was an opportunity. She and Chu had made a bargain in the Nonex. A plan to see both of their destinies fulfilled. The breach of the Fourth Dimension had at first seemed to put that plan on hold, but now she wasn't so sure. Not so sure at all.

Beneath her mask, she smiled. All she needed was a little rest. The growth of the Void would take some time. She could use a couple days of eating and relaxing and healing.

A couple of days of scheming.

Mistress Jane fell asleep.

Tick waited in the conference room; he was the first one to get there. Master George had said they could take exactly thirty minutes to shower, rest, and gather their wits. Rutger was supposed to be putting together a meal for them all—something Tick couldn't wait to get his hands on. That little guy could *cook*. Tick's stomach rumbled and bounced and gurgled, desperate for anything. Even a slice of boiled cabbage sounded good right then.

He was still worried about his mom. And Lisa. And Kayla. And Dad. He should've ignored George's curt command and gone home really quickly to make sure everything was okay. But then again, maybe not. If he was going to be a Realitant, then he needed to act like one. He'd have to trust that they'd—

He stopped. Suddenly and absolutely, he felt like he'd made the biggest mistake in the world. This was his *family* they were talking about. His family. How silly that he couldn't just wink back to Deer Park really fast, check on everybody, then make it back here. How could his peace of mind and the safety of the four most important people in the universe—to him, anyway—be relegated to the bottom of the stack? In fact, it made him mad. How could Master George expect that of him?

Tick stood up and looked at the door. No one was even there yet. He was supposed to sit and wonder about his own family while everyone else took their time primping and relaxing. The last hour or so suddenly seemed absurd to him. He'd sent off his mom without asking her! Sent away his sister! All so Master George could rest assured that his number one weapon was close by and ready for service.

Forget that.

Tick closed his eyes, focusing and pooling his power. Then he winked himself to the woods that ran along the road to Deer Park. He winked himself home.

⌒⌒⌒

Rutger huffed and puffed as he carried the stacks of plates down the hallway. Why Master George didn't buy him some kind of rolling tray to make this easier was beyond him. Of all the Realitants to be carrying heavy plates full of hot and scrumptious food down the length of hall between the kitchen and the conference room, he was the *least* qualified. But every time he pointed that out to the boss, the old man just said it'd probably be awhile before another event, and that next time, he'd help Rutger personally.

Of course, that never happened. The buzzard always had something more urgent to attend to until the very second. By then, Rutger was all done. Even his best friend, Mothball, would magically disappear when the time came to transport the food. And what food it was.

Savory thrice-baked potatoes. Succulent steak with mushroom sauce. Crisp, bright green asparagus soaked in butter and lemon juice. Freshly baked rolls with honey butter. He expected to hear many, many, many compliments after the meal. The anticipation almost made him forget that the entire universe was on the cusp of being devoured by a giant gray fog. Well, it wouldn't happen *today*, at any rate.

Paul and Sofia were there when he brought in the first round. They offered to help, but he declined, suddenly liking the idea that he did it all himself. Sally was there the next time. Then Master George. Mothball popped in after he'd brought in the last of the meal, giving him an "Oh, would ya need some 'elp there, little man?" He just gave her a knowing look and continued about his business, making sure everything looked nice and pretty on the table. Steam rose to the ceiling, and the smells made his considerable belly ache to be fed.

When all was set, he rubbed his hands together, feeling very satisfied indeed.

"Well," he said, "looks like we're ready to partake. All we need is Tick."

"Forget that," Paul said. "He must've gone outside or something—he left the dorms way before I did. And I didn't see him anywhere. Let's dig in!"

"Absolutely not!" Rutger roared. "After all he's done for us? I won't hear of it. We'll wait until he gets here."

Paul grumbled something unintelligible and put his chin in his hands, staring longingly at the delicious, mouthwatering food—in Rutger's humble opinion, of course.

Master George slowly stood up, then leaned forward and put his hands on the table, a grave look on his face. "Goodness gracious me," he whispered. "I know exactly what's happened."

"What?" Rutger asked, hearing the whine in his own voice. He didn't want anything to ruin this fine meal.

Their leader closed his eyes for a moment before opening them again. "I believe we have a rogue Realitant. Tick has run away, against my orders. And at such a time as this." He puffed out his chest, his face sunken in disappointment. "I guess I can understand his decision, but I certainly hope it doesn't come back to haunt us."

CHAPTER
37

A NICE MORNING STROLL

Sato couldn't remember the last time he'd had a full night's rest. And what a strange time to do it.

After the other Realitants had winked away, he'd led his army—now only a few dozen strong—in a full march around the perimeter of the ruins of Mistress Jane's castle. He didn't really know what he was looking for or wanted to find, but they'd searched all the same. And saw nothing unusual—except for the ever-present, massive gray cloud of mist and lightning that spun in the middle of the ruins, growling as it got bigger and bigger. Sato guessed by the end of the next day that it would cover every last inch of fallen stone.

It had grown dark by the end of their long walk, and he'd given his soldiers the entire evening to get some sleep. Tollaseat had seemed the most appreciative, though he never would've admitted it. But the way he collapsed on the ground and started snoozing said it all.

Now it was early morning, and the world was full of that purple, chill air that comes right before the sun begins to show its light. Sato had slept soundly and peacefully, and when he woke up, he'd felt refreshed and filled with strength. As he sat and stared out at the distant horizon, determined to catch the moment when the sun *did* pop over the edge, he thought about what Master George had said. The old man thought there was something to the fact that all the creatures of Mistress Jane had disappeared somewhere, then reappeared in some altered state out of the Void.

Sato hadn't thought much about it at the time, but there *was* something weird about it. When he'd first caught sight of the castle, hordes of fangen and other nasty creatures had been crawling all over the surface of the structure and its grounds. And Sato had also seen some of them fleeing when the weird breach in Reality had first split the air. But there should've been more creatures. Many, many more. Where had they all gone? And why weren't their bodies strewn all over the place if they'd been killed? There'd been some bodies inside the passageway by the stream, but none anywhere else. Had they been . . . cloned? Transformed? What?

The more Sato thought about it, the stranger it seemed. Well, it was his job to find out the truth, and he meant to do it. He was glad to have a specific task to keep himself occupied.

He stood up and stretched, allowing a big, loud yawn to escape that sounded like a demented ghost.

"Get your bones all nice and rested, you did, I 'spect?"

Sato turned to see Tollaseat, who was stretching and

yawning himself. "Slept great, actually. I've been thinking a lot about what we're supposed to be doing for Master George. About the creatures and how they all disappeared."

"Been thinkin' myself, I 'ave," the giant man said. "Remembered you tellin' us all about how them nasty little buggers were runnin' toward the middle of the castle when the mess started and all. Well, mayhaps we should be lookin' there? Only checked the roundabout yesterday night, we did."

Tollaseat was right. Yes, they'd walked around the entire ruins of the castle, but Tick had told everyone that the fangen and all their ugly cousins had been screaming and sprinting deeper *into* the building. Why would they have done that with the whole thing about to come down?

"You might be on to something," Sato said. "Why don't you and I go take a look before everyone else wakes up?"

"Could use a nice mornin' stroll, I could."

The two of them set off again for the destroyed home of Mistress Jane. Sato tried to ignore the huge, churning cloud of gray fog and lightning in the middle of it, but that was one task that proved impossible.

Tick stepped out of the woods near his home just as the sun tipped over the horizon and spilled bright morning light across the old, cracked road that he'd walked down a million times before. He was still disturbed by the long swath of broken, mangled trees he'd seen in the forest. They were leftover from the time he'd let loose his powers without even realizing it. Dissolving and reconstructing mass in his panic.

He'd wanted to forget those episodes, but maybe it was a good reminder that he had a vast amount of power inside him. He needed to make sure he kept learning how to control it.

As he set off down the road toward his neighborhood, he started feeling the inevitable guilt. Master George had been very stern in ordering him to return to headquarters with the other Realitants and to save this reunion for another time. But it made Tick mad. His family was the most important thing to him right now, and he needed to make sure they were safe. He'd tried to wink directly to his house, but the pull of the deep Chi'karda pool in the forest had brought him there instead—exactly where he'd first seen Mothball disappear so long ago. It felt like a lifetime ago.

So this wouldn't quite be as quick of a trip as he'd hoped. He imagined his leader and his friends sitting in the conference room, waxing on about what a poor example Tick had shown. What a bad Realitant he was. How selfish he was. But a few hours wouldn't matter. Plus, he was pretty sure Paul and Sofia would defend him no matter what.

Tick suddenly filled up with cheer at the thought of seeing his family again. He broke into a run down the long, straight road.

⁓

Reginald Chu was scanning through a few more of the data reports Benson had wired to his reading tablet when there was an abrupt pounding on the wooden slab he called a door in his makeshift office. He almost dropped the device from the shock of the interruption, and half of him was angry, the other half relieved no one had seen his embarrassing reaction.

It took him another second to realize that the number of knocks—as hard and frantic as they were—matched the first part of his secret code. After a pause, the knocks started again. Chu quickly reached down and deactivated the lazbots.

"Oh, come on in, already!" he shouted.

Benson slipped through the door, looking as nervous as ever; trickles of sweat ran down both sides of his face.

"What, pray tell, could be so urgent?" Chu asked sternly.

"The boy. Atticus. For some reason, he left the Realitant headquarters and is all alone. I know it's earlier than you expected, sir, but this is too golden of an opportunity. We have him tracked and know exactly where he is! With no one around him to fight off!"

Chu stood up. "Amazing—what a fool that kid can be. But let's not forget, he doesn't really need an army with all that Chi'karda boiling inside his body. We'll have to tread carefully."

"He's heading toward his house, sir. He might be alone for only a few more minutes."

"Oh, please," Chu said with a laugh. "It'll be even easier if he's surrounded by his family. He'll be . . . more distracted."

"Whatever you say, boss. I mean, sir."

Chu hardly noticed the slip. "But maybe haste is best. Ready the Bagger. We leave immediately."

CHAPTER 38

A TENSE CONVERSATION

The conference room had been silent for at least five minutes.

Paul kept fidgeting in his seat, worried about Tick and wishing he hadn't left. All his friend wanted to do was check on his family—they all did. How could anyone blame him? Just because Tick was a freak and could actually travel on his own without a Barrier Wand didn't make him a monster. If Paul could do that fancy trick, he'd be on a beach in the Bahamas sipping lemonade and waiting for the world to end.

Oh, forget this, he thought. Time to speak up.

"Hey, Tick will be back soon. Quit looking so sad." Everyone in the room was staring at the table or the floor like hypnotized zombies. Sofia seemed distraught, and Mothball looked even more sullen than usual. Rutger was eating, the little stinker, but that was probably just how he dealt with things.

"You don't understand, Master Paul," George said. "I could see the rebellion in your friend's eyes, and I knew he was tempted to do things that he wasn't even thinking about yet except on a subconscious level. I knew he'd see his family, remember the horrors he's been through, and begin to think selfish thoughts. Feel tempted to stay with them, run away, keep them safe. How can we have our Realitants run off willy-nilly when we need them the most? He shouldn't have gone. I'm terribly sorry to say it."

Paul understood but didn't want to admit it. "How can you blame him for winking away really quick just to check on his family? I'm sure he'll be back any second. You're making too much of it!"

George slammed his hand down on the table. "I will not have you speak to me this way! I am your leader and I demand respect! We're on the cusp of something that could kill every single living person in every Reality! Each of us have higher callings than running off to check on mums and dads!"

He stopped, and the entire room fell dead silent. Even Rutger had frozen with a piece of steak halfway to his mouth. Paul's anger had vanished, replaced by pure shock. He'd never seen *this* before.

"I know I sound harsh," George finally said in a much calmer voice, "but I feel as if our organization has slowly gone down the pits, so to say, since Jane embraced her evil ways and Lorena Higginbottom decided to leave our ranks. We used to be disciplined and strong and willing to sacrifice all for the greater good. But now I can't even convince any of our members to leave their homes and come to help us. We've fallen apart, I swear it."

The old man suddenly slumped down in his chair and buried his head in his hands. Paul half-expected him to sob, but he just sat there, perfectly quiet and still, for a long minute. Then he looked up, and his face was as determined as Paul had ever seen it.

"Never mind all that," George said. "We have a job to do, and I expect us to do it. If I have to go it alone, I will. And if . . . *when* I defeat the Void of the Fourth Dimension, I'll build the Realitants from the ground up. I stake my life on this promise to all of you."

Paul blinked, not sure what to say.

"Ya won't be alone s'long as *my* heart's still tickin', you won't," Mothball said. "I'll be by your side to the bitter end, warts and all."

"Me too," Rutger added. Then he finally finished off his bite of juicy steak.

Sally wasn't about to be upstaged. "Ya'll ain't havin' all da fun, I can promise you *that*."

"Paul and I—we're in too." Sofia said. She shot Paul a look that said he better shape up. But something in her eyes let him know that she understood his frustrations about George's reaction to Tick leaving.

Paul groaned. "You guys know very well that I'm not quitting. But after all that Tick has done, I think it's really lame to just snap your fingers and accuse him of being a traitor. It's about the most unfair thing I've ever heard."

"It wasn't a snap of my fingers," George said sadly.

"Master Atticus chose to go against my direct order. If my words were harsh, I apologize. But I don't want someone by my side in the very last battle of these worlds who might turn his back on me."

"Tick would never do that," Paul said in a low growl. "You know it. He just went for a quick trip to check on his *family*."

"Sorry to be the one to point this out," Rutger said, "but he hasn't come back yet, now has he?" His eyes darted around the room as though worried he'd said something wrong. "But no one likes the boy more than me. I hope you'll be a little forgiving, Master George."

The leader of the Realitants nodded slowly. "We will deal with him how we must, I assure you. However, I already have a very bad feeling that we may not see him for a while. A very bad feeling indeed."

~~~~~

Tick's heart lifted when he passed a clump of trees close to the road and saw the turn into his neighborhood come into view. He'd been lightly jogging and now picked up his pace to a full sprint, eager to run up the steps of his porch and rip the door open. He knew everyone would be there. Safe and sound and happy. He knew it. He was completely ignoring the small part of him that worried something horrible had happened. That they *wouldn't* be there. Or worse.

This was why he had come. He needed to know for sure. Master George was probably ranting and raving by now, but he'd deal with that when he got back. Soon. He was just about to reach the street, less than thirty feet away, when he heard a loud noise from somewhere above him.

It was a bang, instant and piercing, like the clang of two giant iron pots. Times a thousand. Tick was so startled that he cried out and fell to the ground, rolling off the road and down the slight decline. He came to a stop in the dirt, on his back, looking up to search for what could have possibly been the source of such an awful sound. He saw a blur of flashing light and something silvery and long above him, accompanied by a great whooshing sound, like the thrust of rockets. Wind tore through the air and ripped at his clothes, sending dust and pebbles scattering down the slope.

Holding up his forearm to shield his eyes, his vision finally cleared enough to see the thing that had suddenly appeared in the sky over his head. It was a thick rectangle of silver metal, roughly the size and shape of a coffin. Its surface was smooth, without any seams, and the lights that flashed around it made no sense to Tick, as if they were being created by invisible protrusions from the flying object. Whatever it was, the push of air from the silver coffin was like a hurricane blast, growing stronger as it hovered in the air.

Then it slowly descended toward Tick.

He flopped onto his stomach, got his hands beneath him, and pushed up to jump to his feet. He slipped and slid as his arms windmilled, fighting to gain his balance on the small hill. He'd just gained solid purchase when there was a clicking sound right behind his ears. The noise sent a burst of terror through him, though he didn't understand why, and he burst into a sprint, not even taking a chance to look back.

He'd only gone a few yards when a thin cable of something strong slipped around his stomach, coiled tight, and ripped his body up into the air.

CHAPTER
39

A REBOUND OF POWER

Tick's initial shout turned into a strangled grunt as the cord pinched into his stomach and he vaulted away from the ground. His body doubled over as he grabbed the ridged metal of the thing that had captured him—it felt like a wire on an old telephone pole. He twisted and kicked with his feet and tried to pull the thing loose, to no avail. He continued to rise, the sight of the road replaced by the tops of trees, all of it making his head spin and his stomach flip. Giving up on the cord, he tried to turn so he could see what held him.

The blocky silver rectangle was pulling him along, the metal cord coming out of a hole just big enough for it to fit. There was a moment where everything seemed to freeze, and Tick searched his mind for a possible explanation of what was happening. If anyone was watching from below, what else could they think except that a UFO had zapped down from outer space to steal the first human they could find in order to perform experiments? It was all just so . . . odd. Tick was surprised at how little terror he felt now—much less than when he'd first heard that clicking sound.

Because he remembered that he had an untapped amount of power inside his body.

He closed his eyes and let the Chi'karda flow into his chest, into his heart and nerves and bones and muscles. The surge of it was like a rushing river, somehow cold and hot at the same time, filling him with a rapturous clarity and a sense of being unstoppable. Like he could crush mountains or drink up the entire ocean and spit it back out. He wanted to roar and pound his chest. When he opened his eyes again, the familiar orange mist spun around him and clung to his skin, particles of light bouncing along his clothes, untouched by the wind.

With both hands, he grabbed the trailing length of the cord that connected his waist to the boxy contraption that flew through the air. He wrenched his body around until he'd twisted enough that he faced the long cube of silver. After pulling in a deep breath, he blew out the power that had boiled and churned inside of him, letting it flow like an open faucet, throwing every ounce of power at the box that had captured him. A great rushing sound filled his ears, and the world blinded him with orange light.

A thunderclap shook the air, along with a massive jolt of power.

Tick was suddenly plummeting, his hearing deafened, his senses completely out of whack. It was like he'd been flooded with numbing drugs. On some level, he felt the tops of trees scratching his back, felt the cord still cinched tightly around his waist, but his vision had gone from orange to bright white, and he could hear absolutely nothing. The pulse of his blood was a pounding in his head, a thump-thump-thump that he could only feel, a vibration that rattled down his spine.

He was still being pulled along. Somehow he knew that. The branches weren't suddenly gone—nothing tore at his clothes or bit at his skin. His eyes darted wildly, trying to see anything but the whiteness that seared his sight. The calmness and sense of invincibility from earlier completely vanished, replaced by a fiery panic that lit up his nerves. What was happening to him? He couldn't see, couldn't hear. He barely felt the motion of flying through the air or the metal rope wrapped around his middle. How could all that power he'd thrown at the long, silvery coffin not have freed him and dropped him to the forest floor?

He didn't know what else to do but try again. Though weakened from whatever had happened the first time, he concentrated on his internal self, pooling the Chi'karda once again. It came as only a trickle, a weak stream of power that barely made a splash compared to what it had been before. It had no form or substance. It couldn't take shape. It wasn't strong enough for him to do anything with it. And he still couldn't see.

His panic erupted into anger. Rage tore through his body and weakened some of the dam holding back the Chi'karda. He screamed and tried again, pulling on whatever lever he sensed that controlled the link between him and the Realities. The surge came, rushed through him like a flood, filling him with relief as strong as the power itself.

Still flying through the air, still attached to the cord, he didn't wait, didn't allow himself even a second to enjoy the swell of pleasure. He threw everything he had at the object holding him captive.

This time he didn't hear the thunderclap at all, just felt it. A thump of violence that jarred his bones and rattled his skull. The blinding light around him brightened even more, intense with heat and pressure. The rope around his waist jerked forward, pulling his body along with it. A sprinkle of pain cut through the numbness, making him reach for his back. But his fingers were numb too, and he felt nothing there. All was blunt and dull and lifeless. Nothing made sense anymore. His brain began to shut down.

His hearing came back just long enough for him to hear that clicking sound again. Then everything exploded in a rush of movement, and darkness engulfed him.

～～

Chu needed a break from his run-down excuse for a temporary office. Maybe a permanent break. He hated the little place, and he missed the power of being in charge, of being *seen* as the man in charge.

Reginald Chu stood in the newly built laboratory, leaning against the railing as he stared down at the massive chamber. It was seven or eight football fields wide and at least three tall. Big. Really, really big. Even larger than the chamber inside the mountain palace, which Atticus

Higginbottom had brought crumbling down right before Chu was sent to the Nonex. Tick. The little rat.

But Chu's people had already been working on this new facility and had even picked up the pace, hoping that someday their leader would return. They were loyal and smart. Benson led the security details, but the real geniuses were Chu's engineers and scientists and physicists. He'd gathered more brain power into one place over the last thirty years than anywhere else in all the Realities. His men shared his goals. Most of them didn't care what the end result might be—let Chu rule the world, other worlds, whatever—as long as they kept getting the funds they needed to do the research that kept their old hearts ticking.

And now they'd built the largest research facility in history. This chamber was only a small part of it. It went on and on and on. And the most amazing thing about it was that the complex had been built entirely underground. It was simply awesome.

And it was time for Chu to finally move back in. He'd had his moments of reflection and his moments of appreciating what had been taken from him. But things were going to move, and move fast, now. Below him, his workers were finalizing the very device he planned to use to harness the immense power of the Void that had escaped the Fourth Dimension.

Right on cue, his earpiece buzzed. It was Benson.

"We got him, sir. The Bagger worked like a charm."

"Excellent," Chu replied. "Let Mistress Jane know at once."

CHAPTER
40

A PULSING LIGHT

Sato picked his way along the top of the rubble, knowing that he could slip to his death at any second. The ruined stone and brick and wood and whatever else Jane had used to build the place lay stacked on top of each other like some kind of fragile toy, ready to collapse at any second. Something shifted with every step, and Sato kept thinking he couldn't possibly feel his heart leap any stronger, but it seemed to do so every time.

The gray mass of spinning air was only a few hundred feet to his left, and that certainly wasn't helping his nerves. Cracks of thunder shook the air and made the debris beneath his feet tremble, and as hard as he tried, he couldn't stop himself from looking over every few seconds at the brilliant displays of lightning. The Void itself was downright creepy. It had a steady roar and a chilling movement to it that made Sato feel as if it were alive and hungry.

And it was growing steadily. Half of the castle ruins

had been swallowed by the entity, and its pace of expansion seemed to be increasing. If they were going to learn anything about what had happened to Mistress Jane's creatures, they'd need to figure it out fast.

Tollaseat tapped him on the shoulder, making him almost jump out of his skin. "What if that blimey thing decides it wants to take a bit of leapin' at us?" Mothball's dad asked. "Takes a fancy at throwin' a lightning bolt or two our way?"

"Then duck," Sato replied. "You're welcome to go back if you want."

Tollaseat laughed, a booming sound that drowned out the thunder and rush of wind for a few seconds. "You make a grouchy grump, you do. Or is it a grumpy grouch?"

"Just keep looking." Sato had enjoyed the tiny reprieve from the noises of the Void, but knew he couldn't admit it. He needed to keep his game face on now. Be a leader. "You go that way, and I'll go this way. But not too far off. We need to be off this big pile of rocks in an hour."

"Can't come soon enough," the man mumbled.

Sato turned his back to him once more and started gingerly walking over the rubble again. According to their best guess, they were currently over the section the fangen and other creatures had been running toward, but everything looked the same from the outside—broken and dusty. Keeping his arms out for balance, he walked across the crooked stacks of stones, looking through the gaps and cracks for any sign of . . . he didn't know. Something.

A few minutes later, he spotted it. Far down below the

debris, just visible through the layers of stone, he saw a glowing blue light that pulsed every two or three seconds, flashing more brilliantly before fading again to a dull glow.

"Hey!" he shouted. "Come over here and look!"

Tollaseat's face lit up with excitement, and he started lumbering his way over to where Sato stood. The man was so much taller and bigger than an average man, and Sato feared he'd crash down in a cloud of dust and rock chips at any second. But he finally made it and raised his shoulders in question.

"Down there." Sato pointed.

Tollaseat put a big hand on Sato's shoulder and leaned in to take a look. Sato flexed his leg muscles to keep his knees from collapsing under the added weight.

"Well, I'll be," the man said, the glow from below reflecting in his large eyes. "Take me spine out and tickle 'er up and down! What in the blazes you reckon that is, sir?"

Sato looked at his friend and best soldier. "I don't know. But this can't be a coincidence. Those nasty things of Jane's were running this way, and then they all seemed to vanish, only to reappear later. And now there's a flashing blue light shining in a place that doesn't use electricity."

"Right, you are. Can't be two toads bumpin' tongues on the same fly, that's for sure."

"Huh?" When Tollaseat opened his mouth to answer, Sato cut him off. "Never mind. Let's get down to that thing. Time's running out."

He planted his feet as firmly as he could then bent over to lift a piece of rock directly above the odd blue glow. He chucked it to the side, the crack of it hitting the rubble barely audible over the noises of the Void.

In the shadow of the huge gray funnel of mist filled with lightning and thunder, Sato and Tollaseat started digging through the ruins of Mistress Jane's castle.

~~~

Paul was curled up in his bed—or the bed he'd been given at the Grand Canyon headquarters—staring at the wall. He'd never felt so low in all his life, and there'd been some freaky, scary moments over the last couple of years. But right that second, he just wanted to sink into the mattress, fall asleep, and never wake up again. Everything had gone so wrong.

How could the whole world—scratch that, the whole *universe* and every single Reality within it—be in so much trouble? *Again?* Mistress Jane and her fancy schmancy Blade of Shattered Hope had almost set off a chain reaction that would've destroyed the universe. Paul didn't care about the specifics, but he knew that Tick had saved them all. Yeah, he'd been sucked away into the Nonex, but deep down, Paul had known the kid was okay and that he'd find his way back somehow. Or, at least, Paul had told himself that.

But now all this? Some big gray cloud called the Void from the Fourth Dimension was eating away at a planet? And then Jane said it would keep on going once that was all done. And then Tick had to make it worse by running off against Master George's wishes. Which wasn't so bad to Paul—what was *bad* was the fact that Tick hadn't come *back.* And Rutger couldn't get a lock on Tick's nanolocator. The Realitant system kept saying that it was blocked, a thing that had obviously bewildered and bamboozled everyone listening.

Not Paul. To him, the news had just made him sick to his stomach. He'd insisted on leaving, going to his room. *Sorry, so sorry, but I don't feel so well.* Which was the absolute truth. They were supposed to take care of Chu and Mistress Jane then have fun exploring other worlds for the rest of their lives. It wasn't supposed to be like this. Paul wanted to shout at the top of his lungs. Maybe pound on some walls while he was at it.

He sat up.

He had to do something. Master George and the others had talked and talked around the conference room table and had come up with absolutely nothing to show for it. Except that they were going to keep researching, keep tabs on things, blah blah blah. Paul couldn't stand the thought of all that wasted time and energy. A big glob of *fog* was eating away at Reality, and his best friend had gone missing.

He had to do something, and he had to do something now, or he'd go completely nutso bat-crazy. Ignoring the ache and nausea in his belly, he slid off the bed and opened his door, stepping out into the hallway. It was right then that an image of a box popped into his head. A little metal box with a green button. And Paul knew exactly where Master George had placed it.

He started walking in that direction.

CHAPTER
41

ILL REUNION

When Tick opened his eyes, the face of Reginald Chu was staring back down at him. It was a face that had once meant so much to him—this terrible man was the Alterant of Tick's beloved science teacher, one of the greatest people ever. It was crazy how two opposites could look so much alike.

Tick was surprised at how little panic he felt. The ordeal that had happened near his home had been terrible. The movement and disorientation from whatever it was that had captured him had caused him to faint. He'd eventually awakened on a gurney of steel in some kind of bright washroom, reeking. He almost gagged from his own smell. He'd barely been conscious enough to have the thought, however, before someone pricked him with something that made him doze off again. His last memory was of a big hose washing him off before the darkness took him away.

And now, here he was again. Waking up. He could feel

242

clean, fresh clothes on his skin. He could see lights in the ceiling. And the ugly, smug face of Chu peering down at him as if he were nothing but an insect specimen.

"Don't even think about reaching for your Chi'karda," the man said. "Before I say anything else, I'll warn you on that front. Do you understand?"

Tick stared at him but said nothing. His mind went back to his failed attempts to escape from that weird silver coffin that had captured him. Twice he'd tried to destroy the object and free himself by throwing out his power, only to have it rebound and practically fry his brain. He still didn't really understand the whole strange turn of events.

Chu continued. "I can see the light of understanding in your eyes. I'm sure you remember when you and Jane came to Chu Industries, invited by yours truly. I wanted the best for my Dark Infinity project, and I knew there had to be something in place to block your Chi'karda levels. Well, obviously it didn't work then—now did it? You destroyed my entire building and ruined Jane's body for life."

"Maybe I'll do it again," Tick responded. His confidence was returning, and he still felt no real fear, despite the situation.

"You're missing my point. Once again your arrogance is preventing your brain from processing my words. I'm reminding you of the measures I had in place because they have been improved upon. My people are very clever, and you would be wise not to try anything. You felt what happened when you tried to use your force against the Bagger."

"The Bagger?" Tick repeated. He lifted his head up and

saw that he was lying on a small bed with several metal cords wrapped around his body, holding him down. The cords were much thinner than the one that had sprung from the long silver box and grabbed him by the waist, but seemed to be made from the same material.

"It's an invention of Chu Industries that I have neither the time or the desire to explain. It uses technology that lies beyond terminology you would understand anyway. But the key is that it was armed with my anti-Chi'karda recoil mechanism. And it worked. Sorry to test it on you—I'm sure you don't appreciate being the guinea pig, considering you could have died. What a pity that would've been."

This supposedly grown man was acting like a child, and it annoyed Tick to no end. "Maybe you can just *tell me why I'm here.*"

Chu's head pulled back ever so slightly, as if he were surprised that Tick would take such a tone considering his obvious disadvantages. "Don't mistake bravery for stupidity, boy. With all the people I've crushed or pushed aside in my lifetime quest to rule the Realities and make them better, it should be clear that I have many, many enemies. But no one comes close to being a target of my sheer . . . animosity as you do. Mr. Higginbottom, I despise you—there's no other way to put it. And your margin of error with me is as thin as a red blood cell. Do you understand?"

"*You* despise *me?*" Tick asked, incredulous. "How do you think I feel about you?"

"I'm sure the feeling is mutual. But it hardly matters

now that I have such complete control over you. I suggest you take a more humble approach."

But Tick wasn't done sharing a piece of his mind. "And what's all that garbage about making the Realities better? All you want is power, and you know it. You don't care about anyone but yourself."

Chu's face flashed with anger, and he leaned in closer to Tick. His bad breath wafted to Tick's nose and made him want to squirm out of the bed. "You shut that mouth of yours, do you hear me? Shut your mouth and show me some respect. You could never possibly understand me or my motives. I'll do what needs to be done, and no one can stop me. Yes, I may have a petty streak in me, and I may have done a few things that I might not be proud of, which is unfortunate for you because when I'm done using you, I'm going to dispose of you in a way that brings me a great deal of satisfaction. It's something you can start looking forward to."

Tick lashed out, but the restraints held his arms in place. He was furious and had never wanted to hit another person so much in his life. But he slouched back down onto the bed, knowing he couldn't be stupid enough to try anything with his power over Chi'karda. He'd just have to be patient and wait for the right opportunity to come along.

But at least he had his words. "You're a pathetic man, Chu. How can you even look yourself in the mirror tonight after standing there and talking like that to someone who's not even fifteen years old yet? Pathetic and sad."

Chu, of course, did the most maddening thing then. He laughed as he straightened back up to stand tall. "Don't goad me on, kid. You can yap all day if you want about how young you are, but we all know the power that's trapped inside your child's body. And we all know why."

Tick paused, surprised by the odd statement. Even though he hated to let go of his anger, he had to know what the man meant. "What . . . why . . . why what?"

Chu raised his eyebrows. "Don't play dumb with me, boy. Reginald Chu knows all—or at least what he cares to."

Tick started to sit up before he remembered the restraints. Groaning in frustration, he closed his eyes then opened them again. He needed to find some humility. "I'm serious. I don't know what you're talking about."

"This is unbelievable. How could he keep you in the dark about this?" Chu looked at him in disbelief. "I'm talking about why *you,* of all people, have this incredible ability to manipulate and control Chi'karda. Don't tell me that old man George hasn't explained it to you yet. He knows. He went well out of his way to confirm it."

Tick was dumbfounded. "*What* does he know?"

Chu folded his arms and peered down at him, slowly shaking his head. "Soulikens, Atticus. It's all about the soulikens."

CHAPTER
42

POOR LITTLE CENTIPEDE

Sweat poured down Sato's face, and it wasn't just from the effort of digging through and tossing aside the countless broken stones that had lain between him and the source of the glowing light at his feet. He was nervous because the massive storm of the Void was growing louder and bigger, its shadow looming over him, Tollaseat, and the dug-out pit in which they stood. They needed to figure out this anomaly and get away from there.

He got down on one knee and inspected the source of the light. It was a slit in the floor, about three feet long and a few inches wide. Although it wasn't really *in* the floor—it was more like the rip in Reality he'd seen before when the gray fog had first appeared beside the castle walls. Blue light shone from behind the odd crack in the air, so intense that it was hard to look at it directly. There was nothing else there, as if it were a small window into a river of radioactive material or something otherworldly. The light continued to pulse, flashing every few seconds so brightly that it was blinding.

"How're we s'posed to figure what she might be?" Tollaseat asked. The man was too long and gangly to try to squat down next to Sato. "Took a bit of work, it did, gettin' down this far. T'would be a mighty shame to go back empty-handed, now wouldn't it?"

Sato thought Mothball's dad had an uncanny gift for saying a lot of words that offered no help whatsoever. "I don't know. Just let me think for a second."

He did try to think, and that didn't help either. He wasn't a scientist. Somehow he'd become the captain of an army, for crying out loud. But he knew without any doubt that this small spit of shining blue light had something to do with . . . something.

Out of the corner of his eye, he noticed a centipede creeping along a broken slab of stone. Testing some theory on the edge of his mind, he picked up the poor little thing and tossed it into the slice of pulsing light. The bug disappeared in a tiny burst of white electricity, tiny jagged bolts skittering across the blue surface before dying out. There was no sign of the critter.

"Well, ain't you a cruel one," Tollaseat chided him from above. "What did that wee bugger ever do to you?"

Sato stood up, letting out a big sigh as he did so. "I was just putting him out of his misery. Pretty soon this whole place will be eaten up by . . . whatever that is out there." He jabbed a thumb in the direction of the tornado, then gave one last glance to the blue anomaly. "It was just an experiment. I thought maybe something would happen. Look, I have no idea what to do here. We'll just have to describe it to Master George and see what he thinks. Come on, let's go."

The two of them started up the pile of rocks they'd burrowed out of before. Sato was halfway to the top when he heard a horrible roar, like something half-mechanical and half-animal. It was followed by shouts from his soldiers.

His heart sank, and his first thought was, *What now?*

He picked up the pace and scrambled the rest of the way, almost falling twice as pieces of stone tore loose or broke off. When he reached the peak of the debris, he balanced himself and stood up, Tollaseat right beside him.

Something monstrous was crawling out of the churning mass of the Void's huge tornado. It was big and long, with lightning arcing along its gray skin. With a terrifying dawn of awareness, Sato realized that the thing looked like . . .

It looked like a *centipede.*

⁓

Paul was just about to slip into the laboratory of the Realitant headquarters when Sofia spotted him from down the hallway. *Great,* he thought. He'd almost made it.

She ran up to him. "What in the world are you doing? I looked all over for you. Master George is *not* happy."

"Hey, it's not my fault those idiots can't figure out what we're supposed to do next."

"Idiots?" she repeated. "Really? You're calling *them* idiots?"

"Very funny. Look, I might not be the smartest tool in this workshop, but at least I don't think it's okay to sit around fiddling my thumbs. I think it's high time you and I figured out something on our own."

Sofia rolled her eyes, but he saw some compassion in there too. She was trying to keep everyone happy on both sides of the fence. "Paul, you know very well that not a single person here is fiddling their thumbs. The rest of them are analyzing data, talking to other Realitants, and researching. They're trying to learn more about the Void and its energy so we can beat it. I was just coming to find you to help. We need every set of eyes."

"I'll tell you what the Void is," Paul said. "It's a big gray tornado that's getting bigger the longer we stand around here. We need Tick to go in there and . . . do whatever it is he does. Our *friend* is obviously in trouble, and that should be our number-one priority. Getting him *back*."

"And you really think Master George disagrees with that?" She folded her arms. "They can't latch onto his nano-locator. Mothball went to Deer Park but saw no sign of him. His dad said he never showed up. We can't go looking behind every rock and tree in the universe."

"Oh . . . oh, man." The news made Paul wilt inside. "There's gotta be a way to find him."

Sofia sighed. "Rutger will keep scanning for him, hope he pops back onto the radar."

"Tick should be our—"

"—number-one priority. I know! Don't you think I'm worried like crazy too? I just think we should all work together, not sneak around like this. What are you doing here anyway?"

Paul couldn't keep a secret from her, not now. "I came for the box."

"The box?"

"The box."

Her mouth was slightly open, her expression saying that she had no doubt he'd gone nuts. "And why are you going for the box?"

"Because I'm going to push the green button."

"No, you're not."

"Yes, I am."

"We don't even know what it does yet!"

"George does, or else he wouldn't have made us go get it." Paul reached out and opened the lab door. He'd seen their leader put the box into a cabinet drawer, even though the old man had tried to keep it a secret. The drawer wasn't a safe, though. It didn't have a lock or anything. Maybe George thought if the box was hidden in a place people wouldn't suspect, it might be safer.

"Paul, don't."

He ignored her and stepped into the room. When she didn't reach out and yank him back by the collar, he knew he had her. Times had grown desperate, and it was time to *do* something desperate. Before either one of them could change their minds, he ran over to the cabinet. She followed right on his heels. Paul ripped open the drawer.

The drawer was empty.

"I thought you might come looking for this," a voice said from behind them.

They spun around to see Master George at the lab door, bouncing the box with its little green button in his right hand. At first Paul thought that Sofia might've betrayed him, but one glance at her showed that she was just as surprised—and disappointed—at their leader's arrival.

"I just wanted to . . ." Paul began, but didn't know how to finish.

"Yes, I know," George said. "You just wanted to help, I'm sure. I guess it's time we had a talk about this very special device. It's time I told you about Karma. And then it may very well be time to push this button."

CHAPTER
43

ONE WITH REALITY

Chu had refused to say another word after announcing that it was "all about the soulikens." Tick knew soulikens were imprints of energy created by life and memories and thoughts. Stamps of life on Reality. They accumulated throughout one's existence until their signature hung around them like an aura. The Haunce—the most amazing creature Tick had ever met—was made up of trillions of soulikens.

Tick had an idea of what Chu meant. Most of his Alterants—if not all—had died at some point. Maybe their soulikens had somehow bled to him. Maybe that could explain the powers he had. He'd never wanted to talk to Master George so badly.

But that would have to wait. The gurney on which he lay had been rolled out of that hospital-like room by a man and a woman dressed in blue scrubs then down a long hallway and into an auditorium with rows and rows of chairs and a stage. Draped behind the stage was a huge screen of white material. The workers pushed him about halfway down the aisle then raised the back of the bed so Tick was able to sit up. His arms, legs, and torso were still fastened tightly down by the thin cords of metal. And his Chi'karda was still being blocked.

Chu had walked the entire way beside them, silent and brooding. He dismissed the blue-clad man and woman, leaving him and Tick alone inside the auditorium. The room was barely lit and cold; it was about as uninviting a room as Tick could imagine.

He looked at Chu, but the man was staring at the large screen, his hands folded in front of him. For at least two minutes he said nothing, which drove Tick batty. But he refused to say anything either, because he knew the man was waiting for him to do so.

Finally, Chu gave in and spoke. "Have you ever seen a fire, Atticus?" He still stared ahead, not turning to face Tick.

It certainly wasn't the question he'd expected. "A fire? Of course I've seen a fire. I've *made* fire. You saw me do it in the Nonex."

Chu seemed unfazed, in full business mode. Eerily, he reminded Tick of the other Mr. Chu, his science teacher, when he was about to begin yet another lecture that he thought would change his students' lives forever.

"So then, you have, in fact, seen a fire before?" the man said.

Tick wasn't going to be baited into anger. "Yes. I've seen a fire. Many times."

"Then you know about matter changing from one form to another. In your own experience, you've seen—and caused to happen—a solid molecular structure turn into a gas. Wood to flame. There are countless other examples of the physical makeup of one substance *changing* into another substance. Water evaporating, the decay of leaves, and so on and so forth."

Tick nodded. He had to admit he was intrigued, and he had no choice but to listen anyway.

"You're going to help me do that, Atticus. You're going to help me harness the power of Chi'karda and the Void that is escaping from the Fourth Dimension. And then you're going to make me—and Mistress Jane—one with them."

Tick felt an unpleasant flutter in his chest. He couldn't find any words. Chu was talking about something beyond evil, even though Tick didn't understand it fully yet.

The man finally turned and faced him, and there was something fanatical in his expression. "*One,* Atticus. You're going to make us *one* with Reality. The universe will never be the same."

<hr />

The creature was as big as a bus. Bulky and thick, with dozens of legs protruding from its gray-skinned body. Sato watched in sick fascination as the monster birthed itself out of the spinning mass of the Void then lumbered its way across the remaining span of castle ruins toward his army. The giant centipede's skin was slick with wetness, arcs of lightning flashing along the surface.

Sato was reckless as he jumped and ran over broken stones and bricks, knowing he might break an ankle at any second. But this centipede creature from the Void was heading straight for the Fifth Army, and he wanted to be there to help fight it. As he picked and leaped his way along, frantically looking for the next spot to land a foot before he jumped again, thoughts tore through his mind. This couldn't be a coincidence. He'd thrown the bug into that blue light, and soon after, only only only a monstrous version of it had emerged from the Void. Earlier, gray monsters that looked like creations of Mistress Jane's had come out of the tornado—most likely after having been sucked into the blue light.

And it scared him that the one place the newest creature decided to go was to a campsite full of people, which meant it could probably *think*. And that it wanted to kill and destroy. At least, he assumed so. A few seconds later, his suspicions were confirmed.

One of the many legs on the creature suddenly ripped off the main body, spinning away like a boomerang, headed for the center of Sato's army, which was gathering for battle. The shaft of gray fog flew through the air about forty feet then suddenly erupted into flames, brilliant and yellow. It struck one of Sato's soldiers, a man standing bravely at the head of the front line, who'd just been pulling up his Shurric into a firing position. There was a violent explosion of sparks and fire that started but stopped almost instantly, leaping out then collapsing in on itself. It was so bright that Sato stumbled and fell, smacking his upper arm on a sharp stone.

With a grimace, he quickly looked back at the front line—amoebas of light dancing in his vision—but saw nothing. The poor man had been incinerated.

Sato heard the shouts of battle as his soldiers surged forward to fight, charging the creature as it continued to come at them. He scrambled to his feet, wincing from the pain in his shoulder—there would be one terrible bruise there before long. Tollaseat was there, helping him get up. The man said nothing, but there was a mix of sadness and fear in his eyes.

Noise filled the air: the rushing roar of the Void's spinning cloud, the cracks of thunder, the battle screams of his soldiers.

The Void monster crashed through the last part of the castle debris, landing on the ground dozens of feet from the charging Fifth Army. It righted itself and shot off another one of its legs, a three-foot-long stub of gray fog that spun through the air until it erupted into flames like its predecessor. The twirling missile of fire slammed into the body of a man, causing an explosion just like before. When the sparks and pyrotechnics collapsed again into a tiny spot and disappeared, there was no sign of the soldier.

Another leg flew off of the creature, doing the same trick. Spinning, erupting into flames, flying toward a soldier. This time it a was a woman. She was ready, though, and held her ground. She lifted her Shurric and, with patience that Sato couldn't believe, took the time to aim and fire her weapon at the heart of the incoming attack. The thump of pure sound wave was too deep to be heard, but Sato felt a rattle in his bones. The force of power slammed into the spinning projectile and ruptured it, sending small spits of flame and sparks in a million directions. But no one was harmed.

Sato grinned. They could do this. They *could* beat this thing.

He picked up his pace across the ruins, watching as his army attacked the creature with everything they had. The creature was dead by the time he got there.

CHAPTER 44

GOOD AND EVIL

Master George had taken Paul and Sofia to a small, private room located in the deepest part of the headquarters, far below the surface of the Upper Rim of the Grand Canyon. Unmarked, it could've passed for a utility closet. It held only a table and four chairs, nothing else.

"I come here sometimes when I need a bit of time to myself," the old man said wearily after they'd taken their seats. He held Gretel's box in his hands under the table. "And to be quite frank, I'm at a loss right now. I can barely face my dear old friends, Mothball and the rest. I've always felt as if I have known the direction to take, even in the most dire of circumstances we've faced. But not now. I'm at a loss, indeed. It's no wonder I wanted to hide in this room. I very much appreciate you taking refuge along with me."

Paul looked over at Sofia. Had the geezer really given up?

Sofia reached out and patted George's shoulder.

"Everything kind of took a crazy turn," she said soothingly. "But we'll figure things out."

"Yeah," Paul agreed. What he really wanted was to find out more about the box. And the button. "So can that box do something to help? Are we really going to push the button?"

Sofia shot him a glare. "Seriously? I guess there's only room enough in that brain of yours for one thing at a time." She winked, then, taking away the sting of her words.

He felt a nice flutter inside. "I'm just saying. Things are messed up beyond belief, and we went on a special mission to get that box, so it must be important. We need all the help we can get, don't we?"

Sofia didn't answer at first, just looked back at Master George. "He's right. It might be time to do something a little drastic."

Their leader nodded slowly as he stared at the table. "I couldn't agree more, Sofia. I fear we've come to a place in our journey where we need something a little . . . beyond the regular means. We know so little of this Void from the Fourth Dimension that I'm afraid we need your minds and skills more than ever. We can't rely on Mistress Jane to teach us about the threat that churns inside the Thirteenth Reality. At least when we faced the Blade of Shattered Hope—and the Dark Infinity weapon before that—there was a path before us. Possibilities. Like I've said, this time around, I'm at a bitter loss. You two need to step it up."

Paul couldn't help the impatience that wanted to burst out of him at the seams. "So . . . then what are you saying?"

George pulled his hands up from his lap and placed the small metal box on the table in front of him. The green button was like a beacon, and Paul had to resist the urge to reach out and push it right that second.

"This is your assignment," George pronounced. "But before I tell you about this box, we need to talk about a very important subject. Very important, indeed. It's something that is almost as beyond our understanding as this Void that plagues us presently. And that subject is . . . Karma."

He'd said that word earlier, but now it had a haunted, foreboding ring to it. Paul leaned forward, eager to hear more.

"There's a reason talking about this makes me . . . uncomfortable," George continued. "I'm a scientist, and I know both of you are well aware of that fact. I'm a scientist above all else. And that means that everything I live for is grounded in a solid foundation of tested theories, facts, and proofs. Many of the things you've seen and experienced since being recruited—goodness gracious me, that seems like decades ago—may appear to be magic to many people. To *ordinary* people. But my favorite two words, *quantum physics,* have always been able to explain it all. *Kyoopy,* I believe it's been coined before."

He paused, a look of blissful contemplation on his face. But then he shook his head and snapped out of it. His expression grew very serious. "But this . . . this is something that is a little less certain. A part of our cosmos that is beyond our capacity to comprehend fully. Or beyond mine, at any rate."

"Karma?" Sofia asked.

"Karma," the old man confirmed.

"Everyone knows what that means," Paul said. "Basically, what goes around, comes around. Right?"

"To put it simply, yes." George looked down at the box then back at Paul. "The notion that the universe pays back what people deposit is something that has been a part of human culture since the beginning of recorded history. Be a good person, do good things, and then good things will happen to you eventually. Be a *bad* person, do *bad* things . . . well, then quite the opposite. One way or another, your actions always come back to you. Repayment of what you've dealt. Almost every civilization has believed in the concept in some form. *Karma* is just the most commonly used word to describe the phenomenon."

Paul was fascinated. "And this button has something to do with it?"

George nodded, holding up the box as if inspecting it for flaws. "Yes, it does. There have been those in our ranks who believe Karma is a scientific principle as rigid as gravity. And, *like* gravity, they accept it one hundred percent, even though they can't quite explain why it happens or how it works."

"*They?*" Sofia repeated. "You mean you don't believe in it like some of the others?"

"It's as I've said. I have difficulty accepting something that's not grounded in solid scientific principle and analysis. But the gravity example is a good one. No rational person could possibly argue that gravity doesn't exist, despite our inability to understand it fully. Likewise, evidence of Karma is rampant. And it's possible—and strongly believed by some, in fact—that it can be gathered and manipulated, just like Chi'karda can be with the Chi'karda Drives we have inside our Barrier Wands that power them and make them work."

"So that's what this box is?" Paul asked. "A . . . Karma Drive?"

George looked at him, his eyebrows lifted in slight surprise. "Why, yes, that's *precisely* what it is, Master Paul. Precisely. This box was built by a small group of Realitants, led by Gretel, with some extremely speculative and revolutionary technology. It took them a full decade—exhausting work. Two of the members of the team went mad and had to be discharged from our society. But Gretel believes strongly that she and her team were successful, and that they've created a mechanism that will harness Karma and concentrate it for one purpose. Just like a Barrier Wand."

Sofia reached out to touch the box, but George pulled it away. "No, no. We must be very careful how we decide to proceed in this matter."

"Karma's a good thing, right?" Paul asked. "Let's just push the button and hope for the best." Even as he said it, he knew he couldn't possibly sound *less* like the scientist he was supposed to be. But he was mostly joking. Mostly.

"My good man, use your brain. After all that effort and work, no one has ever pushed this button before. Gretel believes that the power will swirl and coalesce around the one who holds the box, infusing them and their surroundings with Karma to use for whatever purpose the bearer may need."

"Well," Paul countered, "I'd say we're in pretty bad shape, so maybe now is a good time to try it. You're the one who says you don't really know what to do about the Void. Let's push the button, and then maybe Sofia and I can figure out how to use the power."

George pulled the box back into his lap. "You haven't understood what I've told you if you think we should be so hasty. Remember what Karma does. I believe you said it this way: 'What goes around, comes around.' In a way it magnifies, significantly, good or evil."

"Yeah? So what?" Paul pushed, a little sarcastically.

"That's all very well if the power latches on to something good." George pursed his lips and shook his head dramatically. "And I daresay the both of you are as good as it gets. But if it somehow got into the hands of someone *evil,* then we'd all be in very much trouble, indeed."

CHAPTER 45

BRAINPOWER

The Void was a monster now.

Sato and his troops had retreated to the edge of the forest, watching the gray mass continue to grow.

There was nothing left of Mistress Jane's castle. The churning, spinning cloud was now two or three miles wide, its edges a chaotic dance of lightning and boiling tendrils of gray mist. The vortex was probably half a mile tall, blocking out the sun. Thunder pounded the air, and the darkness of a heavy storm cast a gloomy mood over everything.

No one could have felt it any deeper than Sato. There were things to learn here. Terrible, awful things. He had to talk to Master George, tell him about the centipede experiment.

"Tollaseat!" he called out.

The man was a few dozen feet away, but came running. When he pulled up at Sato's side, he looked haggard and exhausted.

"Yes, Captain?" he asked.

Sato took one last glance at the growing Void, hoping he'd never have to see it again. How were they supposed to fight such a thing? They needed brainpower.

"Let's get everybody deeper into the woods," he said, hearing the defeat in his own voice. "I'll contact Master George and have him wink us somewhere safe. We're done here."

Tick lay in the dark, staring up at a ceiling he couldn't see. Chu had put him in a room with no windows and then turned off the lights. Just to make him angry, probably. Just to show him who was in control. It obviously still rankled the man that a teenager had more power than he did.

What a mess. Tick's chest hurt from holding in so much stress and despair. He longed for those few moments after escaping the Nonex, seeing his mom and sister, thinking that maybe all would be right in the world again. How wrong he'd been.

As if the Void weren't enough of a problem, he'd been captured by a man insane with the lust for power. Chu had explained to him a few things, had even shown him a video feed using a Spinner on the screen in the auditorium. It basically boiled down to one simple fact: Chu wanted to harness the incredible amounts of energy he believed emanated from the Void currently devouring the Thirteenth Reality, then use it to *meld* himself—and, evidently, Mistress Jane—with Reality itself. It sounded similar to what Tick had accidentally done to Mistress Jane—melding *her* with Dark Infinity—so long ago.

Chu claimed that once he'd accomplished that task, it would be easy for him to stop the Void and force it to return to the Fourth Dimension. Then he and Jane would use their godlike powers to rule the Realities in a way no one would have thought possible. It was such an impossible idea that Tick couldn't even grasp it. And he highly doubted those two actually trusted each other. Each one of them probably thought there'd only be one left to rule in the end. Each one probably saw the other only as a means to an end.

But Tick was scared. He knew better than to underestimate Reginald Chu. The man was psycho, but he was a scientist through and through. There was no way he'd pretend he could do magical things. If Chu thought this scheme was possible, then it probably *was* possible. And that turned Tick's fear into terror.

He tried to rest up. He needed to be ready when the time came to act.

CHAPTER
46

A LITTLE HELP, HERE

Mistress Jane was exhausted. Not physically—she'd gotten plenty of sleep over the last couple of days inside her apartment—but her mind was spent from all the research. Every waking moment, she had been poring through her old notes, her computer files, her books. She needed to know everything about the Fourth Dimension, and the Void that had once been trapped within it, before she went to Chu's rebuilt headquarters.

She'd winked herself to a lonely mountaintop in the Thirteenth Reality, a place where she'd come before to meditate and scheme. Two things she did very well and needed to do now. But the main reason she'd chosen the location was so she could see the latest developments of the Void that had ripped her beloved castle to pieces, and, by the looks of it, had proceeded to eat the remains as well. The enormous spinning cloud of gray mist looked almost peaceful from this far away, the thunder just a low rumble rolling across the land. But she knew the Void was terrible, without compassion.

It would grow. And it would destroy. And once this world was gone, the other Realities would follow. The energy and power of the Void was a thing of awe, a thing that would make most people cower and shake with fear. But not her. She'd had her moment of doubt, and it had passed. Now she was here, facing the beast that threatened to destroy everything she'd devoted her life to. She faced it, and saw only opportunity now. Opportunity to build the Utopia of which she'd always dreamed.

Power. Energy. Unlimited.

There was a way to capture that, to harness it. To divert it from its current path and use it for better purposes. But she needed help, at least for now.

Yes, with some help, she could do great things with this Void of Mist and Thunder. This Void that represented the pure power of creation. Great things indeed.

It was time to reunite with Reginald Chu and Atticus Higginbottom.

⌒

Paul was pretty sure he could've talked Master George into taking a risk and pushing that green button, but they were interrupted. Rutger, waddling and sweating like never before, burst into the room, his words spilling out between ragged breaths.

"Good grief . . . people!" he shouted. "Why . . . it took me . . . forever . . . to find you!"

George shot up from his chair and asked what was wrong. Eventually Rutger managed to say that Sato had made contact with headquarters, asking for a good spot of Chi'karda in the Forest of Plague. Rutger, with the help of Mothball and Sally, had been able to wink Sato and the rest of the Fifth Army out of the Thirteenth Reality, and now most of them were down in the valley of the Grand Canyon, washing in the river, eating some much-needed food, resting, and recovering.

Paul sat with Sofia on the couch in George's office, waiting for the old man to return with Sato and the other Realitants. They needed to hear the entire story, and their leader said he wanted to wait until everyone was gathered to do it. But Paul had heard enough of the tidbits to have a sickness in his belly. The Void growing bigger, more soldiers dying, something about a blue light that turned things into monsters.

Yeah, none of that sounded too good.

Sofia's knees were bouncing.

"Hey," Paul said to her. "Chill. We're going to figure out all this junk. You'll see."

She stopped moving, and her face flushed red as if embarrassed. "I'm not nervous."

"Yeah, right."

"And you're not? You just want to *chill*, huh?"

Paul shrugged. "I have a good feeling about this box and its button. About the Karma thing. I mean, that's the definition of Karma! The Realitants have always been good, trying to do what's right. And now things are going to come around for us. We're going to get some help from the cosmos, or Karma, or whatever you wanna call it. All we have to do is push that button."

Sofia scooted away on the couch to face him, flashing her standard glare. "Seriously? You think the world's so simple that you can push a button on a tiny box, and everything will be all better? You thought you were smart enough to join the Realitants?" She folded her arms and looked away. "Unbelievable."

It surprised him how much his feelings were hurt. "I'm just trying to show some hope here. There has to be a reason for that box, right? It's supposed to scientifically channel Karma matter. But to me, it's Karma that we even have it in the first place. What's wrong with a little hope? Geez."

Sofia was suddenly at his side, pulling him into a fierce hug, crying into his shoulder and shaking with sobs. When he recovered from his shock, he hugged back, patting her uncertainly.

"It's okay," he said. "Somehow it's going to be okay. Trust your old Uncle Paul."

She pulled away and laughed over her sniffles. "*Uncle Paul?* Please don't ever call yourself that again." She wiped at her eyes and nose then cleaned her hands on her pants, which somehow made Paul like her just a little bit more.

"You can call me whatever you want."

"Oh, man, I'm so embarrassed. I can't remember the last time I broke down like that."

"Please, girl," Paul said. "You've been the toughest one out of all of us. Or did you forget your little jaunt through

Chu's mountain building while the whole thing was falling down, saving Tick, then pulling him out at the last second? You can cry all you want—no one's gonna say boo."

"It just all hit me at once." She'd stopped crying, fully composed just like that, but with puffy red eyes to show for it. "Seems like we can't get ahead before the next bad, awful, terrible thing happens. And now Tick's missing. *Again*. And we still don't know how to stop this stupid Void of Mist and Thunder."

Paul had absolutely no idea what to say to make her feel better. Or how to make *himself* feel better. "I just . . . I don't know. Tick can take care of himself—I'm not as worried about him anymore. Maybe he just wanted to be with his family for a while. Or if he's in trouble, he'll get out of it. As for our other problems . . . well, all we can do is hope for something. Right? Karma. A breakthrough. A brilliant idea. Maybe the Fourth Dimension will call and make the Void go home."

Sofia laughed again. "I vote for that last one."

She'd just spoken when the door opened and Master George came through, Muffintops perched on his shoulder like a parrot on an old sea pirate. Paul didn't know if it looked creepy or hilarious. Mothball came next, then Rutger—his face red from the exertion of coming up from the canyon floor, even though it was mostly via elevator—then Sally. Finally, Sato, who had cleaned up and eaten but still looked like he'd been dragged down a mountain by a billy goat.

Sofia jumped off the couch and gave him a hug. He didn't respond much, his eyes cast to the floor.

Man, Paul thought. *That is one haunted dude.* "Hey," he said. "I'm glad you made it back safely."

Sato gave him a weary look, and it was obvious that he wanted to say something, but he held it back and took a seat on one of the plush chairs. The others did the same as Master George went over and lit up the fire. The guy loved his fires. Then he turned to face his small group of Realitants.

"My dear friends and associates," he announced gravely. "I'm afraid that our deepest fears regarding the Void have only skimmed the surface. It's now time for action, and we're all going to do our part. But there's something we need to do together before we split up."

"And what's that?" Paul asked.

George looked at him for a long moment. "I believe with all of my heart that I've found the two people I trust most with the power of Karma. We're going to push your favorite button, Master Paul. And we're going to do it this very minute."

Paul realized he was smiling.

"And then," George continued, "I'm going to trust you and Sofia to figure out what to do with its power."

CHAPTER
47

I AMAZE EVEN MYSELF

A light went on, blinding Tick even though he had his eyes closed. After opening them on instinct, he had to squint until he finally got used to it. A shadow crossed his vision, then there was the scrape of a chair across a tile floor then the settling sounds of someone getting comfortable. Tick could finally see that it was Chu sitting next to his bed. Tick had to twist his neck uncomfortably to see him because of the restraints holding down his arms and legs and torso.

"What do you want?" he asked, trying to sound angry but having lost all of his spirit after being held captive in a dark room for hours. He'd been tempted to try his powers of Chi'karda, but he couldn't quite bring up the nerve. The memory of what had happened to him the last time still scarred his thoughts.

"It's almost time for us to act," the man said calmly.

Tick looked back up at the ceiling so his neck wouldn't

hurt, and because he couldn't stand the calm expression on Chu's face right then.

"Jane will be here soon," Chu continued.

"To act, huh?" Tick asked. "We're just going to grab some ropes, lasso the Void from the Fourth Dimension, mix it up with some sugar in a glass, then let you drink it? Piece of cake."

Chu remained unfazed. "That's a very unscientific way to put it, but I guess it's not too far from the truth. Great things, Atticus. You're going to be a part of great things in the next couple of days."

"You *do* realize this is crazy, right?"

"There have been those throughout history who have misjudged brilliance for madness. I can assure you this is not the case. Most men simply can't comprehend the speed and level at which someone like myself utilizes the functions of my brain. It's something I've grown to appreciate and admire about myself."

Tick laughed—he couldn't help it. "You didn't really just say that."

"How can anyone not admire greatness?" Chu asked in a sincerely astonished voice. "Can I help it that the greatness is within my own being? No, I can't. I don't deal in such things as pride and humility. I'm a scientist, and things are as they are. No more, no less."

"You keep telling yourself that," Tick muttered.

"If you're done with childish discussions," Chu said sternly, "then perhaps we can move on to the important matters at hand."

"Do you really think I'm going to help you?" Tick asked. It really did baffle him. "I might be a little shy right now about pulling out my Chi'karda, but when push comes to shove, you *know* I'm going to do whatever it takes to stop you."

"I have ways to change your mind. But I don't think I'll need them. By the time we're ready, I think you're going to do exactly what I ask. Voluntarily. You'll *want* to, in fact."

Tick decided to quit talking. It was pointless, and the man was probably trying to manipulate him anyway. *Let him think whatever he wants,* Tick told himself. He knew that in the end, he'd die before he let Chu follow through with his schemes.

"Silence," the man said. "Maybe that's the best thing for you now anyway. You can shut your mouth, but not your ears. Nothing like a . . . *captive* audience. There are a lot of things I need to—"

whomp

A thrumming vibration shook the air, cutting off Chu's words.

Tick instinctively tried to sit up, but the metal cords dug into his skin, and he slammed back onto the bed again. That sound, that tingle in the air . . .

whomp

Chu had frozen, his face caught in a look of childish fear.

whomp

Tick had heard this noise before. *Felt* it before. He'd been walking on the road that led to his house in Deer Park when a wave of power and sound and feeling had reached him. It had been coming from his house, and when he'd run home, he'd discovered Mistress Jane in his basement, scheming very bad things.

whomp

"Does she always have to make such a grand entrance?" Chu whispered, having lost all of his bravado from a minute before. Tick thought the woman must still scare him, even though she'd obviously agreed to work with him.

whomp

The sound was getting louder, the vibration stronger. Things in the room rattled.

"It's Jane, alright," Tick said, seeing an opportunity. "She told the Realitants how dangerous you are. She'll betray you the second she doesn't need you anymore."

WHOMP

This time, the entire room shook as if struck by an earthquake. A cabinet in the corner of the room fell over, tossing supplies everywhere. Chu stood with his arms outstretched, as if he could ward off the threat.

"You can't trust her!" Tick yelled at him. "Let me go so I can help!" He almost felt ridiculous—it was obvious he'd say anything to be released.

WHOMP!

This time the sound and vibration was followed by a hissing noise, like sand running down a metal slide. Tick looked over at the door to see it *dissolving*. He'd seen Jane use the power of Entropy before; he'd done it himself too. The particles of the door decayed toward chaos and vanished, leaving an empty hole. Mistress Jane stood in the hallway, wearing a new robe, its hood pulled over her head, hiding the red mask in shadow.

"Impressive," Chu muttered under his breath.

Jane stepped into the room then reached up and pulled back her hood. The scarred tragedy of her head looked pitiful, but the mask held no expression.

"Sorry I'm late, Reginald," she said in her raspy voice. "But I'm excited for the three of us to be working together again. And so soon after our last adventure."

CHAPTER 48

BOX IN A CIRCLE

For some reason, Master George had decided to sit on the floor, something Paul had never seen the old man do before. It didn't seem proper for such a gentleman in a fancy suit, but he'd done it, and so the rest of them had followed his lead. The room was barely large enough for the group to fit between the couches and chairs—and the roaring fireplace at the head of it all.

But there they were. George, sitting with his legs crossed. Mothball next to him, her long, gangly legs somehow folded up into an impossibly small spot. Then Rutger, perched precariously as though he might roll away at the slightest push. Sally sat by him, looking like a lumberjack taking a long-needed break. Sato was next, all business. Sofia and Paul completed the circle, and Paul kept having the urge to reach out and take her hand. He fought it off, but kind of hoped she was feeling the same way.

A complete circle of Realitants, sitting on the floor.

The Karma box, with its enticing green button, sat on the carpet in the middle.

"I'm sad that Gretel couldn't be here with us," Master George said. "She was needed in the Third Reality. But I've decided to put my trust in her findings and research and . . . this invention . . . at this time of dire need. The box will channel the Karma that she so dearly loved to study, and once we have it within our grasp, I believe we'll be able to figure out the best way to use it."

He shot a glance at Paul, then Sofia, then at the stack of Gretel's notes piled next to them. Paul was thrilled that the two of them were being entrusted with something so important.

"I need everyone in this room to understand the gravity of the decision I've made," George continued. "Karma is nothing more than a concept. A theory. Even those I deemed experts on the mysterious substance were making educated guesses at best, dreamy wishes at worst. But they are people I trust implicitly. I believe their educated guesses may be more reliable than the most researched, documented theories of the world's renowned scientists. In my heart, I believe this complicated device is going to do something extraordinary. And that it will help us."

"Then let's get on with it," Paul muttered, trying to lighten the mood. "Time's a wastin'. Isn't that what they say?"

"Better to waste time than people's bloomin' lives, it is," Mothball countered drily, her eyes not even looking up from the floor.

George cut in before Paul could respond. "I wouldn't take this risk unless I thought the *risk* was worth it. I fear we've reached a time of desperation, and if we wait much longer, the damage may be too great to reverse. Especially with the troubling observations Master Sato made in the Thirteenth Reality."

"Sofia and I will figure out what to do with it," Paul urged. His hands were sweaty with anticipation. "Please just push the button. *Please.*"

"I need everyone here to—" George began.

Rutger cut him off. "Boss. You're stalling. We wouldn't all be sitting here on the floor like kids at bedtime if we weren't committed. The boy is right. Push the button. We can trust Gretel that it will work."

"Very well."

George fidgeted in his seat, wrung his hands and cracked his knuckles, then wriggled some more. No one said a word, and Paul leaned forward. Their leader finally reached out and picked up the small metal box, gingerly, as though it were a bomb that might accidentally go off. He placed it on the floor again, right in front of his crossed legs.

"Here goes nothing," he said. "Now, something I chose not to share with you, Master Paul, is that only two people in the Realities can push the button—me and Gretel. The device was built to read our DNA signature before it will compress. I must say, I'm quite proud that you didn't fail my test and try to do it yourself."

"Oh," was all Paul said in response. Relief filled him from top to bottom.

"But once it's pushed," George continued, "I want you and Sofia to take it and keep it with you at all times as you study the power. The Karma will be focused on the source—the box itself—and, therefore, on whoever holds it." He waited for Sofia's nod. Then Paul's. "Right. Here we go, then. May the Realities smile upon us on this troubled, troubled day."

"And Karma," Paul added.

Master George reached a hand to the box, pressed his thumb against the top of the button, waited a second, then pushed it all the way down.

CHAPTER
49

BENDING AND WARPING

There was a very distinct *click* when the button went down. It was louder than it should've been, it seemed to Paul, the quick bang echoing off the ceiling of the room. There were no other sounds but the crackling of the fire. Everyone else was too busy holding their breath to make a noise, waiting to see what happened.

Master George had a wide look of expectation on his face, his eyebrows raised to their fullest. He slowly and carefully removed his thumb from the button and pulled his hand back into his lap. The button didn't pop back up but instead remained inside the box, so that only the green circle of its top was visible. He handed it to Sofia.

"Hide this away," the man said. "Guard it with your life."

She nodded. "I feel something tingling across my skin."

Paul felt it, too, just barely. He strained his ears to hear anything and his eyes to see anything. Sometimes Chi'karda presented itself in the form of an orange cloud or misty sparkles. He wondered if Karma would do the same sort of thing. He hoped so—he wouldn't be able to stand it if all he felt was this tingle, no visible confirmation that something was happening. He stared, and listened, and felt with his other senses. Waited.

"I don't think it—" Rutger began to say, but he was quickly silenced by shushes from the others in the room. Chagrined, the little man seemed to roll up into a tighter ball.

Master George held up a hand, palm out. "I believe something else is happening."

There was a light rumbling in the distance, like the growl of thunder in an approaching storm. Paul and the others looked at each other with wide eyes. He wondered if they were as spooked as he was. He had a shivering chill going up and down his spine, as if someone had just said they'd seen a ghost walking down the hall and they were all now waiting for it to appear at the doorway.

The rumbling grew louder, and then the room began to shake. Just a slight tremor at first, barely noticeable. Paul put his hands on the carpet and felt a vibration that shot right up his bones. It strengthened until there wasn't any doubt that something unusual was happening—the windows to the balcony rattled, and the picture of Muffintops that hung over the fireplace suddenly fell off its nail, crashing onto the floor. The glass in the frame broke.

Master George let out a little cry of surprise and struggled to his feet. Mothball helped him up as her long bones straightened out to stand up as well. Paul got up, he and Sofia leaning on each other for support. The shaking had escalated to an all-out earthquake, the floor jumping up and down as the walls seemed to bow in and out. There was almost something unnatural about it, as if the room was bending and stretching in impossible ways. He looked at the balcony, where the glass in the windows appeared to have had melted into a liquid, bubbling inward then back out again toward the canyon.

An uneasy feeling replaced the immediate panic from the quake. If this was the good Karma Paul had hoped for, then he wanted to go back in time and throw that box in the river.

The room swayed side to side, up and down, with no sign of stopping. The small group of Realitants had so far stood together in a daze, balancing, maybe hoping it would end. The distant sound of thunder had been replaced with something more sinister: a long, shrill whine like the high-pitched whistle of an old steam train. But intermixed with that were more disturbing noises that cut in and out—moans and groans and screams that weren't quite human.

Paul was beginning to feel dizzy and queasy, and not just from the jolting movement. He was sick that maybe he'd talked George into doing something terrible.

As if on cue, their leader finally took charge.

"Keep hold of each other!" he shouted over the increasing noise. "I don't think—rather I *hope* this isn't related to the Karma box. I'm quite sure of it. I believe we are experiencing a disturbance like the ones that have been happening since the incident with the Blade of Shattered Hope. I want to look outside, see what's going on. But we mustn't separate! Does everyone understand?"

The scene was absurd. The whole room was shaking and bending and warping in impossible ways, and the Realitants looked like old daredevils trying to balance on a high tightrope. But they all nodded their assent and held hands with each other: Mothball, Rutger, Sally, Sato, Sofia, and Paul, all in a row. Mothball held on to George as he started making his way to the balcony.

As they stumbled toward the sliding glass door, everything intensified. The walls bubbled in and out more deeply, the sight of it so disorienting that Paul was starting to wonder if maybe they'd been drugged or something. The floor bounced and rippled, making it impossible to walk a straight line. If they hadn't been holding hands, each one of them would've been sprawled across the carpet. And the noises, awful and disturbing, were also increasing in pitch and volume. It was like a soundtrack for a haunted house, moans and groans and squeals.

George reached the door and paused. With the glass bending and warping, it seemed impossible that it could slide open. But he reached out anyway, grabbed the handle, and pushed all of his weight onto it. The door opened easily, sliding all the way to the left—even as it continued to ripple in crazy ways.

The old man turned and shouted back at them over the terrible chorus of sounds. "I've never seen anything quite like this! Something is *wrong* with Reality!"

"Ya think?" Paul murmured, but he was pretty sure no one heard him. What had they done? What had pushing that button done to Reality? It couldn't be a coincidence.

George turned back to the balcony, which looked like something seen through a sheen of water. It definitely didn't seem like a safe place to go right then, but George walked out onto the wavy, bouncy surface of the balcony floor, still holding hands with Mothball behind him, reaching out with his other hand to grab the railing. It was as shifty and rippling as everything else, but it had to be better than nothing.

When he touched the railing and took hold of it, an odd thing happened. Beginning at his hand, a distinct bulge of warped Reality shot up his arm and through his body like a wave of energy. It went down his other arm then hit Mothball, doing the same thing to her. The ball of power proceeded to go through every single Realitant like a snake swallowing a baseball until it passed through Sofia and shot up Paul's arm. He almost let go of Sofia's hand but didn't. He felt nothing more than a tickle and a surge of static electricity along his skin, his hair shooting up on end. But then the energy traveled down his other arm and disappeared.

Master George was still clasping the rail of the balcony, and even that was a weird sight. The rail was moving, wavering like a mirage, but the old man's arm seemed to be solid. Two things happening at once? That wasn't possible. George faced the open air of the canyon, and looks of confusion passed down the Realitants. Clearly no one understood the anomaly that had passed through their bodies.

"Everyone!" George snapped, his voice muted against the awful noises that still haunted the air. "Everyone up here to have a look! Quickly, now!"

The motion of the room—the entire building, in fact—was still intense, jumping and rippling, an earthquake mixed with hallucination. But Paul and the other Realitants fought against it and surged forward, through the open door to the balcony. They crowded close, maneuvering so that each person could look over the railing and see what Master George saw.

Two seconds earlier, Paul had thought there was no way things could get worse. But he'd been terribly wrong. He stared out at the valley of the Grand Canyon and forgot all about the rocking movement around him.

Slicing its way through midair, running between the tall, rocky walls, was a floating river. Just a hundred feet or so above the raging waters of the Colorado River, there was a wide, bright gap of intense blueness. It was long and stretched in both directions, as if a giant knife had cut through Reality and the wound bled glowing blue blood. It was the same blue glow that Sato had described dropping the centipede into.

"The Fourth Dimension has ripped open into this Reality!" George shouted.

People started falling from the rent in the air.

CHAPTER
50

ODD COUPLE

There'd been a very long talk.

Tick lay there awkwardly, feeling like a spectator at a silent film, as Jane and Chu whispered with each other. His face was tense, and hers—the mask—showed no expression at all. On and on they talked, but Tick couldn't hear a word they said. He was getting closer and closer to giving in to his instincts and just unleashing his Chi'karda with every bit of strength he had. How could it be any worse than letting Chu do whatever he wanted with him?

Finally, Tick couldn't take it anymore.

"You two need to listen to me," he said, trying to sound more patient and reasonable than he felt. "Bad things are going on, and we all know they're getting worse. It's just like in the Nonex. We can't fight each other until we make things right again in the Realities. I promise not to fight if you will."

Tick didn't like saying the words; he didn't *want* to work

291

with Jane or Chu, but maybe he had no other choice. He wished he could find a way to get out of his restraints so he could use his Chi'karda again.

Both Jane and Chu looked over at him. Jane's mask actually pulled up into a slight grin.

"Let me go," Tick pleaded. "I swear on my family I won't try anything. I won't hurt anybody. And I'll stay here while we talk everything out." He winced at that last sentence. Now he was trying too hard.

"Pipe down while the adults talk," Chu said. If he'd said it angrily, or meanly, Tick would've been okay with it. But he said it like he actually thought of Tick like a child, and that boiled his insides. He almost felt steam coming out of his ears.

"Please," Tick said. "You know I can help."

Chu looked back at Jane as if he hadn't heard him. "Ever since this . . . *opportunity* presented itself in your Thirteenth Reality, my people have been working on a device that can harness the power of the Void, adapting it. We can do it, Mistress Jane. We can become one with it. We can *meld ourselves* to Reality. Just like we discussed. Things have come to fruition faster than we could've ever dreamed."

Jane nodded her head slowly. "Don't double cross me, Chu. I'm warning you."

Something snapped inside of Tick. It was like a bunch of valves had been holding back the flow of Chi'karda inside him, and they all broke at once. The power almost burst out of him, but somehow he grabbed it at the last second, held it at bay. But he couldn't keep the words from tumbling out.

"That's enough!" he yelled. "I swear, if you two don't stop acting like I'm not here, I'm going to let it all out, no matter what happens. It's like a dam over here, and it's about to break! Take these straps off of me. Now!"

His heart raced, and he could feel his limbs shaking, the blood rushing to his head and face. Heat ebbed along his skin, as if his pores were straining from exertion, the orange might of Chi'karda trying to burst through.

"Let me go!" he shouted.

He saw a flash of fear in Chu's eyes before the man tried to hide it. Jane was no longer smiling. But neither one of them moved.

"Let me—"

He didn't finish the sentence. A sudden jolt hit the room, shaking it so intensely and violently that all other thoughts vanished from Tick's mind, as instant as the flip of a light switch. The overpowering surge of Chi'karda disappeared as well, making him feel empty and scared. The room slammed toward the side, then sprang back the next second. Chu and Jane both fell down, sprawling over each other in a tangle of arms, legs, and the folds of her yellow robe.

It all happened so fast, like a speed bump in time. The room had barely stabilized before it began to shake again, this time more steadily, growing in strength. Chu and Jane were scrambling to get to their feet, reaching out to hold on to Tick's bed. Things fell off the shelves, rattled across the floor. Tick was helpless, holding on to the sheets as if they'd give him any protection—the straps held him down as firmly as ever.

And the Chi'karda really was gone. Completely. He even reached for it again, wanting to feel its power and comfort, but it was like something had blocked it *within* him. He couldn't find a single trace.

He was looking at Chu when everything in the room went completely crazy. Walls started bubbling outward, and the floor looked as if it had turned into liquid, waves running through the tile without breaking them. The bed jumped up and slammed back down again, and Jane and Chu lost their balance, sprawling out on the rippling floor once more. The ceiling bulged in the middle, as if water were collecting there. None of it seemed physically possible.

And then the horrible sounds started.

CHAPTER
51

HOLDING HANDS

Paul had never seen Master George move so fast.

The old man seemed to lose thirty years in age once he spotted the frightening and impossible sight of bodies falling from a long, blue rent in the air. He turned on his heels and bolted back through the balcony door, pulling everyone else along with him as best he could. They eventually all made it—struggling against the disorienting sights that continued to warp and bend all around them—Sofia and Paul at the tail end. The Realitants were still holding hands, helping each other as they took turns losing and regaining their balance.

"We must get down there straightaway," George called over his shoulder as he headed for the hallway. "After a quick detour to grab my Barrier Wand, as we may have to get ourselves far from this place."

Sofia stopped, and everyone looked back at her. "You guys go. I need to head to the operations center. I can feel

. . . it. I can *feel* the Karma. I think if I can study Gretel's notes—the whole team's notes from that time—I can figure things out."

"I'll help you," Paul added immediately. He felt it too. Even as Reality broke up all around him, he felt a power like electricity trickling through his veins.

Master George looked proud, shockingly not offering one ounce of protest. "Rutger," he commanded. "Take them there at once. Give them access to everything. The others— with me."

Paul's heart leaped as Sofia grabbed the notes from the floor. They followed Rutger, fighting to keep their balance the whole way there.

~

Chu's face was pale with terror.

Tick didn't understand it. He'd thought the man was brave and ruthless, but now he looked like a toddler who'd lost his mommy at the shopping mall. He swayed on his feet as the entire room shook and wobbled, his eyes darting this way and that in a steady flare of panic. Jane was close to him but seemed much calmer as she mildly took a step when needed to keep herself from falling to the floor again.

And then there was Tick. Strapped to the bed, unable to even touch the slightest bit of his Chi'karda. The madness of everything seeming to have lost its solid structure was made ten times worse by the sounds of moaning and wailing that flew through the air. That, and the fact that Tick couldn't do anything, not even run.

"You've gotta let me go!" he yelled at Chu, hoping to take advantage of the man's obvious terror. "Something really bad is happening, and I can probably help stop it! Take these stupid things off of my body!"

"He's right," Jane said.

She didn't shout the words, and Tick barely heard them, but Chu looked at her as if she'd gone crazy.

"You can't be serious!" the man yelled. "You've seen what he can do! He'll escape before we can count to three! You know that we need this boy's power for our plans! He has to be contained until we're ready!"

"And *then*?" Tick asked. "You think at the very end I'm just going to agree to do whatever you want?"

The disturbing sounds of people in pain and dying and suffering swirled through the room, joined by the creaks and groans of the building that shook around them. Everything in sight was twisted and bent, moving in impossible ways. Nothing made sense.

Jane's mask remained expressionless as she stood there, trying to keep her balance. She looked back and forth between Tick and Chu. Back and forth, as if pondering some monumental decision.

Tick kept his eyes on her, feeling so helpless he thought his chest might implode from the rage and panic trapped inside him.

"Reginald," she finally said, her raspy voice somehow cutting through the cacophony of haunts that floated in the air. "We need to leave for a few minutes to talk privately.

We'll come back and get him when we're ready for his contribution."

Chu nodded absently, his eyes showing that his mind was lost in deep thought.

"What?" Tick yelled. "What are you talking about? This is crazy! You guys have to let me go!"

Jane held out a scarred hand to Chu, and he took it. Both of them were still fighting to maintain their balance amidst the quaking, but managing well enough. Hand in hand, swaying, they walked to the door of the room, opened it, then exited into the hallway. Chu swung it closed behind them.

Leaving Tick all alone.

Paul was shocked he hadn't fallen down yet, or tripped over Rutger. The entire headquarters shook like a baby's rattle, and Paul's brain was feeling like the stuff on the inside of the rattle. He stumbled left and right as he tried his best to move forward at a sharp clip. The three of them reached the data center, where Rutger was king. The short man pushed his way past Paul and Sofia and entered the room first, turning on lights and flipping the switches on monitors and machines.

"We'll get to the bottom of this," Rutger said, all business now that he could actually contribute again. "It's always in the numbers. Always."

He climbed up onto his specially-made raised chair and focused on the largest screen in the room, which was several feet wide and already filled with flashing data and colors. Sofia stood right behind him, Paul at her shoulder.

"O . . . kay . . ." Rutger said slowly, drawing out the word as he quickly scanned the data splattered across the monitor. Paul did the same, but he knew the other two would come up with something interesting before he did.

Right on cue, Rutger started in with his findings. "Chi'karda levels are extremely low in a three- to four-mile radius around the canyon headquarters, and the pocket appears to stretch along the river in both directions—probably in line with that blue streak of . . . whatever we saw in the air. There's also some kind of reading for a substance that our sensors can't identify. It has mass, and it's everywhere. My goodness, it's *everywhere*. But . . ."

He spun around in his chair and looked up at the others. "I'm not sure I can . . . I mean . . . it'll take me some time, but . . ."

Paul knew the man was probably ashamed that he didn't immediately know the explanation for the foreign force that permeated the air around the Grand Canyon. But Sofia latched on to the answer right away, excitement shining in her eyes.

"It's Karma, Rutger. It has to be!"

CHAPTER
52

DOWN BELOW

Going down the elevator had been just about the scariest thing Mothball had ever done. The long ride to the bottom of the canyon floor had been riddled with sudden jolts and constant shaking, and even an unexpected drop of twenty feet or so that made everyone scream. Sally may have been the loudest, as shrill as the youngest girl on a roller coaster.

And those sounds. Like a crowd of people with the plague, waiting on death. She wanted the sounds to end, no matter what. Being in the tight confines of the elevator car made it that much worse, the noise amplified and echoing off the walls, ceiling, and floor.

Mothball had never felt such an instant rush of happiness as when they thumped onto the bottom and the doors of the lift slid open. Sunlight spilled in, though even the brightness of it looked somehow . . . *off*, like everything else. As if the light was too yellow, too disproportionate to the shadows it created.

Master George slipped through the opening as soon as the elevator doors opened wide enough, holding his Barrier Wand before him like it was a weapon. On the trip down, he'd done his best to examine the device and make adjustments to the dials and switches that ran along its one side. The button at the top—the one that would initiate the Chi'karda Drive and wink them to somewhere that was hopefully a lot safer—looked so enticing to Mothball that she almost reached out and pushed the ruddy thing herself.

They filed out of the elevator and stumbled their way along a narrow section of towering red and orange rock, finally emerging into the vast expanse of the canyon floor. Things looked just as wild there, but on a grander scale. The mighty cliffs that rose up from the rugged valley wobbled and bent and bubbled just as much as the walls inside the headquarters had, but the terror of the sight was magnified. If those cliffs cracked and crumbled, it'd be the end of the Realitants. And the end of the members of the Fifth Army, who bustled about the banks of the river, looking up at the one anomaly that outshone the rest.

The long rip in Reality ran the length of the valley, disappearing at both ends, and hovering in the air at least a hundred yards above the ground. It shone with a glowing blue light that pulsed every few seconds, its luminescence flashing more brilliantly before fading again.

And what Mothball and the others had seen from the balcony was still happening—odd-looking bodies were falling from the blue gash, but none of them had reached the canyon floor yet. About halfway down, they were whisked away—as if caught in a stiff wind or the gale of a hurricane—toward the cliff walls on both sides of the canyon. They perched by the hundreds on jutting rocks or held on to crevices in the stone with gangly arms and legs.

And they weren't human.

⁓

Tick had finally closed his eyes, unable to take one more second of the troubling sights all around him as he lay helpless, strapped to the bed. But there was nothing he could do with his ears. Unable to use his hands to cover them, he had no choice but to listen to the awful wails and moans that streaked through the air and pounded his senses. It was as if he were in some experiment run by a madman to see how much he could scar a kid's brain for life.

He tried his best to focus his mind on other things. On the odd exchange between Jane and Chu before they'd left him alone. She'd obviously been scheming inside that head of hers and had come to a big decision—something that obviously didn't involve him yet. He hated to admit it, but he felt as if he had to place some hope in Jane, that she might turn back to those feelings she'd expressed before to him of wanting to do good. Tick didn't see how it was possible to survive this mess unless she joined forces with him against Chu and all the weird things going on with Reality.

But the sick feeling in his stomach told him the chances of that happening seemed awfully slim. There'd been something sinister about the way she'd been looking back and forth between him and Chu right before they left. And the words she had said—and the way she'd said them—made it sound as if she was up to no good at all. Maybe she'd finally slipped past some threshold from which she'd never come back. Maybe Mistress Jane was finally evil through and through.

The door popped open to reveal Chu. His face was draped in shadow, but there was something about the way he stood in the midst of the shaking that told Tick that the man had moved past his panic attack and was back to business. His next words, shouted over the terrible sounds, removed all doubt.

"We're putting you back in the Bagger, boy. Time to go for a little ride."

~~~~~

Sato was finally getting his spirits back. He'd been in a daze since leaving the Thirteenth Reality, trying to come to terms with everything that had happened. But ever since George had pushed the button on that weird little box and the world had turned into a freak show, he'd slowly awakened back to his normal self. And now his first concern was the army he called his own; they were in obvious danger from the nightmare that had ripped open in the sky above them.

He ran forward a few steps, squinting against the sun to look at the creatures that had flown out of the blue gash and attached themselves to the side of the canyon cliffs. They were dark and gray and gangly, almost humanoid . . .

And then it hit him. They were too far away for Sato to

get the greatest of looks, but he knew what they were. The remainder of Jane's creatures, transformed by the Fourth Dimension, were here.

Even as he had the thought, the gray monsters started scampering—and flying—toward the floor of the canyon.

CHAPTER
53

OVERRUN

Mothball didn't like the sight of all those gray creatures descending toward them. She didn't like it at all.

"We need to get out of here!" she yelled at Master George.

But the old man was already swinging into action, holding the Barrier Wand up with both hands as he started barking orders. "Sato! Get your army over here, and quickly! We need to pack together into a group, everyone touching someone else!"

Mothball thought Sato had seemed like a new person since taking over leadership of the soldiers from the Fifth Reality. Unshakable, a true leader. But even *he* hesitated, probably in awe and fear of the weirdness of it all. There was a river of blue light running through the sky, the world was shaking, monstrous creatures of the Void were descending toward them, and it sounded like a haunted house at an amusement park.

Sato sprang into action.

As he ran around, shouting and pointing and herding his people toward where Master George stood with the Wand, Mothball and Sally huddled close to the old man. The gray creatures were almost to the canyon floor now, seeming to pick up speed the closer they got.

The army almost made it to Mothball and her group. Sato was in the very back, encouraging and pushing people away from the river toward the canyon wall, when the first wave of Void creatures overran him.

~～

Tick didn't fight it when Chu's lab rats wheeled him out of the small room, down a hallway, and into a large chamber that looked like a massive laboratory. He didn't fight it when the lights started flashing and the banging, whirring noises overcame the now-constant and familiar sounds that haunted the air. He didn't struggle when the Bagger wrapped its cords around him again.

He didn't fight, because he wasn't able to fight. His body was strapped down, and he couldn't feel the slightest trickle of Chi'karda. He was helpless.

All the while, Jane and Chu marched along nearby, whispering to each other and making frantic arm gestures. Tick didn't know what was going on and didn't bother to ask. His heart and will were starting to give up with everything else. He needed to snap out of it, find a spark somewhere. But as with the elusive Chi'karda, he was empty.

At some point it all became too much, and, like before,

when he'd been trapped inside this machine that he didn't understand, his mind sped away to a cold and dark place.

There were no dreams in that lonely place.

Sato didn't scream or cry out for help when the first claw dug into his shoulder. The sharp nails pierced his shirt and raked across his skin, slicing pain through his nerves, but it was the last straw to snap him out of his momentary dazed state and lunge him back into the soldier he'd become. He dove forward, curling into a ball and flipping over at the last second. He kicked out with his feet—landing a solid hit on something soft but solid—then jumped back up to see that the creature had tumbled across the ground. Even as Sato watched, the monster's form dissolved into a swirl of mist and was whisked up toward the sky.

Sato didn't have time to follow the path with his eyes. Dozens more of the scary things were already on him. The closest one leaped into the air—gray wings unfolding like an umbrella—then swooped in, claws reaching for his face. The unmistakable thump of a Shurric pounded the air, and the creature was ripped away before it could hurt Sato. More thumps followed from behind him. His soldiers to the rescue.

Someone threw a few Ragers at the line of fangen and other monsters, mounds of dirt and rock compacting into a giant ball of destruction before it slammed into the creatures. Most of the ones on the ground—those close to Sato, anyway—were annihilated, dissipating back to mist and swimming toward the sky in a streak of smoky haze. The fangen that leaped into the air to escape the Ragers were caught by a ruthless volley of pure sound from the Shurrics.

Sato and his army had survived the first wave of attack. He wasted no time.

"Get to Master George!" he yelled, waving his arms to direct his soldiers. He didn't stop until every soldier was running. "Form circles around the Realitants! Face them—a hand on the person in front of you! Quickly!"

Faithful and brave, they did exactly as he commanded.

Mothball was amazed at how quickly Sato had assembled his soldiers into a formation of circles radiating out from the center, where George and the Realitants huddled as a group. Each person in the rings placed a hand on the shoulder of the person in front of them. They were ready to wink away.

"Everyone closest to me!" Master George barked when the Fifth Army was settled. The madness around them continued, and more creatures were coming, but Mothball and the others were still and silent. "Put your hands on the Wand! Its power will flow through all who are connected!"

He made a quick couple of adjustments to the dials and switches as the other Realitants reached out and gripped a spot on the cool, brassy surface.

"Do we have everyone?" George bellowed out in a loud voice.

There was a chorus of assents, but no way to confirm it

for sure. Mothball knew they'd just have to get on with it and hope they didn't leave anyone behind.

"Alright, then," George said, though Mothball could only read his lips because he spoke so quietly.

The old man pushed the button at the top of the Wand.

Nothing happened.

CHAPTER
54

A HORDE OF CREATURES

Sato had learned an amazing amount of patience since becoming the leader of an army. But it was being tested like never before now. They'd formed up; hands were on shoulders; they'd all faced the old man like he'd told them to. Why wasn't George pushing the button already? Sato tried to look over the shoulders of the giant soldiers he called his own, but it was pointless.

The creatures were coming.

"What's he *doing* up there?" Sato finally shouted, the frustration ripping through his throat, rubbing it raw. He coughed for a few seconds. There had to be something wrong. Had to be. "Report back to me! Send it up the line! I need to know what's going on!"

The soldiers started whispering furiously to those in front of them. Sato kept his hand on the back of the woman who was crouched before him—she was still almost as tall as he was when he stood up straight—but he took a look behind him to gauge the situation. Void-twisted fangen were flying in fast, and other creatures were splashing through the river and loping across the ground. They had only a few more seconds until they'd have to battle.

"Hurry it up!" Sato screamed, even though he knew it was pointless. He was about to explode with impatience. He remembered their first visit to the Thirteenth Reality, when the Wand they'd stolen from Mistress Jane had refused to work because the witch had taken out the Chi'karda Drive. Those moments waiting for something to happen had been agonizing. Tick had winked them out, showing for the first time what a phenomenon he was. The powers he had.

But Tick wasn't here. And everything had gone nuts all around them.

The woman in front of him leaned forward to hear the message being passed backward, then snapped her head to face Sato.

"It's not workin' rightly," she said simply, as if talking about a leaky faucet.

Sato hadn't really needed to be told. "Yeah, figured that," he mumbled to himself. Then he stood up and sucked in a huge breath, ready to scream orders. The world tilted and shook and bent. "Arm your weapons!"

He turned around to face the horde of creatures coming at them.

⌇

Tick wasn't sure when it ended. Or how much time had passed. But he woke up and looked up at a cloudy, gray sky.

He felt a hard, gritty surface beneath him. Jane and Chu stood next to him, peering down impatiently, as if it were *his* fault he'd been out of it for a while. The ground shook, and his vision bent and twisted. Things were still wrong with the world, but at least he was in a different place. Red rock and dusty land, sprinkled with scrub brush and cacti, stretched away from him.

He sat up, not realizing at first that he hadn't been able to do that for a while. Hard, silvery bands were still fastened around his arms and legs like bracelets, but other than that, he was free to move. When all this dawned on his still-foggy mind, shock swam through him, and he looked at Chu sharply, expecting some sort of trick.

The man appeared numb to emotion at the moment, giving a quick nod and scrunching his eyes. All scientist. "The bands will still repress your Chi'karda, boy, so I wouldn't try anything. But I think you'll work with us regardless, once you take a peek over the edge of this canyon."

Chu clicked a remote-control device in his hand, and the bands around Tick's arms and legs sprung loose like coiled wires, popping off him and landing several feet away. On instinct, Tick reached for his Chi'karda, searching for that spark inside of him that was becoming more and more a part of his instincts. As simple as taking a deep breath. He sensed it—could feel it pooling deep inside of him—but barely, as if the pipe between him and the power was clogged.

But he wouldn't have fought back anyway. Not yet. Not until he knew the best route to fixing all the things that had gone bad in the Realities.

He stood up slowly, fighting the imbalance caused by the never-ending quake that rattled the scorched land to which they'd come. He saw the coffinlike silver box that Chu had called the Bagger off to the side, a small opening on one end creating a window into darkness. He swore to understand what the thing was and how it worked some day. But again, not now. Not yet.

Chu was looking at him, his face hard and pinched. But there was also understanding there, as if he wanted to say that things were worse than any of them had imagined and that they needed to work together or die.

Jane stood next to him, her mask a blank expression.

"Something is blocking the Chi'karda here," she said, her raw voice sounding full of pain. "The closer we came to this place, the weaker it got. Neither one of us is completely sure what's going on, but it does remind me of something we'd studied long ago . . ." She nodded to her left, and Tick looked in that direction.

The Grand Canyon. At least, a part of it.

A few hundred feet away, the flat land beneath them ended in the jagged lip of a cliff. Tick only knew this because beyond it was open air and the sight of canyon walls. A sea of stratified rock, layer upon layer, every shade of red and brown and creamy white. Gray clouds churned in the sky, thicker and more erratic over the abyss closest to them. There was a strange blue light reflecting off the bottoms of the boiling vapors of clouds.

"Go and have a look," Jane said, her tone sad and filled with dread. "We wanted you to know what's at stake."

Tick knew he had no choice. Feeling as if someone had draped a hundred pounds of wet cotton across his shoulders, he started walking toward the upper edge of the looming cliff.

CHAPTER
55

LET'S MOVE

Sato fought furiously. Wielding a Shurric provided by one of his soldiers, he aimed and fired the thumps of sound energy at creatures as they came close, barely having enough time to see them catapult away before he had to do it again. And again. The monstrous forms from the Void were relentless and numerous, and they seemed to have no concept of death as they charged in. As each one died, they dissolved into a wispy stream of smoke and shot toward the sky. Up there, they joined their dead in a massive, churning pool of clouds. The bright blue streak of the floating river cut through the gray.

The Fifth Army had spread into battle formation, still braced in a rough circle around Master George and the others in order to protect them. Many of the fangen—or creatures that had once *been* fangen and had been transformed into something worse—leaped into the air and tried to fly toward the middle, as if they knew the precious lives that

315

waited there. The heart of the Realitants, and maybe the last hope in defeating this indescribable new enemy of Voids and mist and thunder and blue light.

Sato's soldiers kept steadfast, picking off the creatures one by one. But they kept coming.

They kept coming, and there was no end in sight.

⁓

Tick looked down into the valley of the canyon and couldn't believe what his own eyes reported back to his brain. The assault on his senses made him think it couldn't be real. So many things were going on at once, and none of them made much sense. A thick, pulsing streak of blue light cut through the middle of the air like a floating river, running the length of the canyon just as the real river made of water did. A battle raged down there, and it appeared to involve the Fifth Army, judging from the tall human figures standing their ground in a circular formation. They fought creatures of gray, Voids no doubt. When they died, wisps of smoky mist shot up from the ground like ghosts trailing gray rags until they reached—and joined—the churning storm clouds that hung over everything.

Tick reached for his Chi'karda again, and it was even weaker than before. There, for sure. But mostly blocked. He could pull it out if he wanted to, try to use it, but only a little would come out at a time. It'd be pointless. The strangeness of everything around him was also affecting Chi'karda. A scary thought—he already felt helpless enough.

"The situation is even worse than we thought."

Jane's voice made him jump. He turned to see her standing right behind him, the wind whipping at the folds of her hood and robe. Chu was right next to her. Tick had been so engrossed with the haunted vision before him—and the sounds of thunder, so loud—that he hadn't noticed them creep up.

"What's going on?" he asked, hoping for answers but knowing they didn't have them.

"The Realities are being ripped apart," Jane said. "Things have escalated."

"Escalated?" Tick repeated. "I'd agree."

Jane nodded. "This is why you need to work with us. Chu and I can stop this madness. With your help."

"So you guys keep saying," Tick said spitefully. "I'll only promise to help if you promise to quit being so . . . *evil*."

A look of hurt flashed across Mistress Jane's mask, but it vanished quickly. Chu rolled his eyes and chuckled, a sound that was thankfully whipped away by a surge of wind.

"Your word means nothing to me anyway," Tick said, hearing the defeat in his own voice. "I'll do whatever I can to help stop this craziness. But I swear I won't let either one of you hurt more people in the end. I won't!"

Jane looked at him with hard eyes, glaring through the holes of her mask. "So are you committed then?"

Tick wanted to howl mean words at her, but he simply shouted, "Yes!"

"Reginald?" Jane turned her gaze to the man. "Are you ready?"

"Of course."

Jane pointed back in the direction from which they'd come. "We need to get a couple miles out at least, I'd guess. We can't do anything—especially here—until we can find the full strength of Chi'karda. Come on."

She pulled up the lower edges of her robe and started running, a sight that for some reason made Tick want to laugh. Instead, he shot a dirty look at Chu and sprinted after her, wondering if the old man could keep up.

CHAPTER
56

THE FURIOUS BEAT OF WINGS

We need to make it to the wall!" Sato shouted.

His throat hurt like acid had been poured down his gullet; his voice was raw and scratchy as he continued to encourage and command his Fifth Army. The creatures of the Void kept coming in their onslaught of an attack, threatening to overwhelm Sato and the rest with sheer numbers. But the soldiers kept their composure and maintained their positions, firing Shurrics and throwing Ragers. With every monster killed, another wispy streak of mist shot toward the sky to join the ever-growing mass of storm clouds that boiled above them.

The ground shook beneath them; screams of pain and anger pierced the air; thunder rumbled and lightning flashed; things bent and twisted and bubbled in unnatural ways. And the gray creatures kept coming—fangen through the air and the others loping and leaping across the dusty canyon floor.

Sato aimed his Shurric at a lanky, six-legged beast with a head that was all gaping jaws and teeth. He fired, then watched the thing disintegrate and swirl into smoke and be whisked away, flitting upward out of sight. He aimed at another monster—three legs, three arms, two heads. Fired. Killed it. Another one—a blur of arms and smoky fur and teeth. Shot and obliterated. Another, then another. The beasts of the Void were everywhere.

Sato was taking aim when claws ripped into his shirt, scratching his skin. He looked up at a fangen just as its claws clenched into a fist and gripped the material, yanking him upward. The Shurric slipped out of Sato's hand. He reached out to grab it, but he was too late. It clattered against the head of one of his soldiers.

The creature flew farther up, keeping a tighter hold on him now with two clawed fists, its membranous wings flapping against the twisty, windy air. Sato flailed with his arms, trying to beat at the beast, to no avail. He changed his focus to the thing's two-handed grip and tried to loosen the claws. They didn't budge.

Sato reached up with his hands and gripped the fangen's forearms. He held on tightly for leverage, then kicked up with his legs, smashing one of his feet into the beast's face. It wailed a piercing cry and shook his body while it plummeted several yards, almost crashing into the soldiers below. But at the last second, it swooped up again, furiously beating its wings. Sato's stomach pitched and twisted as badly as the morphing shapes of Reality all around them.

He gripped the fangen's forearms again, kicked up with

his legs. His foot connected again, and this time he threw his hands at the wings, catching one of them by the thin stretch of skin between two bones. He yanked on it with all of his weight, pulling downward.

The creature shrieked again as they both fell toward the ground once more. This time, they came within reach of two tall soldiers, who quickly dropped their weapons and grabbed the fangen, slamming it to the ground, freeing Sato. And then they took care of the beast.

Sato jumped to his feet, adrenaline screaming through his body.

An odd sound suddenly tore through the air, overpowering everything else. It wasn't just that—all other noises seemed to cease at once, replaced by an overbearing, all-consuming sound that made everyone pause in whatever they'd been doing. Sato couldn't help it any more than the others. He faced the open canyon that towered above him.

A tonal thrum, mixed with a sound like bending metal, rang throughout the valley, giving Sato the strange sense that his ears had been stuffed with cotton. He didn't see anything different or unusual at first, other than both sides of the battle had stopped fighting. The soldiers of the Fifth Army had lowered their weapons, searching the sky to figure out what was going on. Most of the Void creatures had disappeared—when, Sato had no idea. But trails of mist were everywhere, all of them snaking their way toward the clouds.

His gaze lifted; he felt almost hypnotized by the warping and the bell-like sounds clanging through the valley. He was looking directly at the churning gray storm when it suddenly divided into countless tornadoes, funneling down like a hundred gray fingers.

And then Reality itself started to split at the seams.

CHAPTER
57

GASHES IN THE WORLD

Paul's eyes hurt from looking at so many screens in the operations center, and his stomach was queasy from the shaking—though he was getting used to it—but his heart had swelled about three sizes. They were making progress. Real progress. And he could *feel* the power of Karma working inside of him. His mind was filled with images that he knew didn't originate from his own thoughts.

Sofia had worked the hardest of the three of them, searching and reading every last line of Gretel's notes. She looked exhausted and had finally taken a seat across from Rutger and Paul.

"Karma," Sofia said, almost reverently. She held the gray box with the pressed green button in her hands. "I thought Chi'karda was like magic. Karma's even beyond how we thought the world worked."

"It's pretty cool," Paul agreed. "I think you're right that it's the cause of all the weirdness around us. For some reason,

Karma wants things escalated. Like maybe our window of opportunity is going to be short. Whatever it is."

Rutger slapped his thighs. "Are we all agreed on the findings, then? Our theories about what's happened so far, and where we think it's leading us?"

Instead of answering, Sofia looked at Paul. "What do you see in your mind, right now?"

"The place where Jane's castle used to be," Paul said with a smile. They'd had this conversation a dozen times already, and the answer was always the same.

"The Thirteenth Reality," Sofia responded. "Me too."

"Me too," Rutger added.

They all kept seeing the same vision in their heads. Karma was communicating with them. And they knew what it meant.

"Let's run through our data one last time," Sofia ordered.

⁓

Tick had jogged or walked at least a couple of miles when everything changed again. At first, it was just an odd feeling, his ears popping, the drop of his stomach. But then a sound like bells and twisting metal filled the air and everything went dead silent for a few seconds; the quiet almost made him fall down, he'd grown so used to his eardrums being pounded. But then a new noise started up, and he and Mistress Jane and Reginald Chu stopped moving and looked back toward the gaping canyon they'd left behind. There was something incredibly mesmerizing about the . . . *music* that floated along the wind.

"What's going on back there?" Chu asked, his voice full of irritation as if all the crazy stuff was putting a chink in his plans. Which was true, Tick admitted.

"It's changing," Jane announced.

Chu scoffed. "Thank you for that scientific assessment."

Tick ignored them both, staring at the massive disk of clouds that spun above the canyon in the distance. Lightning flashed, but no thunder rumbled away from it. The bluish light that shone out of the strange floating river—which was not visible from where he stood—reflected off the bottom of the brewing storm. A buzzy, relaxed tingling went through his body and across his skin. A part of him wanted to lie down and take a nap.

"Atticus," Chu said, his words muffled slightly as if he were outside a bubble. As if they weren't worthy enough to overcome the sweet sounds wafting from the canyon. "What's that look in your eyes? What do you know about what's happening over there?"

"Nothing," Tick said softly, though he doubted they heard him. "Nothing."

Things changed then, so abruptly that Tick stumbled backward, falling to the ground as his eyes widened in astonishment. The slowly spinning mass of clouds instantly transformed into countless towering funnels, the roar of the twisting tornadoes wiping out the peaceful sounds from before. The clouds dropped then, falling like arrows toward the valley floor below. Quick bursts of lightning arced through the gray mist of the funnels, and this time, the thunder was loud and cracking. When the tornadoes vanished from sight beneath the upper lips of the canyon walls, Tick readied himself to stand and pull himself together.

But another sight in the sky made him stop cold. Gashes in Reality ripped open all over the place, streaks of dark and light that tore across the air. Some were a few feet long, others in the hundreds. The ground shook, and the sounds of breaking and cracking rocked the land.

Tick pressed his hands against the hard dirt to steady himself as he focused on the gaps that littered the sky. At first he'd only noticed that they didn't look the same, that they had varying shades of color and light, but as he got over his initial shock and peered closer, he could see that the rips in Reality were actually windows to other worlds.

Through the one closest to him, he saw buildings and cars and people—a city at night. The darkness of the scene made it hard to see much, but there seemed to be a huge traffic jam and people running down the sidewalks. Another gash nearby revealed a field of crops and a farmhouse during the brightness of day. Yet another showed a jungle or rainforest, thick with trees and vines and foliage. All the rents in the sky showed something different: a desert, a mountain peak, a neighborhood with damaged homes, people packed inside a mall—many of them huddled together as if they were cold, several views of lands with broken trees or floods.

Tick's mind was overrun with all the information he was witnessing. He tried to process it, understand it. A blue river of light that hovered above ground, creatures from the Void, Reality looking warped and weird, churning clouds and lightning and tornadoes, rips in the air that led to other

Realities, more earthquakes. His Chi'karda being held back from him somehow. What did it mean? What did it all mean?

Someone shook his shoulders and snapped him out of the trance he'd fallen into, gaping at the gashes in the air. He looked up to see Jane, her red mask pulled tightly into a look of concern.

"We need to get out of here," she said, her scratchy voice somehow cutting through the din of terrible noises that rattled the world around them.

"What's happening?" Tick asked. In that instant he almost forgot all the things he hated about the woman kneeling beside him and holding on to him with scarred hands.

Her mask relaxed into a neutral expression, but with her so close, Tick could see directly into her eyes behind it. And there was cold, hard fear there. She leaned in closer to whisper in his ear.

"I can sense a force here that we studied long ago. A project that I was led to believe had been abandoned because of its danger. Apparently not. And that only makes our mission more paramount."

After a long pause, the noise and shaking and ripped seams in Reality glaring at the forefront once more, she finally spoke again. And even though Tick didn't really know what she was talking about, the icy tone in her voice made his blood run cold.

"It's Karma, Atticus. Karma's been unleashed. And it's only making things worse."

CHAPTER
58

A REASON

Mothball gawked at the tornadoes and the splits in Reality—at a brief glimpse at one of the impossible gashes that showed a boy and a girl running down a beach, a moving image that hung right in the middle of the air—as she and Sally fought to protect Master George from the onslaught, taking him to the wall of the canyon.

The rents in the air—long gashes that appeared to be windows to other Realities—were all over the place, as if the world was a sheet of canvas and someone had taken a sharp knife to it, slashing uncontrollably. Behind each rip was a different scene. Forests and oceans. Cities and farms. Close-ups and faraway views. The people she saw looked frantic and scared, often running from or toward something. It was all a big nightmare.

But at least the creatures from the Void had all vanished. Sato stood nearby, his soldiers lined up behind him, facing the valley floor.

"Those tornadoes are dropping," Sato announced. "I don't know how to fight tornadoes."

Mothball glanced up and saw them, dozens and dozens of spinning coils of gray air. Even as she looked, she felt their wind against her face and clothes. And it was getting stronger. They had maybe two minutes before most of them touched down.

"I don't either," Master George said glumly.

⌒

Jane moved surprisingly fast, saying that they had to get farther out of range. She yelled at Tick that they needed Chi'karda so they could wink away before it was too late. The three of them—Tick, Jane, and Chu—ran across the dusty land, ignoring the rents to other Realities that floated magically around them, glimpses into an endless display of worlds and settings.

Tick moved as close to Jane as possible without a risk of his legs getting tangled with her robe as it swished, swished, swished.

"What's keeping us from Chi'karda?" he yelled at her. "We could use it just fine back at your castle!"

"It has to be Karma," she replied without slowing or looking his way. "It's a power that's both unpredictable and immense. If it's suppressing Chi'karda, then it has a reason. Either way, we need to hurry and get where we're going. I think we're almost far enough out."

Tick knew exactly where they were heading. Felt it in his bones. "We're going back to the Thirteenth Reality."

This time, she did turn her head toward him, a look of surprise on her mask.

"Yes, Atticus. We need to go back to the source of it all. To its heart."

They kept running.

CHAPTER
59

WALL OF WIND

When the leading tips of the tornadoes touched down on the dusty, rocky floor of the canyon, a wild wind erupted. It ripped through the air, picking up dirt and pebbles as it went, coming at Mothball and the others like a wall. She could barely see through it or past it, but she noticed the funnels of the tornadoes joined together, creating one huge cyclone of gray.

Soon that wall of wind and debris burst over the soldiers then swept across the rest of them. Mothball shielded her eyes as it hit her and the others in the back. The wind was like a solid thing, a bubble of air that had a giving but strong membrane, pressing her against the hard rock of the cliff. George and Sally were next to her, fighting to breathe clean air.

Particles of dirt and dust beat at Mothball's face, scratching across her skin. The fierce wind tore at her hair and clothes, seeming as if its force would rip all of it off and bury them in the solid rock. She screamed, but dust flew into her mouth, choking her and making her cough. She closed her lips and looked to the side. The hurricane blast didn't stop—it just grew stronger and stronger. Pressed her harder and harder against the rock at her back. The world had become a haze of brown, swirling and churning.

It stopped without any warning.

The wind pulled back as if it were being sucked in by the gray cyclone like a giant vacuum. Mothball saw the visible wall of debris suddenly sweep away from her. Before long it was gone, completely, and the churning gray mass of fog and mist was lifting up from the ground. She thought it looked alive, and angry, being sucked toward the sky against its will. Even as she watched, it narrowed and compacted, rising, getting smaller and more tightly woven. Most of the others around her had recovered and were standing or sitting and observing the show. She felt Master George's hand squeeze her upper arm.

"What . . ." she started to say, but stopped. Any question would be pointless. And George certainly didn't try to answer. They watched, together.

A few seconds later, it became apparent what was happening. The fog and mist of the Void was being *consumed* by the floating river of blue light. Every drop of the gray mist whooshed into the still-throbbing blueness, disappearing as soon as it did so. The long sapphire streak across the sky didn't change or grow thicker. It just kept pulsing, kept sucking up everything in sight. Not just the Void, but sticks and loose stones and any lingering clouds that had tried to stick to the sky. Mothball was surprised that she and the others hadn't flown up with the rest of it.

And then, just like that, the air was clear. The only things visible above them were the strange river of blue light running between the walls of the canyon, and the gashes in the air that were like windows to other worlds. They hadn't moved or changed, and there were probably a hundred of them that Mothball could see, all shapes and sizes. But the ground had quit shaking, and all the bending and twisting of Reality had stopped as well. The world seemed to have gone back to something a little more close to normal.

"I'll be darned," Sally said.

"That sums it up right nicely," Mothball replied.

Master George was straightening himself, dusting off his clothes. The Barrier Wand lay on the ground, dull and dirty. "Let's get upstairs straightaway. I hope Paul and Sofia have learned something valuable."

Even Tick was out of breath when Jane finally called them to a halt. He figured he was younger and in better shape than the other two, but somehow they'd all kept up and together, although Chu was sucking wind, hard. Tick turned back to look at the canyon. There wasn't a sign of any clouds or the gray mist of the Void anymore, but those rips in Reality that looked in on countless scenes and settings from all over still hung in the air like decorations.

"I think . . . we've gone far enough," Jane said, her voice even more raw than usual with the heavy breathing that scoured her throat. "In fact . . . it's odd. I can feel every ounce of my Chi'karda. And I don't think it's because of the distance we ran."

Tick immediately probed his inner self and saw that she was right. His power was there, as strong as ever. "You mean whatever's been blocking it is gone? What do you think happened?"

"Like I said, if it's Karma, the force obeys its own rules. We need to wink to the Thirteenth before anything changes."

Chu looked at Tick with narrowed, suspicious eyes. "I should've kept you in those bindings. We can't trust you now."

"We can trust him," Jane said. "He knows he has no choice but to work with us right now. Ready yourselves— since I'm most familiar with the Thirteenth, I'll wink all three of us there. I want us to be a nice, safe distance from the Void. And we will need time to meditate and regroup."

"My people are ready when you're ready," Chu added.

"One step at a time."

Chu had no response, but right before Jane winked them away from the outer reaches of the Grand Canyon, Tick saw something in the man's eyes that he didn't like. He didn't like it at all.

PART
4

THE
TRANSFORMATION

CHAPTER
60

ROUND TABLE

Paul had never seen such a captive audience.

Mothball, Sally, Sato, and Master George—Rutger was busy in the operations center—sat at the conference table, looking at Paul and Sofia with wide, though tired, eyes. The group had made their way back up from the canyon floor after the strange events had subsided, discussing what had happened in drained, weary voices. They looked awful—dirty and windblown and scratched and bruised. But thankfully, they were alive, and every last one of them—including those who'd been researching—were eager to talk about what needed to happen next.

"We know some things," Paul said to start it off. "And we've made our best guesses about a lot of others. But time is short, so I'm going to let Sofia fill you in."

Sofia looked more determined than Paul had ever seen her before. She cleared her throat and started talking.

"This all began when Tick and Mistress Jane had their

battle outside the Factory. The Haunce had helped Tick heal the Realities from the disaster that was the Blade of Shattered Hope, but the boundaries and barriers and seams were still really weak. Sealed, yes. But weak. When Jane and Tick battled, using extreme amounts of Chi'karda to do so, they . . . broke things. Things we might not totally comprehend, but were certainly never meant to *be* broken."

"We're talking about the rips in Reality," Paul added.

"Exactly," Sofia continued. "We believe Tick and Jane created a situation in which conduits between Realities opened up. Not only that, but conduits between *dimensions* as well. And ultimately that's what allowed the Void of the Fourth Dimension to begin bleeding through to the Realities themselves. Whatever Tick did to escape the Nonex was kind of the last straw."

"You mean he stirred the dadgum pot once and for all is what yer sayin'," Sally said.

Master George raised his hand like a kid in school. Sofia tried to hide a smile and pointed at him.

"Perhaps the situation would've been much more manageable had the Fourth Dimension not been so . . . agitated. There may very well be a bees' nest outside your open window, but it'll get much worse if you swat that nest with a big stick. I think that's what happened here."

"Something like that," Sofia agreed. "Whatever the explanation, we are where we are. Which brings us to Karma."

There wasn't a sound to be heard in the room.

Sofia took a deep breath. "We need to gather all of our forces. All of them. Load up on weapons and ammunition.

And then head back to the Thirteenth Reality. It's what Karma wants us to do. Rutger has already started trying to contact all of our Realitants out in the field."

Paul half expected shouts and complaints. He also wondered if Master George would feel as if his authority had been challenged, but if anything, the old man looked proud. He had, after all, given them the assignment to figure things out.

"I know we're short on time," their leader said. "And I trust you both implicitly. But give us an explanation as best you can."

"Of course," Sofia replied. "For starters, we believe that the blue anomalies seen by Sato in the Thirteenth and the one out in the canyon represent the Fourth Dimension itself. Conduits for the Void to reach into *our* dimension. And it's a little scary that the blue river outside these walls decided to suck everything back into itself. It's like the Void was reaching out to gain strength and ammunition and has now pulled it all back to its main force."

Paul hated this new enemy. Shapeless, mysterious, seemingly without any kind of mind or conscience. No fear of death or consequences. "Which is why we have to go to the Thirteenth," he said. "That's where it all started, and it probably has something to do with the unique power of the place and its abnormal links to Chi'karda. We think the Void is gathering its forces there until it can unleash an attack we could never stop."

"Which is where Karma comes in," Sofia said. "It's hard to describe it, but I can't get the image of the Thirteenth—

the place where Jane's castle used to be—out of my mind. Paul and Rutger feel it too. It's more than just a thought or a daydream. It's almost like something is putting it there . . . *inspiring* us. We're getting better at understanding Karma's power and how it communicates. But we know this: Karma escalated events, put pieces in place, so that we'd all head back to the source of the Void's birth in our dimension."

At that moment, Rutger stepped into the room, his face lit up with excitement.

"I've reconnected with Master Atticus!" he shouted. "Found his nanolocator! He's just winked to—"

Paul cut him off. "The Thirteenth Reality."

Rutger nodded with a huge smile.

"I guess that seals the deal," Sofia said.

Master George stood up, a fierce and proud look on his face. "My good friends. I'm sure I'm not alone in saying that I'm scared of what awaits us there. And I believe it's quite alright to feel a bit of fear now and then. We can use it as a weapon. But know this—our society was created for such dark times as these. And the Realitants are about to have their most shining moment of all."

Paul's hands clenched into fists, and his heart started to thump.

"Sato," George continued, "go and ready your army."

CHAPTER
61

A GOOD-BYE

At some point while Sato had been upstairs in the conference room, the blue river floating in the air had disappeared. But the rips into other Realities remained. Like slashes in a great invisible curtain, they peeked into countless other places. It gave Sato the creeps.

He stood on top of a big rock in front of his army, staring them down, having remained silent for at least one long minute on purpose. He wanted them to contemplate, to gather their thoughts, to have a last moment of peace. Trouble waited for them ahead. The worst they might ever face. Master George had no doubt that their fate would be settled in the Thirteenth Reality, and Sato trusted the leader of the Realitants like he never had before.

Finally, Sato spoke, his voice rising up to echo off the walls of the canyon.

"I've asked you all to do a lot lately," he began. "Too much. And we've lost some of our soldiers along the way.

I'm sorry for the sacrifices you've had to make, for the pain and injuries and suffering. I'm sorry for those who gave their lives. I'm sorry for a lot of things. But I accept the responsibility. It's all on my shoulders. And I just have a few questions for you."

He paused again and took a moment to sweep his gaze across the eyes of the crowd. He was glad he'd stepped up on the rock so he could see them all—their tall, weary bodies and their haggard faces.

"Are we ready to give up?"

The resounding boom of their collective *"No!"* made his heart soar. Adrenaline pumped through his body.

"Are we ready to quit fighting?"

"No!"

"Do we fear an enemy we don't understand?"

"No!"

"Will we go and fight no matter what fate brings?"

"Yes!"

"Will we fight?" He screamed it now, energy surging through the air like electric charges.

"Yes!"

"Will we win?"

"Yes!"

"Will we win?"

"Yes!"

"Will . . . we . . . win?"

"YES!"

Sato's chest heaved with heavy breaths. "Then let's go and do it."

Master George was back in the operations center with Rutger, and he felt a deep sadness in his heart. There was a part of him—deep down, hidden, but there for sure—that was telling him he was saying good-bye to his longtime friend for the very last time. He tried to ignore it, but it was shattering his heart.

"I'm sorry to leave you here," George said. "But I fear we can't win this battle unless we gather all of our forces. Keep trying until you've found them. All of them. Can you do that for me?"

"Of course I can," Rutger said. The short man put on a brave face that hid nothing. "I give you my word that I won't rest until every living Realitant responds and we come to help you in the Thirteenth. I'm already about halfway there."

George nodded slowly, his lips pressed together. "Good, then. You'll know where to send them—we'll stay in constant contact."

"I know, boss. I know."

George reached out and put a hand on his old partner's shoulder. "My dear Rutger. We've been through a lot together, haven't we?"

"We sure have." He grinned, as genuine an expression as he'd ever shown.

"I . . . just want to thank you for being there for me all these years. I want to thank you for . . . for being my friend. Whatever happens . . ."

Rutger held up a hand. "Not another word, boss. Please. Not another word. It's not needed."

The two of them locked eyes for a long moment, a thousand memories bouncing between them. It was true. They needed no words.

"Very well. Then we'll see you and the rest of the Realitants on the field of battle. Whatever form it takes. Now, I have a lot of winking to do. My Barrier Wand is going to be very hot indeed."

Master George turned away and walked out of the room, hoping Rutger hadn't noticed the tears that had begun to well up in his eyes.

CHAPTER
62

REST AND RELAXATION

Jane had winked them to the top of a mountain, a craggy peak of black stone that had no vegetation whatsoever. Tick had felt the cool rush of thin air when they'd arrived almost an hour ago and hadn't stopped shivering since. Once there, Jane had insisted on taking some time to meditate and prepare herself for the difficulties that awaited. Chu had grumbled, and Tick had asked questions, but she'd refused to say another word.

Tick was glad for the break and for the time to collect his own thoughts. Everything had been such a mad rush. But instead he'd fallen into a restless sleep, shivering all the while. When Chu woke him up with a light kick to the ribs, Tick was instantly awake, and thankful his body had gotten a break.

"It's time we get moving," Chu barked. Tick wondered if there'd ever been a more unlikable person in the Realities.

Ever. The man turned his attention to Jane, who was up and ready to go. "Why'd you wink us so far out anyway?"

Instead of answering, Jane pointed to a rise of rock to their left with nothing but cloudy sky beyond. Then she walked toward it briskly, obviously expecting the other two to follow her. Which they did—Chu a little begrudgingly, mumbling something that Tick couldn't hear. They reached the spit of rock that rose about thirty feet above their heads, and began to climb the slope, a gradual one with plenty of handholds and footholds. As they neared the top, Tick heard a noise like the rushing sound of water in a swift river. It grew in volume, becoming a roar when he finally poked his head over the upper lip of the jagged black stone.

What he saw before him, stretching from one side of the land to the other, was something that his brain couldn't compute at first. It seemed impossible, an image he'd only seen in weather reports and videos of massive storms out in the ocean. Miles and miles across, a wide whirlpool of gray clouds slowly spun in a giant circle, an enormous hurricane of fog and mist, with tendrils of lightning flashing within. Thunder rumbled across the windswept fields between Tick and the unbelievable sight in the distance. And even as he watched, he could tell that the storm was growing, as if with every sweep around the churning circle, the vaporous gray air pulsed outward.

The Void looked ready to consume the entire planet.

"Because I thought it'd be a bad idea to land in the middle of the belly of the Void," Jane finally said after everyone got a good look at the beastly storm. "Let's be glad I'm in charge."

"You're in charge?" Chu laughed. "I'm the only one here with the technological means to accomplish what we both want. And you know it."

"We all need each other right now. And that's that."

Chu didn't answer, but his eyes showed a fanaticism that scared Tick. Something was up with the man.

"We *will* capture the power that rages within that storm," Chu said slowly, evenly. "We will harness it and use it to accomplish the greatest feat ever known to mankind. We'll become one with the fabric of Reality, see all things, be able to *do* anything we imagine. My team has it all calculated. We're ready to move, even though we haven't done the testing I'd normally demand."

"My goodness," Tick said. He barely heard his own voice over the increasing sounds of thunder booming across the land. "You've completely lost it!"

"Lost it?" Chu replied with a bark of a laugh. "Boy, you have no idea what we've planned! When we add the consciousness of my great mind and soul to the infinite power of the Void and then to Reality itself, I'll become like a god. All suffering, all crime, all hunger . . . I can make it end. *We* can make it end. Jane will have her Utopia. Finally."

Tick looked over at the red mask of Jane, which showed no expression. The wind ripped at her robe and hood. She said nothing, which, for some reason, filled him with dread.

"Am I the only left here who's sane?" Tick finally asked. "We're talking about wild experiments and fantastical ideas when we have a hungry storm out there about to eat everything? Including us, by the way!"

Jane turned sharply to him. "Atticus, you don't understand. You don't."

Just then, not too far away—toward the bottom of the slope of the mountain—a host of people suddenly appeared, winking into existence in a quick series of flashes. Tick's jaw dropped open—it was Master George, Paul and Sofia, Mothball and Sally, Sato and dozens of tall soldiers. They spread out before him like . . . like an army. Tick couldn't believe it.

"It was just as we feared!" Jane shouted at Chu.

The man took a few steps back, a suspicious look on his face, one of his hands reaching for his pocket. His fingers slipped inside.

"What are you doing?" Tick asked.

Chu's voice suddenly boomed through the air as if he were commanding an army through a loudspeaker. "It's time, Benson! Bring them all in. Bring them all. The entire force. The Metaspides, the Ranters, the Denters. It's time for war."

Tick leaped into motion, running toward him, not fully understanding, but determined to stop whatever he was trying to do.

"I'll be right back," the man said with a last glance at Tick.

Reginald Chu disappeared.

CHAPTER
63

A GIFT FROM FRIENDS

As soon as Chu disappeared, Tick had only one thought consume his mind. Reuniting with the Realitants. But he'd barely taken a step when he felt a tingle shoot down his back, and suddenly he and Jane were on the far side of them, off the mountain and between his friends and the churning Void. Jane had winked them there.

The wind tore at their clothes, and the cracks of thunder coming from the lightning within the Void made the world seem as if it were about to split open. Which, Tick realized, was actually happening, in a way. Though there weren't as many rips in Reality as he'd seen back at the Grand Canyon, glimpses to other worlds dotted the air.

"Why'd you do that?" he yelled at Jane.

She stepped up close to him. "No matter what you think, you have no choice but to help me now. Call it a trap if you'd like, but you are out of options. Help me, or the Void will kill everyone. Everyone!"

They stood on grassy fields that had seemed far away just a minute ago. The massive hurricane of the Void churned in a grand circle next to them. It was easily the most frightening thing Tick had ever set his eyes upon.

He knew she'd won. Only he had the power to stop such a horror. "How can I even trust you?" he yelled at her. "I'd be better off doing it alone!"

She leaned into the fierce wind, her gaze glued to the monstrosity in the near distance. She finally looked at him. "And if you succeeded, I'd still do whatever it takes to build my Utopia. Do you understand? You might as well join forces with me now."

Tick glared back. He wanted to ask how she could still be thinking of her Utopia when so much was on the line. But he chose to let it go for the moment. He was going to turn the tables on her. Use *her*, for a change. He'd rely on his instincts, pool their powers just like when they broke out of the Nonex. And somehow he would destroy the Void and sever the link with the Fourth Dimension.

"Then let's do it," he finally said.

"It's the right decision, Atticus!" she shouted. "Be prepared to use every ounce of our Chi'karda once the time is right! Stick together every step of the way!"

Tick nodded, refusing to give in to the fear that wanted to cripple him on the inside. "Then there's only one thing to do."

She nodded, pointing at the spinning mass of the Void. "Walk straight into it."

"Tick!"

He looked back to see Sofia and Paul running straight toward him, sprinting at full speed. Part of him wanted to tell them to go back, to leave him, that it was too dangerous this close to the Void. But he wanted to see his friends. Desperately. He started off in their direction to close the gap.

"Atticus!" Jane shouted. "We don't have time for this!"

"I'll only be a second!"

He ran until they met, and then they were all hugging each other, fiercely, even laughing. Right then Paul and Sofia were his tie to everything that he cared about in life. Seeing them filled him up, something he'd needed so badly. He'd been running on empty for a long time.

"What's going on?" Tick asked them. "How did you know I was here? Why are *you* guys here?"

"No time to explain," Sofia responded, shouting into the wind, leaning close to his ear. "We finally connected with your nanolocator, and . . . we figured some things out. Karma, Tick. There's a thing called Karma that's going to help you. It's made things happen so that we'd all end up here. Right here, right now."

Tick squinted his eyes in confusion. "Karma?"

Sofia put a small bag with a hard, boxy thing inside it into his hands. Paul had tied a string to Tick's wrist before he could even vocalize the questions in his mind. He felt a buzz inside of him, a surge of feeling that gave him goose bumps.

"There are things we don't totally comprehend yet," Sofia said, smiling. Actually smiling. "Take this with you for whatever it is you . . . and she have to do. It's going to work out, Tick. Paul and I know it. Sato knows it. We all know it!"

"But . . ." Tick was speechless.

"We've trusted you a billion times," Paul added. "Trust us now. See you when all this is over!"

He swatted Tick on the back, and then the two of them ran back toward the other Realitants and Sato's army.

CHAPTER
64

THE MAGIC SILVER CUBE

It was almost impossible not to stare at it. The massively huge storm of the Void, roiling in a giant circle as lightning cracked and whipped through its fog and mist. A gray, monstrous thing that was growing by the minute. Master George thought he was being more than careful when he'd winked them several miles away from the spot of the once-great castle of Mistress Jane, but they had still ended up way too close for comfort.

At least they had no excuses, now. No time to look and wait and grow more fearful. The nearest wall of the Void was close, and they'd have to start fighting soon. Though *how*, exactly, you fought a storm was anyone's guess. What could they do but try? Follow the path of Karma and buy time for Master Atticus to do what he must and meet his own destiny with the Void. Paul and Sofia had given him the Karma Drive and returned safely.

They were all together now—Sally and Mothball. Paul

and Sofia. Sato and his Fifth Army. Only Rutger was missing, having stayed in the command center in order to gather in the other Realitants. It was a ragtag group, but the best hope the Realities had at the moment.

Sato stepped up to him. "No time like the present."

Master George could tell that the boy wanted to show him some respect, allow the leader of the Realitants to issue the first command. But George was no fool. He was here to fight, as old and frail as he may be, not command. He wouldn't send all these people to their most dangerous task yet without being by their side. Not this time.

"You're in charge now," he told Sato. "Especially since you've fought this . . . thing before."

Sato was trying to hide a look of disappointment on his face. "We only fought the things that came *out* of the Void. Not the Void itself."

George shrugged his shoulders. "Well, they're bound to be related, connected. I know of nothing else we can do but to take our weapons and attack it as you did the monsters it unleashed. If nothing else, perhaps we can at least stop it from growing. We need to buy time until Atticus can do what he has planned."

"We'll do it," Sato said. "We'll beat it, or we'll die trying."

"Oh, goodness gracious me. Don't talk like that." He patted the boy on the shoulder. "All right, then. Take charge, my good man. I'll be right here fighting with you—though I may linger in the back." He gave him a smile. "And we'll hope that others come to help soon enough."

Sato nodded, a different countenance spreading across his face and demeanor. He suddenly looked like a cold, hard leader. He gave a long, lingering glance at the nearby wall of churning fog then turned to his army and the other Realitants.

"Line up!" he shouted. "Rows of twenty, staggered by four soldiers on the ends!"

The orders were followed, and soon the formation was complete, each person facing the Void. Paul and Sofia, and Mothball and Sally, were mixed into the group, new members along with Master George.

Sato shouted a command that was lost in the wind, but his hand signals were clear enough.

The Fifth Army started marching toward the Void of Mist and Thunder.

Tick refused to tell Jane anything, saying simply that his friends had given him a good-luck charm. He felt the string tightly wound against his wrist, felt the bulk of the box inside the bag. He was doing exactly what Paul had asked him to. Trusting them. He could use all the help he could get anyway.

His eyes stung from the ripping winds that tore across the fields away from the Void, picking up dust and rock and debris along the way. All of it pelted him from head to toe. He wiped at his face and kept going, determined to stay by Jane's side as she marched toward the towering wall of spinning gray fog, leaning into the stiff wind. They were almost

355

there, and the sight of the Void up close was frightening, all lightning and thunder and swelling power.

Jane didn't slow. And neither did Tick. He did look back every once in a while, and it seemed as if Sato's army was massing for an attack on the Void itself, which seemed ridiculous.

Just let me handle this, guys, he thought. *I can do it.*

They were a few hundred feet away, Tick's entire vision filled with nothing but gray mist and flashes of light, his ears numb from the pounding noise, when Chu abruptly appeared right in front of them. Winked in, flashing into existence. He held a large, silver cube about the size of a microwave oven in his hands. The wind pushed his black hair all over the place in a frenzy and riffled his clothes, but Tick noticed his eyes. They were sane and clear, which, for some reason, scared Tick.

Chu held the metallic box out in front of him. "This is it!" Even though he was obviously screaming, his words were barely audible over the deafening roar of the Void. "The work of more than a hundred scientists! It will change the Realities forever, and I plan to be the guinea pig this time!"

"Get out of our way!" Tick yelled back at him.

"Atticus," Jane said. "We need him, remember?"

"No!" Tick was done being told how things would be done. "Chu, we don't need you; I don't care what Jane says. Get out of my way."

"I have an entire army about to wink in!" Chu responded, shouting his every word. "With all my greatest

creations at their disposal! They have orders to annihilate anyone and everyone in the fields behind us unless you do as I say! Don't let their deaths, and the end of the Realities as we know it, be on your shoulders! My plan is the only way!"

"What is that thing?" Tick yelled, nodding toward the silver cube.

Jane didn't let Chu answer. "It doesn't matter!"

"It does! I want to know!" Tick replied. And he did. He *wanted* to know. Something told him it was important.

Chu lifted the cube up a couple of feet, and then he screamed out his words to be heard over the storm of the Void. "It's made of the same matter that binds the universe together. A science that only a precious few understand. We need simply to utilize the almost infinite energy of the Void to break it apart, dissolve it—and *me*—into trillions of atoms. Then, with the power of your Chi'karda—both of yours—we can meld and bind myself to the very fabric of Reality. And Jane, too, if she still wishes. We can do this!"

Tick had been leaning forward, focusing with all his concentration to hear and compute every sentence as it came out of Chu's mouth. It sounded like the ranting of a mad scientist, but Tick knew better. He couldn't underestimate Reginald Chu. There was something here, something unprecedented in human history. And it scared Tick.

He'd have none of it. "Get out of my way!"

"Please, boy!" Chu shouted, sincere pleading in his eyes. "I swear to you, this is real. This can work. My intentions are noble! I can make the Realities better with a human side! We can finally create Jane's Utopia!"

Tick thought the man had gone too far—losing every ounce of the scant credibility he was shooting for—when he claimed he was trying to be noble. Did Chu really expect him to *believe* that?

Tick looked over at Jane, and he saw the most human expression he'd ever seen on her mask. She was torn, through and through. He felt pity for her, then, shocking himself. He could see that the promise of her elusive Utopia had gotten to her.

"Mistress Jane," Tick said, but not too loudly. Working with Chu was the worst idea possible. And yet he had no doubt the threat that the man had made was real. And something—some feeling deep within him—told him what to do.

He lurched forward and grabbed Jane by the arm, pulling her along as he walked toward Chu. Tick grabbed him by the arm with his other hand, letting Sofia's bag dangle from his wrist. Then he broke into a run, dragging the other two along with him, fighting the monstrous winds.

A few seconds later, they slipped through the outer wall of the Void, swallowed by the gray, angry mist.

CHAPTER
65

ENLISTED IN THE ARMY

The noise was unreal. A level that Tick had never experienced before. Loud, pounding, relentless. Gray darkness surrounded the three of them as they walked through the outskirts of the Void. Each flash of lightning was followed immediately by a brutal crack of thunder. Tick figured he'd be deaf within a half hour, if not dead.

At least the wind had stopped. Jane had used her Chi'karda to put a bubble of protection around them, more to prevent being struck by lightning than anything else. It was invisible, but had an orange sheen to it that mixed oddly with the gray, boiling mist that seethed along its edges. It was all so strange, so surreal. But Tick knew they probably hadn't seen anything yet; it was about to get a lot weirder and a lot scarier.

Chu walked alongside him, hefting that large silver cube. Tick wanted to ask him more questions but didn't have the heart to attempt it. He'd have to scream at the top of his lungs, and who knew if even that would work.

Out of the corner of his eye, he noticed Chu balance the cube in one arm and reach his other hand into his pocket. He opened his mouth to say something—exactly what he'd done earlier when he'd communicated with someone in his own Reality—but an odd expression came over his face, and he seemed to reconsider his decision. He pulled his hand out of his pocket and gripped the cube firmly once again. Was it because of the noise? Or had he changed his mind on something? Decided not to do what he'd planned after all? Maybe the device didn't work in the middle of the storm.

The three of them kept moving, protected by a bubble of clear orange, going deeper into the depths of the gray storm.

The heart of the Void waited.

⸻

Master George had emptied the last of the Realitants' arsenal to arm Sato's army for one last battle.

Paul held his Shurric steady, its butt end pressed against his chest, handle gripped firmly, his finger ready at the trigger. He had Ragers and Slicers in both of his pockets and another Shurric strapped across his back in case the first one ran out of juice. He was ready for battle as they marched toward the wall of the Void. Streams of mist jumped out and swirled back, and plumes erupted from the surface then were sucked in again; the entire storm boiled and fumed. All while lightning danced and crackled within and without.

Somehow he and Sofia had been jostled and pushed

about by the much taller members of the Fifth until they found themselves along the back line. It seemed like chance, but Paul had a sneaking suspicion that the Fifths were trying to protect them, since they were young and small compared to the rest of the army. That made Paul mad—even though he couldn't help the small part of him that was relieved. His scared side. His terrified side. He was ashamed of the feeling and swore that when they got into the heat of battle, he'd do whatever it took to prove he wasn't a scaredy-cat chicken.

Sofia was next to him, stepping stride for stride, gripping her own weapon, staring straight ahead. She seemed too focused, or maybe even too lost in thought. Paul had the sudden urge to grab her hand and run away from the danger. Shame filled him again. What was wrong with him? He was a *Realitant*, for crying out loud.

"Hey!"

The sharp bark of a man's voice came from behind him, loud enough to be heard clearly over the rumbling sounds of thunder. Paul stumbled to a stop and turned around, even though the rest of the army kept marching. Even Sofia. A man stood about twenty feet away, dressed in shiny clothes and black boots. He was stocky and had a balding head and a red, angry face. He looked like the kind of guy you'd see in a parking lot and turn around to walk in the opposite direction. Had no one else heard him shout?

"Sofia!" Paul yelled, turning back to look at her. She stopped and saw him, then the stranger who'd appeared, her eyes widening at the sight. *At least I'm not crazy,* Paul thought. "Make sure someone tells Sato!"

As she grabbed at the soldier closest to her, Paul faced the visitor again, who still stood in the same spot. "Who are you?"

The man walked up to him, an arrogant smirk on his face. "I'm from the Fourth Reality. Name's Benson. Who are you?"

"Uh . . . Paul. What . . . why are you here?" Something weird was going on, and Paul hoped Sato would send some people back quickly to help him out.

The stranger smiled, though it was full of anything but kindness. "I work for a very important man, kid. His name is Reginald Chu. Ever heard of him?"

Paul swallowed, the weirdness of the situation turning to fear. He took a step back and pointed his Shurric at the man. "Don't move."

Benson laughed. "No need to shoot, son. Just letting you know that my boss—he doesn't like me to call him that, which is a shame, don't ya think?—well, my boss said that if I don't hear from him, I'm supposed to come in here and start attacking anything and everything I see. You understand?"

"You?" Paul asked, his finger itching at the trigger. "By yourself?"

"Yeah, me and what army, right?" Benson laughed again, but then his face suddenly creased into an angry, angry look. "Guess what, little man? I *haven't* heard from the boss. Which is very bad for you."

The man snapped his fingers like a magician, and

machines started appearing behind him, dozens and dozens of machines and other contraptions, filling the fields.

Paul took a step backward in shock, then another as he scanned the area with his eyes, dazed. But he stopped when he recognized some of the objects lining up behind Benson. A nightmare from what seemed like another lifetime.

Metaspides.

CHAPTER
66

TWO DIFFERENT ENEMIES

Sato's thoughts churned as he marched toward the Void, wind ripping at his clothes and hair.

It had taken all of his willpower not to charge after Mistress Jane when he saw her standing near Tick earlier. His anger toward her had been building for many years, and this time, something inside of him snapped as if he suddenly knew this was his last chance to seek revenge for the death of his parents. When all this was over, surely one of them— either him or Jane—would be dead. And if it was *her,* he wanted it to be at his hands. He had dreamed of it for years.

But something had stayed his hand. Calmed him. Brought a peace that almost didn't make sense. Almost on a subconscious level, he made a decision. And, just like that, all the anger and the hate and the thirst for vengeance went away. Gone. He didn't understand it, but he felt it all the same. He had a calling in the world now. And he swore to never think of Jane again after he watched her disappear into the gray mist with Chu and Tick.

A murmuring behind him interrupted his thoughts. A rumbling of whispers and movement as people talked to each other, leaning close to speak ear to ear. He looked back at his soldiers, wondering what they could be excited about. He didn't see anything on the other side of the tall soldiers who made up his army, when he heard a different sound coming from the Void. A series of thumps and roars, like drums and wind. He quickly whipped around to take a look.

The giant wall of churning fog was only a couple hundred feet away now, and forms of mist were separating from the main cyclone. Pockets of swirling gray air popped out all over the place and coalesced into more human-shaped bodies than any Void creatures they'd encountered before. They formed in the air then dropped to the ground, landing on two feet that were suddenly solid. The ones closest started walking toward the Fifth Army.

On some level, Sato knew that these creatures were people who'd been stolen by the Void, sucked in from who knew where by the pulsing blue substance that was somehow related to the Fourth Dimension. It didn't make sense to him, probably never would. But the Void had turned them into monsters, and now more than fifty had already been created. They were coming toward him, as if they'd zeroed in on him specifically.

He remembered all too well what those things could do. His army would need to attack hard and fast before the beams of pure flame came shooting out of the creatures' mouths.

He was just turning to face his army and shout commands when Tollaseat interrupted him, something he'd never done before.

"Got major trouble, we do," the giant man said.

"Yeah, I'm pretty aware—"

"No, sir! I 'spect you don't! Not talkin' about the fog things! There's an army of machines revvin' up on the other side of us. Looks a might nasty, too."

Sato lifted up on his toes and saw a few traces of silver and what looked like mechanical arms. He didn't understand it at first, didn't know what was going on. But he knew three things.

His army was small. And surrounded. By two different enemies.

~

Tick guessed they were about two miles into the massive storm of the Void when everything fell apart. It started with the wind, a visible, monstrous thing mixed with the gray mist. It grew to an unnatural level, so fierce and mighty that the sound of it drowned out the booming thunder. And the bubble of protection created by Mistress Jane finally became worthless.

It stayed intact, but suddenly became a victim of the wind, whipping up into the abyss of the Void with Tick and the other two still inside of it. They smacked into each other, rolled around, tossed back and forth like pebbles inside a bouncing beach ball. Chu's cube flew out of his hands, and its corner hit Tick just above the eye, sending a sharp lance of pain through his skull. An inch lower and he might have been blinded for life. Chu called out, frantically trying to maneuver his way through the chaos to grab his precious device once again.

But movement was impossible for any of them. Tick finally curled up into a ball and quit trying to fight something he couldn't change. He bounced up and down, wincing each time he slammed into Jane or Chu, hating the feel of chins and elbows and feet digging into his flesh and bones. The temptation to unleash his Chi'karda was overpowering, but he held back, realizing that flying around in a bubble was better than getting separated and lost, each of them swept away by the brutal winds.

The shiny orange bubble of Chi'karda hit the ground and rolled. Grunts and shouts and barks of pain filled the air as Tick closed his eyes and squeezed his arms and legs into an even tighter ball. The bouncing finally settled, and everything stopped moving. Tick, filled with nausea, looked up to see that not much was different from before. The orange sheen of the bubble was still around them, the swirling mist of the Void raging on the other side. His first thought was that maybe a particularly strong gust had caught them from underneath to throw them through the air like that.

He saw Chu crawling toward his silver cube. Jane was trying to stand up, obviously woozy, her robe in disarray and revealing her scarred hands and arms.

"We need to move," she said in a hoarse voice that Tick

barely heard. "The Void is going to keep trying to stop us. We need to move! Now!"

Tick nodded. Chu picked up his precious device. Jane pointed, making Tick wonder how in the world she could possibly know which way they'd been walking before. But he had no better ideas. They picked up where they'd left off and started moving.

They'd taken maybe ten steps when the ground exploded upward, throwing them all in different directions. The bubble vanished for good.

⁓

Benson winked away as soon as his army of machines showed up. Paul couldn't blame him. What good would one human do when you had the kind of technological might Reginald Chu had at his disposal? The metallic machines—some boxy, some round—littered the flattened fields in front of Paul, and each one of them looked ready to kill. The only ones he recognized were the Metaspides, spherical, with long legs and nasty weapons. They had attacked him twice before; they weren't very nice.

The other machines out there were new to Paul, but just as vicious-looking. A big, boxy robot on wheels with two arms that resembled bulldozers but had fists of steel with nasty spikes on the end. Hovering, disk-shaped metal plates that were several feet across and came to a razor-thin edge along the outer circle.

In the long pause that seemed to float through the air like an air-bound virus between when Benson winked away and when the inevitable battle would begin, Paul could see labels on the closest machines. All of Chu's inventions were marked, starting way back with the Gnat Rats.

The bulldozer-robot was called a Denter. And the flying saucer weapons were Ranters. The phrase "Manufactured by Chu Industries" was printed on every machine.

Beautiful, Paul thought. *Just beautiful.* Like fighting a massive storm called the Void of Mist and Thunder from the Fourth Dimension wasn't going to be a big enough challenge for the Realitants.

The moment felt like an eternity but couldn't have been longer than twenty seconds.

Sofia finally broke the silence. "How did it all come to this? The smallest army ever caught between two impossible enemies."

Paul had never heard such sadness in her voice. That's what hit him with a rush of fear—the realization that they were probably about to die. Not seeing all the machines in front of him. Not hearing all of the terrible sounds of the Void behind him. If Sofia was feeling hopeless, they must be in bad shape.

Paul shot a glance back at the Fifth Army. They seemed confused, milling about as if deciding which front to fight first. There was a commotion on the far side, but it was hard to see over the tall bodies of the soldiers. It all added up to equal one major downer.

"We just have to fight," he finally said. "That's all we can do. Fight until we either win or die. Until Tick does whatever he's going to do. Maybe Rutger will find us some more people. But all we can do—me and you—is fight."

Sofia looked at him with something like awe, which swelled his chest up with pride. She even had the beginnings of a tear in one of her eyes.

"One of these days, I'm going to realize just how much I like you," she said. "Maybe once you're old enough to quit making fart jokes."

He smiled, a ridiculous thing to do when you were about to die. But he did it anyway. "That's a deal right there. I'm gonna hold you to it."

She smiled back.

The machines of Chu Industries started whirring and chirping and revving, a chorus of awful sounds. Then they all moved at once.

CHAPTER
67

A GLIMPSE OF RUTGER

Sato barely had time to assess the situation. On one side of his army, a horde of machines were about to attack with technology far beyond a few Shurrics and the other meager weapons the Fifth had at the ready. And on the other—on *his* side—at least a hundred gray soldiers were marching toward him, their mouths already beginning to open up. The abyss inside matched the fiery sockets of their eyes. Pure flame and heat.

They had no time to wallow in despair or wish for better days. It was fight or die.

"Attack!" he yelled, as loud as he possibly could. "Slam them with Shurrics before they can fight back!"

A series of thumping concussions rocked the world as every one of his nearby soldiers started firing. Sato felt a quick burst of pride at seeing a dozen or so of the Void creatures obliterated into wispy trails of mist. But more came.

And beams of brilliant fire shot out of their mouths, like

a volley of arrows, streaming up toward the sky then back down toward the Fifth Army.

"Take cover!" Sato shouted, but the screams had already begun.

⁓

Master George was in the middle of the fray, wondering desperately why in the name of all that was good and green on the earth he'd decided to pretend to be a soldier. He could barely hold the Shurric in his arms, and he didn't know what to do. He stood there, looking to Mothball and Sally for direction. He'd do whatever they did.

The sky was suddenly lit up with streams of fire, coming from the direction of the Void. The sounds of revved up machinery came from the other side, where that nasty ogre Chu had sent some of his inventions. But for what purpose, George had no idea. What in the dickens was going on?

"Whichaway should we be a-fightin'?" Sally asked.

"I'm a bit bamboozled, I am," was Mothball's reply. "Paul and Sofia are back there." She nodded toward where Chu's attack was starting. "I reckon we best go that way."

The two of them charged behind other soldiers, bringing up their weapons to take aim. Master George followed, fighting the temptation to wink himself straight out of there.

Come on, Rutger, he thought to himself. *Don't fail me now. After all these years, don't fail me now.*

⁓

Tick's body bounced, something he didn't think was possible for a human body to do. But he did. With the protection of Jane's Chi'karda bubble gone, he'd flown through the air when the ground erupted from below, then landed fifty feet away and bounced. At least twice. He rolled to a stop, dazed and bruised. The winds were fierce and hard and loud around him, lightning flashing everywhere, the sounds deafening. All was a gray blur; he might as well have been blind.

He got to his knees, then tried to stand up, but the gusts ripped at his body and made him fall again. Back to his knees, he squinted his eyes against the wind. He looked in every direction, saw nothing but the mist and fog of the Void swirling and churning like boiling water.

"Jane!" he screamed, though the sound was caught up and whisked away before even his own ears heard it. "Chu!"

He tensed his leg muscles and tried to stand up once more. He'd just gotten his balance when the surface below him exploded outward again, throwing his body forward. After flipping and flailing, he bounced and rolled again. Every inch of him hurt.

Chi'karda. He needed to use his Chi'karda.

Power filled him at the thought, consumed his insides with alternating waves of hot and cold. Orange sparkles mixed in with the gray that filled his vision. With a thought, he replicated Jane's protective bubble of air. It formed around him and cut off the wind and a lot of the sound. But there were thumps that he felt through the ground. Those eruptions were happening all over the place. And it dawned on Tick what was happening.

The Void didn't want them to find its core, its heart,

or whatever represented its essence. The Void was trying to protect itself.

Filled with the raging power of Chi'karda, Tick went in search of Jane and Chu.

~~~~~~

Paul tried not to fall apart inside as utter chaos ruled around him. Metaspides cut across the ground with their spindly legs and jumped on top of soldiers, who had to fight with all four limbs to keep from getting hurt. The Denter machines stomped around, shaking the ground beneath them, swinging those massive, spiked arms at anything that moved. The Ranters spun and flew through the air, trying to cut a path to victory.

But the soldiers of the Fifth weren't giving up. Not by a long shot. They fired their Shurrics and threw their Ragers and tossed their Squeezer grenades at the creations of Chu Industries. They battled with their arms and legs when their other weapons failed. It was an all-out war, and Paul found what little bravery he could and did his part.

He slowly moved forward, legs bent in a crouch, sweeping his Shurric left and right to fire at any machine that came close. A Metaspide leaped into the air, came down at him. A quick jerk of his arms, a hopeful aim, a pull of the trigger. A thump of pure sound sent the thing catapulting away.

Sofia was at his side, skipping Ragers in strategic locations. One of them balled up into a sphere of ground and rock and destroyed two Denters and a Ranter in one fell swoop.

But people were dying, getting hurt. The Fifth Army was getting smaller and smaller. How much longer could they hold out?

Paul shot a Metaspide to his left, a Ranter spinning in from the front, and then blasted a Denter to his right. Sofia threw an entire handful of Squeezers at a pack of machines that had somehow slipped behind them. Paul gave her a quick cheer.

They kept fighting.

～～○

Sato pushed out of his mind the screams that kept piercing the air and invading his thoughts. They were an army. This was a battle. People would die. All he could do was try to prevent as many deaths as possible. He ran across the fields, shooting his Shurric at the creatures of the Void, aiming for any that looked ready to open those mouths of theirs and spit out fire. The other soldiers had caught on as well, taking care to kill the monsters of mist before they sent out streams of flaming heat that were almost impossible to defend against.

A beam of fiery orange came sailing through the air, straight for Sato's head. He dove to the ground, spinning onto his back just in time to see the terrifying flames swoop over his body and land in a patch of flattened grass. It caught fire but was soon put out by his soldiers running across it, looking for something to shoot. Some soldiers tossed Ragers, which proved very effective, often taking out five or six of the Void creatures in one destructive roll.

Sato leaped to his feet and rejoined the fray.

⁓

Master George had given up on doing much other than shooting his confounded Shurric weapon when he had a very clear shot. Otherwise he was too scared he might lop off the heads of his own people. He was no soldier, and he had begun to greatly regret thinking he could help. If anything, he felt as if he was a terrible hindrance.

Mothball and Sally fought ferociously beside him, attacking any threat that came close. He knew they were trying to protect him, and it touched his heart. Though if they died doing so, he'd never forgive himself.

The battle raged all around him, an awful experience that made his insides tremble. Beams of fire shooting through the air from Void creatures on one side, horrific machines stomping and scuttling and spinning all over the place on the other. Brave soldiers fighting with everything they had; brave soldiers dying. Shurrics pounding, Ragers smashing, Squeezers breaking apart machines, people screaming.

The battle was everywhere.

There was a squeal of metal against metal next to him, followed by a solid thump and the quake of earth at his feet. He stumbled as he turned to see what had happened then almost fell at the sight of a huge machine, silver and black with dark rubber wheels, appearing at his side. The robot had two huge mechanical arms that ended in spiked fists of steel. George looked in fright at the letters written across the chest of the beast:

DENTER
Manufactured by Chu Industries

He'd barely read the last word when the robot raised an arm up into the air and swung it back down. The metal fist and its spikes dug into George's chest, and then lifted him up and threw him through the air like a discarded piece of trash. Pain erupted through every single cell of his body, a flashing burn of hurt that made his mind want to shut down. He flailed with his arms as he flew, saw blood dripping from his skin, watched as the ground rushed up at him. He slammed down, and every last ounce of breath escaped from his lungs.

He landed in a way that turned his face to the fields beyond the battle, toward a spot that had been empty when the fighting started. But now he saw a sight that lifted his heart despite the pain that ripped through him. A short, round ball of a man, waving his little arms frantically, as if giving orders. Behind him, hundreds—maybe even thousands—of people had appeared, wielding all manner of weapons.

Rutger had done it. He'd found the other Realitants and come to the rescue.

Master George ached like the end of the world. He closed his eyes, wondering if it might be the last time he ever did so.

CHAPTER
68

A DEAD BODY

The Void was throwing everything it had at Tick. He doubted if he'd ever understand how the thing worked—if it was alive or a mindless pool of unchecked power. But it seemed to be thinking now, and it didn't want him to take another step toward the elusive core that made up its heart.

The ground exploded all around him, like the spray from a breaching whale. The bubble he'd created with his Chi'karda did nothing against that, throwing him left and right. He'd get up only to have it happen all over again.

Great spouts of flames and lava rained down from above, like descending angels of fiery destruction. Tick had to stop and focus each time they hit, throwing his power out to keep the shield from breaking down. Lightning split the air in any direction he looked, its sound like a thousand locomotives next to his ears. His head felt numb through and through.

Balls of mist solidified, pounding on his protection like

an angry kid trying to break through a piggy bank. Each wallop sent a vibration of pain through his bones, and he threw even more of his thoughts into controlling the flow of Chi'karda. All while the ground continued to explode and throw his body around, all while fire rained from the sky, all while lightning tried to strike its way into any opening it might suddenly find. All with the horrible, horrible noise of the world breaking in half. Tick was rattled, and he knew it. But he forced himself to keep his wits intact, to not let the fear and panic win over his nerves.

He dealt with the chaos, doing his best to keep moving in the general direction he thought Jane had indicated, and relying on his instincts. Relying on some inner sense that he didn't even comprehend. He was just moving now. Moving forward, not backward. Guided by what, he didn't know. But guided by something.

A body lay up ahead, its arms and legs sprawled in impossible positions. Lifeless. A silver cube was perched in a pile of rubble right next to it.

Tick walked up to the spot and stood over the dead form of Reginald Chu.

⁓

Paul heard the shouts and cheers first. Then he noticed that most of the machines had stopped in the middle of whatever havoc they'd been inflicting. His soldiers turned to look at something in the distance.

Haggard, beat, exhausted. That was Paul. His arms and legs felt like rubber, and he hurt in roughly seventy-five places. He'd run and jumped and dodged and dove and shot both of his Shurrics almost to their limit. He'd been hit and swept aside by machines. A spinning Ranter had almost taken his head clean off, but Sofia had saved him with a quick burst from her Shurric. It had been her last charge, because she then tossed the weapon aside and started throwing the few Ragers she had left.

It was a miracle, but both of them were still alive. And now something new was happening. Something was going on.

He ran up to her, grabbed her by the hand. She was filthy and bloody and bruised. But she didn't protest and went with him as they zigzagged their way through the crowd of tall soldiers from the Fifth Reality. It was as if the very air had changed—gotten brighter. The mood had visibly lifted.

He saw why, when they finally made it to a break in the people and machines. Hundreds and hundreds of people—dressed in oranges and reds and browns and blacks and turbans and robes and jeans and sandals and every color and type of clothing he'd ever imagined, and many that he hadn't—were charging the enemies on both sides. Somewhere in the middle of all that, he thought he saw Rutger.

Rutger.

He and Sofia exchanged a glance, then turned to look at the churning hurricane of fog and mist and lightning. It was still growling and angry. Getting bigger.

Then Paul spotted Master George, lying on his stomach. Not moving.

⸺

Sato had been on the verge of giving up. He hated to admit it to himself, but the truth was the truth. Cold, hard Reality. They were outnumbered, outmanned, and almost out of weaponry. The creatures from the Void kept coming, shooting their beams of flame. The world rocked with thunder and screams.

But now they had help.

A sea of people, dressed in all kinds of clothes, surged forward. They carried all kinds of weapons, some of which Sato had never seen before: red tubes looped around shoulders, connecting a backpack to nozzles held in both hands; long poles with electricity sparking on the end; cubes of blue metal that glowed with a brilliant light. The people came down the slope to join the battle, most of them roaring, eyes aflame. Sato saw Rutger in their midst, cheering them on.

The tide had turned.

⸺

Jane limped up to Tick as he stared down at the lifeless face of Reginald Chu. She slipped through the protective bubble of his Chi'karda and put a scarred hand on his shoulder. He turned to face her and saw the mask, which was half-melted. There was only one eye now, half a mouth. Everything else was a smeared ruin of metal. He probably would've gasped from shock if he hadn't felt so numb inside.

"He never had a chance," she said.

Tick looked over at the silver cube, a third of it buried in a pile of rock and dirt. Something had taken ahold of him inside. A presence. An unmistakable feeling in his heart and unexpected thoughts in his mind that he knew weren't his own. It was pure power—a lot like Chi'karda in how he could sense it. Where it had come from, he had no idea. But a clear path had suddenly opened before him. It hurt him— hurt him deeply—but he knew he couldn't stray from it.

Karma. Sofia had called it Karma. He touched a finger to the bag she and Paul had tied to his wrist. Everything in the world was now crystal clear in his mind. He knew his destiny and how to find it.

He walked over and picked up the cube. He turned to Jane.

"I need your help!" he shouted.

She nodded, and he wondered if she felt the power's presence as well. It was like electricity in the air, and warmth in his veins. Unmistakably *there*.

Jane pointed to her right. "The heart of the Void is that way. We're close now."

Tick and Mistress Jane headed for their destiny—and their doom.

CHAPTER
69

BECOMING ONE

The ground trembled and shook as they walked across it. Tick's mind was more focused than ever now, as if some miracle drug had been pumped through his veins. His hold on Chi'karda was absolute.

He was ready for anything.

The winds swept past in torrential gusts, but they did nothing to even stir his clothes. Without hardly thinking about it, his bubble of protection stayed true, as did Jane's. They'd even learned to control the earthquakes beneath them, squashing their force before they could lift their feet off the ground. The Void noticed, and quit trying. Fists of fog continued to form in the mist, pounding at their shields, thumping and bumping. Nothing broke through.

They kept walking. Tick hugged the silver cube to his chest. That unseen presence that had filled him left him with no doubt that the object was vital to what awaited. Everything was about to come to a head.

384

A brightness began to lighten the air, like the beginnings of dawn. It had a blue tint to it, and it either thinned out the fog and mist or just made it easier to see. But the feel of the air around them was changing. And then it appeared before their eyes. Not gradually, and not from a distance, growing in size. It was suddenly just *there,* as if they'd been catapulted three miles forward without feeling anything.

A thick shaft of pure blue light, blinding in its brilliance. It came from the sky and tunneled into the ground, running in both directions as far as Tick could see. The perfectly round cylinder was at least fifty feet wide, the radiance within its core pulsing like a heartbeat.

Tick squinted and held up his hands, peeking through his fingers. It was impossible to look at the light for more than a second or two, but there was something incredibly beautiful and mesmerizing about its steady beat of flashing brightness. The purity of its blue. The hum and buzz emanating from it. Tick felt it in the air and in the ground beneath his feet. The steady roar and pounding of a thousand waterfalls.

It was energy and life and power, unlimited and daunting. Tick had to fight to not lose himself to the awesomeness of it all.

"The core of the Void!" Jane shouted.

Tick nodded. He knew that already. Just as he knew what needed to be done. Just as he knew that Mistress Jane would never leave this place, and that he'd never be the same.

He turned to her, finally breaking his trancelike state.

"I need your help to harness its energy! I need you to break apart the cube. And . . . me."

Her half-melted mask stared back at him, saying nothing. Showing nothing.

"You know it's the only way!" he yelled. She *had* to know.

"It's going to fight us," she finally replied.

Tick nodded.

She paused again. "You have to promise me, Atticus! Promise me!"

"What?"

The roar of the Void shook the air.

"You know!" she shouted. "You *know* what my heart has always envisioned! It's always been about the end, Atticus. *Tick.* Always the means to the end!"

"Utopia."

"Utopia!" She stepped closer to him, only inches away. "I need your word if you want me to do this. Otherwise nothing matters!"

"I give you my word that I'll devote everything to it. But in my own way."

"Swear it!"

"I swear."

She stared at him a long time before nodding. "Then let's go."

She didn't wait for him to respond. She turned and sprinted for the blinding, brilliant shaft of pulsing blue light. Tick ran after her, hefting the cube in his arms. The Void immediately retaliated.

Things started flying out of the core, all shapes and sizes, some alive and some not. Dozens of man-shaped creatures like the Voids who'd attacked them at the ruins of Jane's castle came first. Their mouths gaped open as soon as they appeared, yawning wide to reveal the furnaces that burned inside. Beams of lava and flame shot out all at once in an organized volley of heat.

Jane stopped to face the threat, as did Tick. With flicks of his eyes, he directed the power of Chi'karda—bursts of brilliant orange—to shoot forth and meet the attack in mid-air, obliterating the streams of lava before they could fall toward the ground. The two forces met in a shower of sparks and a burst of explosive sound. Jane and Tick swept their gazes left and right, destroying them all. Then they focused on the creatures themselves, wiping them from existence with one brutal assault of Chi'karda. Wisps of fog flew in all directions.

Jane moved forward again, and Tick followed. They'd only taken a few short steps when all kinds of animals made from the same gray substance emerged from the blue core. There were tigers and dogs and snakes and mad bulls. Alligators. Giant scorpions. They mixed together into a crowd of monsters, scurrying about the ground, all of them bent on attacking the two humans close by.

Jane and Tick stopped again and fired away with Chi'karda. The creatures' eyes had that same bright look of flames, vicious and angry. Snakes slithered across the ground; tigers leaped forward; everything came at them.

Tick could feel pressure mounting inside him as he

picked apart the unnatural creations with his power. Sweat poured down his face. Every blast that took down one enemy seemed to reveal three more—they just kept coming and coming. Jane's arms were whipping around, back and forth as she aimed and fired, like her hands were weapons. Tick just looked, killing with a glance. Zap, zap, zap. The sounds of explosions and the roar of the core filled the air.

Heaving deep breaths, Tick wiped away all of the enemies on his side then helped Jane destroy the last few on her side. They ran a few steps closer to the blue light.

A massive tree trunk, gray but looking solid enough to smash a truck, came hurtling out of the core, end over end. Tick dissolved it into wispy nothingness with a burst of Chi'karda. Next came a huge chunk of steel and concrete, the jagged and broken remains of an old skyscraper. Jane destroyed it. Cars came flying out. Busses. More trees. Homes, ripped from their foundations. Boats. Planes. Telephone poles.

Now yelling with each blast, Tick attacked the objects coming at him, annihilating them all. Nothing came within ten feet of him. Jane seemed just as strong, throwing her spurts of power out like grenades. Chaos reigned, noise battered the world around them.

Still the core continued to throw things at them, and on some level, Tick understood that the Fourth Dimension sucked things away from the Realities and transformed them into these projectile weapons. All of the matter they were fighting against had once been real and whole in a world somewhere.

He'd had enough. He couldn't keep it up forever. Exhaustion was creeping in.

"Jane!" he yelled. "We need to rush the core! This has to stop!"

She answered by moving forward, still waving her arms as she directed her powers. Tick followed, taking step after slow step as he focused with all his might. One slip, and he'd have a crushed head.

Still enemies flew at them, relentless and unstopping. Huge rocks. Giant Dumpsters. More beasts and man-like creatures. Some monsters shot back with streams of lava flames.

Tick wiped them away with nothing but his thoughts, exploding Chi'karda out of himself. Jane did the same.

They made it to the blindingly bright core, its pulsing blueness as hot as the thrusters on an alien spaceship. Tick couldn't look at it directly. He screamed as loud as he could and sent out one last detonation of pure Chi'karda, obliterating every single gray creature and monster within sight.

And then there was only the light and the roar of the core.

Jane quickly stepped next to him and grabbed the cube from his hands. For an instant, he wanted to rip it away from her, but he knew what she was doing. What she had to do.

"It's the only way!" he yelled at her.

"The only way!" she shouted back. "Atticus Higginbottom! Don't you dare forget your promise! Don't you dare!"

She backed away from him until she was at the very edge of the core, the shaft rising above and below her to infinity, visible as if they stood on a plane of glass surrounding it. Then she turned and thrust the cube directly into the light.

A concussion of sound and power rocked the air, making Tick fall down. Jane's robe burst into fire, and she screamed, an awful noise of things ripping and tearing. Tick had to shield his eyes. He could barely see what was happening, but he knew her entire body was being consumed. She kept screaming. Louder and louder. Then she suddenly turned back to him, her mask gone, her face a mess, her whole form burning. Where the cube had once been was now a spinning vortex of blue and gray and white lights.

"Now!" she shouted with a strangled, ruined voice.

Tick got to his feet and ran to her. He put his hands into the swirling lights. They immediately jumped out and began to spin all around him, growing brighter and thicker, encompassing every inch of his body. He barely had time to see Jane's destroyed body fall backward into the core and disappear forever. Then he was consumed by light and energy and a million other things he didn't quite understand.

Time stretched forward before him. He felt himself breaking apart, dissolving into molecules and atoms. There was a great rushing noise, and there was pain. He suddenly saw the entire universe before him, all at once. He saw the eyes of every person in every Reality, all at once. He saw fields and houses and forests and mountains and waterfalls. Oceans and deserts. But he had no eyes—his body had been ripped apart, thrown to the very edge of existence.

He and Reality—the fabric of Reality itself—were becoming one. The transformation lasted for infinity, yet was instantaneous. He was everything and nothing. Everywhere and nowhere. He was the space that filled the gaps, the barriers. He was matter and antimatter. He was Reality.

Tick had no idea how it worked. Not yet. But he knew that understanding would come soon.

A thought formed in his head. He pictured the core of the Void, the Fourth Dimension, the rips in Reality, and the link between them all. The chaos that reigned throughout all the worlds—even the countless ones that had yet to be discovered—filled him. His consciousness brought it all in, saw it all before him. The things that needed to be healed and the things that needed to be severed. Like the answer to a riddle popping into his mind, he *knew* how to heal and sever.

With powers no human had ever known before, Tick started fixing the wounded universe.

CHAPTER
70

AN ABSENCE OF SOUND

Paul sat on the ground, holding Master George in his arms. Sofia was there, too, weeping just like Paul. The battle still continued around them, but Paul could tell it was almost over. Most of Chu's inventions had been obliterated by the new armies brought in by Rutger, and everyone had now turned their forces on the monsters from the Void. They were being destroyed almost as soon as they came out of the churning hurricane of mist. But the Void still raged, still grew. How could they ever stop it?

Master George barely had any life left in him. Each breath was a struggle, and his body was well past healing. Their leader was about to die.

The old man sputtered a cough, and his eyes blinked open. They focused on Paul, then Sofia, then filled with tears.

"I'm so sorry," Paul whispered. His heart crumbled inside of him.

"Master George," Sofia said through a lurching sob.

"No . . . no . . ." the man said through another coughing fit. "It's . . . okay. My good friends . . . you'll carry . . . on."

"Why?" Paul asked, feeling a sudden bubble of anger. "Why didn't the Karma work? The Void's still there! And . . . look at you . . ."

Sofia squeezed his arm but didn't say anything.

George reached out and grabbed both of their hands, seeming to gather one last surge of strength. "Oh, but Master Paul. I believe it *did* work. I have no doubt of it. You'll see soon enough."

The leader of the Realitants exhaled his very last breath.

⁓

Sato had just begun to feel some comfort. The influx of armies had turned the tide, at least in the short term. Chu's machines were defeated. The creatures of the Void were being destroyed almost as soon as they emerged from the spinning vortex of mist.

Now they just had to pool their resources and figure out a way to attack the—

The Void disappeared. The entire thing disappeared in an instant.

An abrupt absence of sound popped Sato's ears as if he'd just been sucked into the vacuum of space. His brain tried to process what he suddenly saw before him—empty air and distant mountains and fields and sky. Sunlight.

There was no more wind. No lightning. No thunder. No mist. No creatures of gray.

The Void had vanished.

~~~

It was gone.

Paul sat in the flattened, ruined grass with his eyes closed, feeling the warmth of the sun against his cheeks, still stunned. Somehow Tick had done it—he'd defeated the Void—but there'd been no sign of him after its disappearance.

The Void was gone. But so was Tick.

The lifeless body of Master George lay a few dozen feet away; the soldiers of Sato's army lined up to pay their respects. Mothball, kneeling next to the old man, sobbed uncontrollably as Sally and Rutger both rubbed her back.

Mixed feelings would be the order of things for a while.

Sofia was sitting beside Paul, and he opened his eyes when she nudged him with an elbow.

"Hey," she said softly. "You okay?"

Paul wondered how to answer that. "I think so. I still feel kind of weird, and sad, and . . . weird. There's no way I'm going to accept that Tick is gone. It has to be like the Nonex or something. He'll find his way back."

Sofia's eyes fell a little, but then she seemed to catch herself, as if she was trying to stay strong for Paul. "I hope so. I mean . . . he made it all go away—the Void, the rips in Reality. He couldn't have done that if he was dead, right?

Maybe he's stuck in the Fourth Dimension, battling his way out."

"Yeah. Maybe."

Sofia leaned her head on his shoulder, which made everything just a little bit brighter.

Paul suddenly had a rush of thoughts that he couldn't keep to himself. All his words came spilling out.

"I'm going to be more serious, work harder. Make a bigger difference. Help the Realitants get back to what George was talking about—strong and rigid and organized top to bottom. We'll start recruiting again, find the best of the best. We can build more headquarters, make sure we have a presence in every Reality. I think we should maybe even go public soon, work with governments and universities—make a real difference in people's lives. And I think we should start exploring, see if we can discover and name new Realities. The Fourteenth, Fifteenth, Twentieth, Thirtieth. We've got a lot of work to do, Sofia."

He'd been staring at the empty fields where the Void of Mist and Thunder—and before that, the castle of Mistress Jane—had once stood. But he noticed that Sofia had lifted her head and was staring at him. He looked at her, loved seeing the awe in her eyes.

"I mean it," he said. "I really do."

"I know," she whispered back. "And we're going to do it together, with Mothball and the rest. It's going to be great."

"And fun."

"Lots of fun." Sofia pointed out into the distance. "I think we should build something right there. A branch of the Realitants. Not a gaudy castle—something simple. We should use the power of the Thirteenth like it was meant to be used. Before Jane messed it all up."

"Brilliant idea, maestro." Paul still had a heavy heart, but he couldn't deny the excitement he felt for the future.

Sofia took a deep breath and let it out. "So. We've made some pretty grand plans. What should we do first?"

Paul found a smile. "We'll figure it out tomorrow."

CHAPTER
71

ONE MONTH LATER

Lisa sat on her front porch and stared out at the trees as the morning sun broke through in the distance and lit everything up. She wished she felt that way on the inside. She wouldn't have thought it was possible, but she missed Tick more and more with each passing day. It wasn't getting any better.

He'd vanished from their lives. Again.

But Atticus Higginbottom—her stinky little brother—had somehow stopped the Void before it could destroy everything. Tick had saved the universe. Again.

Despite her worry, she laughed at the thought. It seemed so absurd and ridiculous, and she knew Tick would laugh, too, if he were there. But it was true. Totally true. Tick was a hero for the ages. At least she had that to hold on to.

The front door banged open, and Kayla came sprinting out onto the porch, her head swiveling left and right as she looked for something. When she finally spotted Lisa, a look of excitement spread across her face.

"Come inside!" the little girl yelled. "Quick!"

Lisa was tempted to be annoyed—she'd just gotten comfortable and wanted some time to be alone outside. She wanted time to think about things. How the world was slowly but surely getting back to some sense of normalcy, how people were rebuilding and laying foundations for an even better future. The Realities were sharing information through the now very-public assistance of the Realitants. The universe would never be the same. Things were changed forever.

But she wasn't annoyed. She couldn't be. Kayla was smiling for the first time in a long time.

"Li-sa!" her little sister insisted with a stomp of her foot. "Daddy said come inside right now! Something's in the fireplace!"

That picked Lisa right up out of her chair. The look in Kayla's eyes showed that this wasn't a silly game. The two of them went through the front door and into the living room, where their mom and dad were standing arm in arm, staring at the fireplace. Inside the dark hole within the brick frame were hundreds of orange sparks flashing and snapping, crackling like a fire, though there were no flames.

Lisa stepped up beside her parents and looked at their faces, which were filled with awe. Lorena and Edgar Higginbottom had tried so hard to put on a brave front since Tick had gone missing again, to be strong for Lisa and

Kayla. But they hadn't been able to hide the devastating sadness within them. It was in their eyes. Like death itself.

"What's going on?" Lisa asked.

"It has something to do with Tick," her dad replied. "I know that much. It has to."

Lisa's mom patted her husband on the arm. "Let's not get our hopes up, Edgar." Her face showed she wasn't following her own advice.

The dancing orange lights suddenly stopped, winking out of existence. Lisa was shocked to see a piece of paper resting on top of the logs—she was certain it hadn't been there a second ago.

"Grab it," she whispered to Kayla.

Her little sister ran to the fireplace and picked up the paper, took a look then ran to their mom and handed it to her. Everyone crowded around to see.

It was a letter. Lisa's mom read it aloud.

Dear Mom. And Dad. And Lisa. And Kayla.

You're probably wondering right now how this letter was created. Or how it got to you. More importantly, you're probably wondering where I am and what I'm doing. What I've become. There are things in the universe that are beyond our comprehension—I've still got a lot to learn myself. Someday I hope to understand it enough to explain it fully.

Something amazing has happened. A combination of so many things. The soulikens of an infinite number of my Alterants somehow bled to me. Filled me up. The

power of Karma was involved. So was the unbeliev-
able energy of the Void from the Fourth Dimension.
The inventive mind of Reginald Chu and the sheer will
of Mistress Jane. It all added together to make this pos-
sible—I've become an entity, like the Haunce, a force to
help watch over the Realities.

But the details and the complexities of it all don't
matter. Not right now.

This is what matters:

Know that I'm alive in so many ways. That I will
always be with you in some form or another. That I'll
devote every ounce of my energy to making life better in
all of the Realities. Great things await us in the future.
But most important of all, know that I love you. All of
you. More than the infinite power of Chi'karda and
Karma combined could ever express. I love you. I love
you guys so much.

I will always be near. Always.

> *Your brother and son,*
> *Tick*

Lisa's mom finished reading, and silence filled the room except for a few sniffles, most of them coming from Lisa's dad.

"Go get Tick's *Journal of Curious Letters*," he said. His voice trembled a bit, but there was a smile on his face and the unmistakable spark of life in his eyes. "It's under his bed. This letter will make an excellent last page to the collection. Don't you think?"

EPILOGUE

THE FIRST MEETING

P aul sat at the large conference table, feeling a little bit as if he'd finally awakened from a long, long dream. Things felt surreal and kind of strange. Different. But good. Mostly good. Today's agenda had an item listed that would never be forgotten. He took a second to look around the room at his fellow Realitants.

There were a few people here he didn't know very well. Not yet, anyway. People like red-haired Priscilla Persiphone, a doctor named something-or-other Hillenstat, or the dude that couldn't speak named Jimmy—the guy didn't even have a tongue. Ew. There were others: Nancy and Katrina and William. A couple more he couldn't remember. All of them had come just in time to save the Fifth Army—along with Paul and Sofia—from being completely wiped out in that last and final battle. So they were definitely his new friends.

And then there were the others. The ones who'd become family.

Mothball, still marked with wounds from the terrible battle in the Thirteenth Reality, but with a smile planted on her long and weary face. Rutger, sitting taller than ever; he'd done the impossible and gathered together all the missing Realitants. Sally, who'd been wearing the same shirt since that fateful day, saying that it'd be bad Karma to put on anything else.

Sato's face was actually a little less stern than it had been of late. Paul knew he was thinking of all the soldiers he'd lost, and the promise he still planned to keep. To take what was left of his army and reclaim the Fifth Reality from the Bugaboos. They'd be leaving soon to do just that.

And Sofia.

Her eyes met his. She didn't say anything, and neither did he, but a lot passed between them in that gaze. The months that seemed like years, the pain and hurt and terror, the thrill of winning mixed with the sorrow of all that had been lost along the way. The ache for those who were no longer there. And an unspoken bond that could never be taken away from them. She smiled, and he smiled back.

And finally, he looked to the head of the table.

To the place where Master George had always sat with his flaky red scalp, his loyal Muffintops on his lap, his three-piece suit, and his Barrier Wand usually somewhere nearby. The old man with the proper speech and the constant twinkle in his eyes. The old man who'd brought them in, trained them, encouraged them. The old man who'd chosen to fight by their side in the end, though he had to know his chances of surviving were slim. Paul had a lump in his throat at the thought, and wished he could say good-bye one last time.

Someone else was sitting in the leader's chair now. Someone very different, having just appeared in a blaze of sparks and the sound of static charges.

A being, roughly in the shape of a human body, a cloudy mix of blue and white light swirling through and around each other, occupied the seat where Master George had once reigned. Little flashes of orange danced throughout the ethereal substance, along with zigzags of bright electricity, like miniature strikes of lightning. The otherworldly apparition glowed warmly and gave off a humming sound. Paul could feel a vibrating buzz in his bones.

There was a face projected on the surface of the wraith-like figure's head. A familiar face that was smiling at the moment. Tick. It was good to see him again. Oh, man, it was *so* good to see him again.

Atticus Higginbottom, in a form that no one else in that room would ever understand, leaned forward and put his ghostly elbows on the table.

"Let's get this meeting started," he said.

A GLOSSARY OF PEOPLE, PLACES, AND ALL THINGS IMPORTANT

Atticus Higginbottom—A Realitant from the state of Washington, in Reality Prime.

Alterant—Different versions of the same person existing in different Realities. It is extremely dangerous for Alterants to meet one another.

Annika—A spy for the Realitants who was killed by a pack of fangen.

Bagger—A large device from Chu Industries that can fly and is armed with Chu's anti-Chi'karda recoil mechanism.

Barf Scarf—The red-and-black scarf that Tick used to wear at all times to hide the ugly birthmark on his neck.

Barrier Wand—The device used to wink people and things between Realities and between heavily concentrated places of Chi'karda within the same Reality. Works very easily with inanimate objects, and can place them almost anywhere. To transport humans, they must be in a place concentrated with Chi'karda (like a cemetery) and have a nanolocator that transmits their location to the Wand. The wand is useless without the Chi'karda Drive, which channels and magnifies the mysterious power.

Barrier Staff—A special Barrier Wand created by Mistress Jane.

Benson—A servant of Reginald Chu in the Fourth Reality.

Bermuda Triangle—The most concentrated area of Chi'karda in each Reality. Still unknown as to why.

Billy "The Goat" Cooper—Tick's biggest nemesis at Jackson Middle School.

Blade of Shattered Hope—A weapon created by Mistress Jane that allows her to harness the power of dark matter and utilize the linking of her Alterants to sever a Reality from existence.

Bryan Cannon—A fisherman in Reality Prime.

Bugaboo Soldiers—The nemeses of the Fifth Reality, these assassins are bent on taking over their world. Often dressed as clowns, they are very unstable.

Chi'karda—The mysterious force that controls Quantum Physics. It is the scientific embodiment of conviction and choice, which in reality, rules the universe. Responsible for creating the different Realities.

Chi'karda Drive—The invention that revolutionized the universe by harnessing, magnifying, and controling Chi'karda. It has long been believed that travel between Realities is impossible without it.

Chu Industries—The company that practically rules the world of the Fourth Reality. Known for countless inventions and technologies, including many that are malicious in nature.

Command Center—Master George's headquarters in the Bermuda Triangle, where Chi'karda levels are monitored, and to where his many nanolocators report various types of information.

Darkin (Dark Infinity) Project—A menacing, giant device created by Reginald Chu of the Fourth Reality to manipulate others' minds. Destroyed by Tick.

Denter—A robot built by Chu Industries that is like a bulldozer with metal fists sporting spikes at the ends.

Earwig Transponder—An insect-like device inserted into the ear that can scramble listening devices and help track its host.

Edgar Higginbottom—Tick's father.

Entropy—The law of nature that states all things move toward destruction. Related to fragmentation.

Factory, The—Located in the Thirteenth Reality, it is where Mistress Jane "manufactures" her abominable creations.

Fangen—A creature created by Mistress Jane, utilizing the twisted and mutated version of Chi'karda found in the Thirteenth Reality. Formed from a variety of no fewer than twelve different animals, the short and stocky creatures are bred to kill first and ask questions later. They can also fly.

Fifth Army, The—Sato's fighting unit, made up of people from the Fifth Reality.

Firekelt—Creation of Mistress Jane. A monster covered in hundreds of cloth-like strips that ignite on demand.

Fourth Dimension—Another dimension that is as different from ours as the oceans are from outer space. Hardly understood, and with limited research available, because it's never been explored before, the Fourth is breached when Tick and Mistress Jane battle it out after the incident with the Blade of Shattered Hope. The Void of Mist and Thunder is spawned from this dimension.

Fragmentation—When a Reality begins losing Chi'karda levels on a vast scale, it can no longer maintain itself as a major alternate version of the world and will eventually disintegrate into nothing. Its cause is related to entropy.

Frazier Gunn—A loyal servant of Mistress Jane.

Frupey—Nickname for Fruppenschneiger, Sofia's butler.

Gnat Rat—A malicious invention of Chu Industries in the Fourth Reality. Releases dozens of mechanical hornets that are programmed to attack a certain individual based on a nanolocator, DNA, or blood type.

Grand Canyon—A satellite location of the Realitants. Second only to the Bermuda Triangle in Chi'karda levels. Still unknown as to why.

Grand Minister—Supreme ruler of the Fifth Reality.

Great Hall—A room within Mistress Jane's castle that has a high concentration of Chi'karda.

Gretel—A Realitant taking refuge in the Third Reality.

Grinder Beast—An enormous, rhinoceros-like creature with dozens of legs in the Tenth Reality.

Halters—A weapon that shoots out tiny darts laced with a paralyzing serum.

Hans Schtiggenschlubberheimer—The man who started the Scientific Revolution in the Fourth Reality in the early nineteen-hundreds. In a matter of decades, he helped catapult the Fourth far beyond the other Realities in terms of technology.

Haunce, The—A mysterious, ghostly, powerful being made up of billions upon billions of soulikens.

Henry—A boy from the Industrial Barrens in the Seventh Reality.

Hillenstat—A Realitant doctor from the Second Reality.

Jimmy "The Voice" Porter—A Realitant from the Twelfth Reality. Has no tongue.

Karma—A mysterious force that has been studied for years by a team within the Realitants, led by Gretel. Its powers are unpredictable, but it's believed to heighten the strength of good or evil, depending on who wields it.

Katrina Kay—A Realitant from the Ninth Reality.

Kayla Higginbottom—Tick's younger sister.

Klink—Guard of the Execution Exit at the End of the Road Insane Asylum.

Klint Tanner—A man living in the Twelfth Reality who helps gather data for the Realitants.

Kyoopy—Nickname used by the Realitants for Quantum Physics.

Ladies of Blood and Sorrow—A mysterious society of women loyal to Mistress Jane.

Lazbots—A robotic device of Chu Industries outfitted with incinerating lasers.

Lemon Fortress—Mistress Jane's castle in the Thirteenth Reality.

Lisa Higginbottom—Tick's older sister.

Lorena Higginbottom—Tick's mother.

Mabel Fredrickson—Tick's great-aunt. Lives in Alaska.

Master George—The leader of the Realitants.

Metaspide—A vicious robotic creature from the Fourth Reality that resembles a spider.

Mistress Jane—A former Realitant and ruler of the Thirteenth Reality, she wields an uncanny power over Chi'karda. Since the accident in which she was "melded" with fragments of the Dark Infinity weapons, her power has increased tenfold.

Mordell—The leader of the Ladies of Blood and Sorrow.

Mothball—A Realitant from the Fifth Reality.

Ms. Sears—Tick's favorite librarian.

Muffintops—Master George's cat.

Multiverse—An old term used by Reality Prime scientists to explain the theory that Quantum Physics has created multiple versions of the universe.

Nancy Zeppelin—A Realitant from Wisconsin in Reality Prime.

Nanolocator—A microscopic electronic device that can

crawl into a person's skin and forever provide information on their whereabouts, Chi'karda levels, etc.

Nonex—When Alterants meet, one disappears and enters the Nonex. A complete mystery to the Realitants.

Norbert McGillicuddy—A post-office worker in Alaska who helped Tick and his dad escape an attack by Frazier Gunn.

Paul Rogers—A Realitant from Florida in Reality Prime.

Phillip—Owner and operator of the Stroke of Midnight Inn in the Sixth Reality.

Pick—Master George's nickname for a major decision in which Chi'karda levels spike considerably. Some Picks have been known to create or destroy entire Realities.

Priscilla Persiphone—A Realitant from the Seventh Reality.

Quantum Physics—The science that studies the physical world of the extremely small. Most scholars are baffled by its properties and at a loss to explain them. Theories abound. Only a few know the truth: that a completely different power rules this realm, which in turn rules the universe: Chi'karda.

Quinton Hallenhaffer—A Realitant from the Second Reality.

Rager—An advanced weapon that harnesses extreme amounts of static electricity. When unleashed, it collects matter in a violent, earthen ball that can shatter whatever gets in its way.

Realitants—An organization sworn to discover and chart

all known Realities. Founded in the 1970s by a group of scientists from the Fourth Reality, who then used Barrier Wands to recruit other quantum physicists from other Realities.

Reality—A separate and complete version of the world, of which there may be an infinite number. The most stable and strongest is called Reality Prime. So far, thirteen major branches off of Prime have been discovered. Realities are created and destroyed by enormous fluctuations in Chi'karda levels. Examples:

Fourth—Much more advanced technologically than the other Realities due to the remarkable vision and work of Hans Schtiggenschlubberheimer.

Fifth—Quirks in evolution led to a very tall human race.

Eighth—The world is covered in water, due to much higher temperatures that were caused by a star fusion anomaly triggered in another galaxy by an alien race.

Eleventh—Quirks in evolution and diet led to a short and robust human race.

Thirteenth—Somehow a mutated and very powerful version of Chi'karda exists here.

Reality Echo—An object that literally exists in two Realities at once, making the object indestructible.

Reginald Chu—Tick's science teacher in Reality Prime. Also the person in the Fourth Reality who founded Chu Industries and turned it into a worldwide empire. They are Alterants of each other.

Renee—An inmate at the End of the Road Insane Asylum.

Ripple Quake—A violent geological disaster caused by a massive disturbance in Chi'karda.

Rutger—A Realitant from the Eleventh Reality.

Sally T. Jones—A Realitant from the Tenth Reality.

Sato—A Realitant from Japan in Reality Prime.

Sato Tadashi—Former Grand Minister of the Fifth Reality, killed by the Bugaboo soldiers. An Alterant of the Realitant Sato.

Shockpulse—An injection of highly concentrated electromagnetic nanobots that seek out and destroy the tiny components of a nanolocator, rendering it useless.

Shurric—Short for Sonic Hurricaner, this weapon is the more powerful version of the Sound Slicer. Shoots out a heavily concentrated force of sound waves, almost too low for the human ear to register but powerful enough to destroy just about anything in its direct path.

Sleeks—Creations of Mistress Jane. Wispy and strong, lightning fast. They guard the forest that surrounds the Factory.

Slinkbeast—A vicious creature that lives in the Mountains of Sorrow in the Twelfth Reality.

Snooper Bug—A hideous crossbreed of birds and insects created by the mutated power of the Chi'karda in the Thirteenth Reality. Can detect any known weapon or poison and can kill with one quick strike of its needle-nosed beak. Pets of Mistress Jane.

Sofia Pacini—A Realitant from Italy in Reality Prime.

Soulikens—An imprint or stamp on Reality, created by natural energy and Chi'karda, that becomes a lingering piece of one's self that will never cease to exist.

Sound Slicer—A small weapon outdated by the much more powerful Shurric.

Spinner—A special device that shoots out a circular plane of laser light, displaying video images on its surface.

Squeezers—A grenade that shoots out strong wires that contract and curl up.

Tick—Nickname for Atticus Higginbottom.

Tingle Wraith—A collection of microscopic animals from the Second Reality, called spilphens, that can form together into a cloud while rubbing against each other to make a horrible sound called the Death Siren.

Tollaseat—Mothball's father, from the Fifth Reality.

Void of Mist and Thunder—An elusive, mysterious, extremely dangerous entity that has been trapped within the Fourth Dimension since before mankind.

Voids—Tick's name for the monstrous creations that are spawned from the Void of Mist and Thunder.

Waterkelt—Creation of Mistress Jane. A monster made completely out of water.

William Schmidt—A Realitant from the Third Reality.

Windasill—Mothball's mother, from the Fifth Reality.

Windbike—An invention of Chu Industries, this vehicle is a motorcycle that can fly, consuming hydrogen out of the air for its fuel. Based on an extremely complex gravity-manipulation theorem first proposed by Reginald Chu.

Winking—The act of traveling between or within Realities by use of a Barrier Wand. Causes a slight tingle to the skin on one's shoulders and back.

DISCUSSION QUESTIONS

1. Tick has to make some really difficult decisions in this book, many of which relate to working with the two people he sees as his mortal enemies: Chu and Mistress Jane. Could you work with someone you hate in order to bring about the greater good? What would that be like?

2. This last book is full of adventure and peril. Which scene did you think was the most intense? Were you ever scared that one of the four best friends would die? How would you react in such scary situations?

3. The bond of friendship between Tick and his friends becomes stronger throughout the series. Why do you think that is so? How do their experiences together create that special bond? Do you have someone you are not related to that you'd be willing to risk your life for?

4. How did you feel about Master George throughout the series? How did his death affect you? Did it seem

inevitable? Do you believe that the next generation is now ready to take over the Realitants?

5. How do you feel about the role of Karma in the story? Is it symbolic of anything to you? Do you believe in any kind of higher power that might give you just the nudge you need when you need it the most?

6. At the end of the book, Tick makes an incredible and ultimate sacrifice to save the world. Would you have had the courage to do the same thing? How do you think he felt?

7. What is your interpretation of what Tick has become at the end of the book? How powerful is he? What do you think his role will be with the Realitants? What would a typical day be like for him?

8. What do you think awaits the Realitants in the future?